Dead

by a

Dead Man's Hand

Phillip Strang

BOOKS BY PHILLIP STRANG

DCI Isaac Cook Series
MURDER IS A TRICKY BUSINESS
MURDER HOUSE
MURDER IS ONLY A NUMBER
MURDER IN LITTLE VENICE
MURDER IS THE ONLY OPTION
MURDER IN NOTTING HILL
MURDER IN ROOM 346
MURDER WITHOUT REASON

DI Keith Tremayne Series
DEATH UNHOLY
DEATH AND THE ASSASSIN'S BLADE
DEATH AND THE LUCKY MAN
DEATH AT COOMBE FARM
DEATH BY A DEAD MAN'S HAND

Steve Case Series
HOSTAGE OF ISLAM
THE HABERMAN VIRUS
PRELUDE TO WAR

Standalone Books
MALIKA'S REVENGE

Copyright Page

Copyright © 2018 Phillip Strang

Cover Design by Phillip Strang

All rights reserved. No part of this book may be reproduced, stored in a retrieval system, or transmitted in any form or by any means (electronic, mechanical, photocopying, recording or otherwise) without the prior written permission of the publisher, except by a reviewer who may quote brief passages in a review to be printed by a newspaper, magazine, or journal.

All characters appearing in this work are fictitious. Any resemblance to actual events, locales, or persons, living or dead, is coincidental.

All Rights Reserved.

This work is registered with the UK Copyright Service

ISBN: 9781980918677

Dedication

For Elli and Tais who both had the perseverance to make me sit down and write.

Chapter 1

Ethan Mitchell, old for his years after seventeen years in prison, knew the exact amount of time since his arrest for murder: eighteen years, five months and three days. After so long in prison, many things confused him on his release, but one thing he was sure of was that people do not come back from the dead. However, one month before his release from prison for the murder of a man, he had received a letter. It had only two sentences.

Time will not save you. St Mark's Church, three in the afternoon, the first Wednesday after your release.

He had recognised the writing. After all, hadn't they grown up together. The signature was unmistakable: it was his brother Martin's.

Ethan Mitchell had good reason not to be in the church, but not the ability to resist the invitation. After all, they had been inseparable as children, even as adults, until that fateful night.

As Mitchell waited in the church, he looked around the place. Nothing much had changed. His brother, if it was his brother… *But that's not possible*, Mitchell thought. *I killed him, spent seventeen years in prison for his murder.*

The church was empty, as Mitchell knew it would be. He and his brother had sung in the choir as children and attended Sunday service with the Boy Scouts. They both knew the church intimately, and they knew the vicar, a man who retired to the rectory every day for an afternoon nap.

A voice echoed through the church; Ethan felt the hairs on the back of his neck stand up. It was his brother; no one else had that distinct tone, that lisp.

'Martin, it can't be,' Ethan said.

The unmistakable voice again. 'It's time to pay for what you did.'

'You're dead. I killed you.'

'That you did, but I've waited for my revenge.'

Unable to move, Ethan Mitchell stood transfixed where he was standing. In front of him, the altar; to the right, the organ that his mother used to play; and somewhere the spirit of a long-dead brother. He remembered back to that night when they had both been drunk. Choirboys they may have been, even Boy Scouts, but in adulthood the recklessness, the crime, and the closeness they had shared had dimmed to disdain. Even so, they were still inseparable, and nobody had expected that one would murder the other. Martin had thrown the first punch, caught Ethan on the face. Ethan had retaliated with the added force of a rock he had picked up. He had hit his brother full-force in the chest before pulling out a knife from inside his jacket and stabbing him. Martin lay dying at Ethan's feet, Ethan proclaiming at the top of his voice, 'You bastard. I've finally killed you, and you deserved it.'

'I told you I'd come back as I lay dying on the ground,' the voice inside the church said.

Ethan looked around, tried to ascertain the direction it came from, but the acoustics were deceiving, the voice echoing off the walls of the empty church. 'Where are you?' Ethan shouted.

'You'll see me soon enough.'

'We were angry and drunk. I didn't mean to kill you.'

'I would have killed you if I had had the chance, so don't pretend it was an accident.'

A man appeared at the front of the church. He sauntered down the aisle, heading towards Ethan Mitchell, a man who had been released just one day earlier from prison. Ethan looked forward, trying to see the man's face. 'I can't see you,' Ethan said. 'Are you dead?'

'You'll see me soon enough,' the man said. He wore a heavy coat with a large scarf wrapped around his face. On his head he wore a hat, its brim pulled down at the front. At ten feet from Ethan he stopped and reached into his right-hand jacket pocket.

'No, don't.'

'It's only right,' the man said. He levelled the gun that he taken from the pocket and emptied three bullets into Ethan, the noise echoing around the church. The man then put the gun into his pocket and walked out of the church and onto the busy street.

***

'Not an easy face to forget,' Detective Inspector Keith Tremayne said.

'Why's that?' Clare Yarwood, Tremayne's sergeant in Homicide, asked.

'Eighteen years ago, I arrested the man. Salisbury's a small place, everyone knew Ethan Mitchell and his brother, Martin.'

'Why's that?' Clare asked. They were a good team: Tremayne closing in on retirement, his sergeant just turned thirty. They'd been together for a few years now in Salisbury, a city southwest of London, close to Stonehenge.

'Identical twins. You couldn't tell the two apart.'

'Where's the brother?'

'Ethan killed Martin, spent seventeen years in prison for the crime. He was released yesterday.'

'I thought twins were meant to be close,' Clare said.

'As children they were, but as they grew older they started getting into trouble, and both of them used to get drunk. If no one else were around, they'd argue with each other. I knew them both. Martin, he was the more easy-going, but you could never be sure who was who.'

'There's a letter in the man's pocket. It seems relevant,' Jim Hughes, Bemerton Road Police Station's crime scene examiner, said.

Tremayne opened the letter and read it. He then showed it to Clare. 'What does it mean?' she said.

'It seems as though his brother invited him to the church,' Tremayne said.

'His dead brother?'

'I saw the body, arrested Ethan for his murder.'

'Macabre,' Clare said. 'Whoever killed the man was not back from the dead.'

'Then why was Ethan here, and who was it?'

Clare could see that Tremayne was pleased to be busy again. There had been a few quiet weeks at Bemerton Road, and Tremayne without a murder enquiry was being subjected to their senior's attempts to retire him. Even though the retirement package was excellent, Clare knew that Tremayne would never retire voluntarily.

'I'll be the last one out of this station,' he had said on a few occasions to Clare.

They were a good pair, a man in his fifties, cynical, seen-it-all, and occasionally cantankerous, and his younger sergeant. Tremayne would never tell his sergeant that he liked and respected her very much. As for her, Tremayne was almost as important as her own father, who was a good man but cold. To Tremayne, she was always Yarwood, and his disparaging, verging on sarcastic, comments did not come with a barb, but a genuineness. She had learnt how to deal with him some years before, give him back what he gave. Some outsiders thought the relationship strange, but Clare did not, nor did Jim Hughes, the CSE. He wasn't much older than Clare, and Tremayne had initially given him the treatment, but Hughes had stood his ground, proved his worth, and now the detective inspector only needed his evaluation of a murder scene to be confident he had enough information to proceed.

'Ethan and Martin had plenty of relatives in Salisbury,' Tremayne said. 'We'd better start visiting a few of them.'

'Good people?' Clare said.

'Middle of the road. Some are no better than the Mitchell twins, others are honest.'

'Did you like the brothers?' Clare knew that even though they were villains, that would not preclude Tremayne from liking them. He wasn't a man who saw those on the side of the law as good, the others as bad. He judged people on their merits, not their criminal record.

'Sober they were okay. Always willing to enjoy a pint of beer as long as someone else was paying.'

'You!'

'Don't look at me like that, Yarwood. I pay my fair share, even buy you the occasional glass of wine.'

'The brothers when they were drunk?'

'Difficult drunks, always wanted to argue, take you outside and teach you a lesson. There were a few pubs in Salisbury that barred them, but to little effect.'

'If the two came in, no one was willing to stand up to them, is that it?'

'A double act. You take on one, you get the other, and you saw Ethan. He wasn't a weakling.'

'No.'

'The two of them had been in trouble with the law a few times, stolen cars, breaking and entering. Small time hoodlums, the pair of them. None too bright, either. They married sisters. We should meet them first.'

'You know where they live?'

'After nearly thirty years in the city, I know where every villain and his family lives, you know that.'

'A warm welcome?'

'Martin's wife, probably. Ethan's wife, she'll not be so easy. She wasn't fond of him, divorced him years ago, and his reappearing will only stir up old memories, old conflicts.'

'And more murders?'

'Yarwood, I don't know. There's enough hatred flowing around, and there is still the van they robbed.'

'What do you mean?'

'Ethan and Martin, they attempted one job too many. They robbed a van carrying gold bars. Somehow they had found out about it. It was out on the Andover Road late at night. They managed to stop it, somehow gain entry into the vehicle, cosh the driver, point a rifle at his offsider. Then Martin, he's in the van and off. Ethan's following behind.'

'The men in the van?' Clare said.

'They're sitting in a ditch, trussed up and in their underwear. Martin, he had more brains than Ethan, is wearing one of the uniforms. They drive down a country road, empty the van, set it on fire, and take off.'

'The car Ethan was driving?'

'Stolen. Once the van didn't call in as scheduled on the radio, the alert went out. The Mitchells had timed it well, and their car was found in ten feet of water not far from Salisbury. After that, nothing. The guards hadn't seen anything, other than two men who said little and wore balaclavas. They were even suspected of being in league with the robbers, but later on they were just found to be incompetent. The driver of the van had a girlfriend down the road, no more than ten miles. He wanted to get there and spend a couple of hours with her.'

'And the other man?'

'He was hopeful that her friend was coming over. They were going to make a night of it, but Ethan and Martin upset their plans. Anyway, as I was saying, Ethan and Martin had pulled off the perfect crime.'

'Why did Ethan kill Martin?'

'Ethan and Martin had hit the big time. They have all this gold, and they don't know what to do with it. You can hardly walk into the local bank and deposit it. The two brothers, ecstatic and confused, stop at a pub to talk it through, make a few phone calls.'

'Did they get drunk?'

'It's in their nature. Within two hours, they're standing outside next to a car with a fortune in the boot. They start arguing. Some of the locals come out from the pub to watch. Ethan tells them to clear off and mind their own business. Martin, he's a bit calmer, telling Ethan to take it easy. Some of the locals take the hint and leave the two men to it. One of the locals, not a good witness, as he was on his eighth pint of beer, leans against the pub wall. The two brothers debate what to do, their voices raised again, and Ethan hits Martin and then thrusts a knife into his brother's stomach. The drunk who was watching vomits on the flowers, and then rushes inside to raise the alarm.'

'You took the call?'

'I was out there within fifteen minutes. Martin's dead and on the ground, Ethan's inside the pub and restrained. The man's unapologetic.'

'He's not concerned?'

'The drunk told us that Ethan had told Martin that he was going to deal with him and that he had had a lifetime of being one half of a comedy act.'

'A clear declaration of premeditated murder?'

'The man was drunk, didn't know what he was saying, but the judge didn't see it that way. All he saw was a villain who had overstepped the mark. The prosecution was crash-hot, the defence was weak, and Ethan Mitchell was found guilty and sentenced to twenty years.'

'And the gold bullion?' Clare asked.

'Half was in the car; the other half the brothers had hidden somewhere, and Martin's dead and Ethan never told anyone where it was. It may have helped with his sentencing, but he was keeping quiet.'

'Does anyone know?'

'Ethan's murderer might.'

Chapter 2

'Tremayne, what are you doing here?' were the first words that he and Clare heard on the door being opened at the council house.

'Betty, long time since I've seen you,' Tremayne said. Clare looked over at her senior, not sure of what to make of the welcome. She had known him long enough to realise he seemed to know everyone in Salisbury. Thirty-five thousand inhabitants, and every villain and his or her family appeared to know her DI, and most, at one time or another, had felt his firm grip on their collar.

'And who's the person you're with?' the woman said. From her mouth hung a cigarette, around her waist, an apron.

'This is Sergeant Yarwood.'

'Pleased to meet you,' Clare said.

'There's no point in you two standing out there. You'd better come in. I've heard by the way.'

'Ethan, it was always going to happen,' Tremayne said.

'I'm surprised he lasted this long. Any idea who it was?' Betty said.

'You were married to him for a long time, what do you reckon?'

'I divorced him over fifteen years ago, found myself another man, hardworking and honest.'

'The opposite of Ethan.'

'Not totally. He likes to drink, as much as Ethan and his brother did, but he's a harmless drunk.'

'No fighting, no roughing you up?'

'Not him. He just wants to sleep after a few drinks. He suits me fine, and he's looked after Ethan's kids, better than he did.'

'How's Gerry and Marcia?'

'Why ask me? Your lot arrested Gerry last week for that jeweller's in the High Street. Marcia, she's doing well, her own shop.'

'We go back a long way,' Tremayne said, looking over at Clare.

'Oh!' Clare's only comment.

'Ethan and Martin, before they went off the tracks, used to go down the pub of a night. Betty always came along.'

'Someone had to get them home,' Betty said.

'Good times,' Tremayne reminisced.

'Good times, but then Ethan's and Martin's attempt at crime became more ambitious.'

'They were always small time,' Tremayne said. 'Until they stole that gold.'

'A curse that's been. If they had stuck with pilfering, the most that would have happened would have been a few years in prison. With that gold, Martin ends up dead, and Ethan's in jail for seventeen years. It was you who arrested him.'

'I had no option. Martin's lying dead on the ground, Ethan's admitting to the crime. Even so, twenty years, out in seventeen, was a stiff sentence.'

'It's past history,' Betty said. 'And besides, what are you here for? To offer condolences to the grieving widow?'

'Are you grieving?'

'I'm sorry he's dead, and he was the father of my two children. I feel numb at the present moment. No doubt I'll sit down later and shed a tear. Do you need someone to identify him?'

'If you could?'

'It's been over fifteen years since I last saw him. Gerry kept in touch, so did Marcia. She used to visit him every couple of months.'

'We'll use her,' Clare said. 'Do they know?'

'They've heard. Marcia will be coming up here later on. You can wait for her if you want.'

'Ethan and Martin hid some of the gold,' Tremayne said.

'Are you here because of that?' Betty said.

'Not us. We're Homicide. Ethan's dead, and we need the person responsible. The gold, it was worth a lot of money, always seems relevant.'

'None of us have it. There were no tip-offs from Ethan as to where it was. As far as we're concerned, it destroyed us as a family, and none of us saw any of the benefits.'

'We found a letter in Ethan's pocket, the reason he was in the church.'

'From who?'

'That's the problem, Betty. It was from Martin.'

'An old letter?'

'It was written recently.'

'But that's impossible. You were there when he was killed. You even attended his funeral, saw him lying in his coffin.'

'Forensics are checking the letter. It has to be a forgery, but someone knew Martin's writing, and the bait to lure Ethan to the church.'

'Someone after the gold?'

'From what we can see it was someone who wanted Ethan dead. There's no sign of a fight, only someone walking up to where Ethan was and shooting him three times. The letter implies revenge by Martin.'

'What's the point?' Betty said. 'Martin's dead, we all know that, and it's not as if he had anyone who cares about him, not after all these years. Gerry was fond of his uncle, but he was just a child back then. If someone was after the missing gold, why kill Ethan? I don't get it.'

'Nor do we,' Tremayne said. 'You've a large family, some villains in there. Anyone you can think of?'

'Not for killing Ethan. There were a few who were angry after he stabbed Martin, spouted vengeance, but that was just the heat of the moment. And the relationship between the twins was always tense. They were always together, almost conjoined, but they had grown to hate each other, although they couldn't stand being apart from each other for more than a few hours.'

'When you were married to Ethan, how did you handle it?'

'Martin was always over. He stayed too often for me in the spare room. A damn nuisance, really, but what could I do? You marry one, you got the other. Tweedledum and Tweedledee, that's what I used to call them. Mind you, Martin hated it, but it wasn't enough to make him move out.'

'Could you tell them apart?' Clare said.

'Are you worried that the other one would be in bed with me and I wouldn't know?'

'Something like that.'

'I could tell. Don't ask me to elaborate.'

'Betty, getting back to something serious,' Tremayne said. 'Martin's dead and Ethan's on trial for his murder. What was the family's reaction?'

'Shock, then anger. Their older brother, Gavin, he's upset, wants to rip Ethan's head off. Their sister's never spoken about it much.'

'I still hold that it was one of your extended family who killed Ethan,' Tremayne said.

'It was the gold we'd have wanted, not Ethan dead,' Betty said.

'That was the problem in the first place. The two brothers had a fortune, didn't know what to do with it. Do you think that Ethan had told someone where the stash is hidden, and his being alive would only complicate the situation?'

'You're the policeman. But why kill him in a church? Why not anywhere else?'

'That's for us to find out,' Tremayne said.

'Any signs of anyone in the family acting differently?' Clare asked.

'Not that I've seen. And if they had the gold, they could have had it for seventeen years.'

Tremayne and Clare realised that there was no more to be gained from Ethan Mitchell's ex-wife. They left the house and headed back to Bemerton Road Police Station.

***

Back at the station, Clare headed up to Homicide to start preparing the reports; Tremayne headed over to Forensics.

'What can you tell us?' Tremayne asked.

'You're a bit premature. The body's in with Pathology, the letter is under analysis.'

'Give me whatever you have.'

'The letter is written on paper you can buy in any newsagent.'

'How about the bullets?'

'Once we have them, give us a couple of hours. We'll not be able to tell you the make of weapon, although Pathology should be able to give you a distance the body was away from the gun when it was fired.'

'We're sure it was about ten feet,' Tremayne said.

'We'll confirm.'

Tremayne, realising that he was not going to get much more, returned to Homicide. In his office, Superintendent Moulton. 'Interesting case you've got here,' he said. Tremayne knew him as a procedures man, keen on reports, pedantic over expenditure.

'I arrested the dead man eighteen years ago,' Tremayne said.

'What's this about his dead brother killing him?'

'Speculation. There's a letter. It purports to have been written by Martin, but it can't be. I was at the scene when he was murdered, and the man was definitely dead.'

'You're not going to try and convince me it's the spirit of the dead man?'

'Superintendent, how long have you known me?'

'It seems forever.'

'Five years at least. We've had a few strange cases, but nothing that couldn't be explained. Spirits and ancient gods and whatever are just pure nonsense and should be filed away with the fairies at the bottom of the garden.'

'Yet you still wear a crucifix around your neck.'

'Force of habit, nothing more. Yarwood, she was freaked out by what happened at Avon Hill. I wear it more for her benefit than mine.'

'Don't pretend, Tremayne. You were freaked out as well.'

'That's as maybe, and we saw things that can't be explained.'

'Yarwood?'

'She's still susceptible. If there's not a rational explanation for the murder of Ethan Mitchell, she'll have me believing it was a ghost that killed him, especially if the letter is found to be genuine.'

'Is that likely?' Moulton said. He had come down to Homicide to talk about Tremayne's retirement. He decided against bringing it up this time, and besides, Tremayne and murder made for an interesting conversation.

'Whoever killed Mitchell was flesh and bones, I know that.'

'His family?'

'We've met the man's ex-wife. They've been divorced a long time. We're working our way around the other family members. There are one or two bad apples in there. None are known for violence.'

Chapter 3

Jim Hughes phoned after Moulton had left. 'Nine millimetre bullet. The gun had been fired at a distance of approximately ten feet. One bullet to the heart, the other two to the body.'

'We have to assume Ethan Mitchell knew the person,' Tremayne said.

'Why? The man was confused. A letter from a dead brother, a church, who knows what he was thinking. The pathologist will send his report in due course,' Hughes said.

Tremayne called in Clare. 'We've a few relatives to see. Are you ready?'

'Which one first?'

'Ethan's and Martin's brother. We'll find him not far from here. He runs an electrical repair shop.'

'What do you want?' Gavin Mitchell said. Clare could see that he was shorter than Ethan. He was behind the counter of his small shop, surrounded by electrical appliances. The place smelt of cigarettes; Clare did not like it.

'Your brother.'

'I've heard. All that money and he left us scratching around.'

'Business not good?' Tremayne said.

'What do you think? It's cheaper to buy new than repair.'

'So why do they?'

'Beats me. They still come in, mainly the elderly. They've not embraced the modern disregard for assets.

Me, I look after my gear, not like Ethan or Martin ever did.'

'Did you ever go and see Ethan in prison?'

'What for?'

'He was your brother.'

'What's that got to do with it? He killed Martin.'

'Would you have been interested in the gold?'

'I've always kept to the straight and narrow, stayed honest.'

Tremayne turned to Clare. 'Gavin, we've nothing against him,' he said.

'Mr Mitchell, your brother is murdered, and you act as though it was nothing,' Clare said.

'I can't pretend to care when I don't. The man could have gone anywhere. But no, not Ethan, he's back here opening old wounds, making people remember. Betty, Ethan's wife, she's got on and made something of herself, although she's got Gerry to worry about. Marcia, Ethan's and Betty's daughter, is fine, got herself a nice little shop, making more money than me.'

'What about the gold?'

'What do you want me to say? None of us has it, although there are a few in Salisbury who would have twisted Ethan's arm to make him talk.'

'Twisted?' Tremayne said.

'Beat the hell out of him, cut him up, stub out lighted cigarettes on him. Not that he didn't deserve it, but the gold that's missing, how much is it worth?'

'Over seven million pounds.'

'And Ethan's in a church getting shot. The man was stupid. He should have just come back, taken the gold and left. He had kept the secret for eighteen years, and the first thing he does is to come back and start chasing ghosts.'

'You've heard about the letter?'

'Is it genuine?'

'Not from Martin, it's not,' Tremayne said.

'Well, who wrote it?' Gavin Mitchell said.

'Among your many skills, how are you with forgery?'

'Tremayne, you're a miserable bastard, you know that. We've known each other for over twenty years, and you can't resist trying it on.'

'I know it,' Tremayne admitted.

'If it wasn't Martin, then who was it?' Gavin asked.

'We've no idea. If I didn't know you so well, you would have been a suspect.'

'Why me?'

'You could have fooled Ethan in that church.'

'Not before I had found out where the gold was.'

'Did you hate Ethan enough to kill him?'

'I hated him for what he did to the family, Martin as well, but murder, not me.'

***

Tremayne was perplexed after the conversation with Gavin Mitchell. He felt the need for a pint of beer. The New Inn in Bridge Street satisfied his requirements, although he had to stand outside so he could smoke a cigarette. Clare, a non-smoker, waited just inside the open door, feeling some of the heat from inside. Tremayne stood outside, shivering.

'You should give them up,' Clare said. 'They'll be the death of you.'

Clare realised a lecture from her was not going to change the man, and not even Jean, Tremayne's former wife, who was now spending increasingly more time with him, could either.

'What did you reckon to the elder brother?' Clare said.

'Let me finish this cigarette, and then we'll talk inside. Order me a pint, a glass of wine for yourself.'

The barman, known to both of the police officers, did not need Clare to place the order; he knew what they wanted. Clare found a place in one corner and waited for Tremayne; he came in soon enough. 'It's a good beer in here,' he said.

'I can't say the same for the wine.'

'Why kill the man and why did he go to the church?' Tremayne said.

'That's two questions. Is there anyone with that much hatred they'd want to kill him?'

'You've met Ethan's ex-wife as well as his brother. Neither of them is flush with money, and Ethan was sitting on a fortune, supposedly.'

'But is he?' Clare said. 'Everyone assumes he had the gold somewhere, but what if it's a story put out by Ethan?'

'Illogical,' Tremayne said.

'Then why the church, the letter? Whoever lured him there had a reason, and that reason was to silence him.'

'Ethan killed his brother. He must have known he wasn't going to meet him unless he believed in spirits from beyond the grave.'

'You knew the man. What do you think?'

'Ethan never struck me as the sort of person who'd believe in such things. You've got to have a better reason for him being there.'

'Whoever it was must have known how Martin wrote, his signature.'

'Which indicates his family.'

'What about the drivers of the van? What did they know? Were they in league with the twins?'

***

Marcia, the daughter of Ethan and Betty, was friendly as Tremayne and Clare entered her shop. It was small but well-presented. Clare remembered buying a blouse there once.

'Marcia, how are you?'

'Detective Inspector Tremayne, it's been some time.'

Marcia closed the door to the shop. 'A few minutes won't make any difference,' she said.

'Your father?' Tremayne said.

'I should just shut up and go and spend time with my mother, but it won't help.'

'That's understood,' Clare said. She had found keeping busy the best therapy when her fiancé had died.

'I used to visit him, but after so many years away in prison, I can't say I knew him that well,' Marcia said. 'Bob's been more of a father to me than Dad ever was. I'm sad, of course, but what more can I say.'

'Bob?' Clare said.

'He married my mother after our father went to prison.'

'The last time you saw your father, what was his mood like?' Clare said.

'It was a few months back, his birthday. He was looking to get out, not sure what he would do,' Marcia, slim, short-haired, and with a mellow voice, said.

'Salisbury?'

'He had nowhere else to go. The family wouldn't want much to do with him. After all, he did kill my uncle. My mother moved on, he hasn't.'

'We've got your brother in custody,' Tremayne said.

'We can't hold it against you,' Marcia said. 'Gerry was always trouble, even as a child. Our father's in prison, you'd think he would have learnt that crime doesn't pay, or at least, the Mitchell version.'

'That's the trouble,' Tremayne said. 'Ethan and Martin never did.'

'Gerry?'

'He never thought it through either. He'd attempted to steal an antique bracelet and a necklace, both valuable, both recognisable. He could have sold them down the pub for a couple of hundred pounds, possibly to a fence for a couple of thousand, but Gerry failed to see the alarm in the jeweller's.'

'Any chance of a reduced sentence under the circumstances?' Marcia said.

'Unlikely.' Tremayne said.

***

'What about this letter? How long before Forensics can give us an update?' Tremayne said as he and Clare were heading back to the police station on Bemerton Road.

'They'll contact us soon enough,' Clare said, knowing that Tremayne was not the sort of man to wait in his office for a phone call or an email. He was hands-on, he wanted to be out on the street looking for people and clues, or else in the interview room trying to get the truth out of someone.

The Forensics department, modern and efficient, its people in white lab coats, did not always appreciate unwelcome visitors, although, with Tremayne, they had come to expect him wandering in the door.

'This is a smoke-free zone,' Louise Regan, the head of Forensics, a studious-looking woman with thick-framed glasses, said.

'Sorry about that,' Tremayne said, putting his cigarette packet back in his pocket.

'Just remember for the next time,' the woman said. Clare and Louise both knew that Tremayne would not. He was a man set in his ways, a man who had entered the police force over thirty years ago when smoking and drinking pints of beer were expected.

'What do you have?'

'Did you have an envelope?' Regan asked.

'Just the letter.'

'Sometimes we can pick up DNA off the back of a stamp where they licked it. We're still conducting an analysis of the dead man's writing.'

'Martin Mitchell?'

'His brother Ethan as well. He wouldn't be the first person to write a letter to himself.'

'We've assumed it was the person who shot him.'

'We'll need handwriting from all the possible suspects. Are there many?'

'The immediate family, no one else.'

'We'll organise it if you give us the details.'

'But what can you give us now?' Tremayne did not require a lecture on how Forensics operated. He needed something tangible.

'The paper is from an A4 notebook, the sort you can buy anywhere.'

'Does that make the letter recent?'

'We believe the letter was written in the last four to six weeks.'

'Any reason for the time?'

'Experience.'

'Was the letter written in Salisbury?'

'The envelope may have helped, but apart from that, impossible to tell.'

'What about the writing?'

'We believe it was written with a black ball-point pen. As to the handwriting, we do have examples of Martin and Ethan Mitchell's signatures, and Ethan's writing.'

'And?'

'The connecting strokes vary, and the slanting is more severe on the letter than the examples we have.'

'Which means?'

'It's not conclusive, but there's a strong possibility that neither of the two men wrote the letter.'

'What can you tell us about the bullets that Ethan Mitchell was shot with?'

'Nine millimetre Makarov.'

Chapter 4

Tremayne remembered the last time he had spoken to an insurance company representative, other than when they were taking his money. It was over thirty years previously. He and Jean had moved into a new house. Even though he was a police sergeant, it had counted for nothing when the house had been burgled, and the claim had been voided.

And now, a man in his mid-thirties was standing before him. 'Paul Rudd, Gainsford Insurance.'

'The bullion?' Tremayne said.

'My company paid out on what was never recovered. With the case now reopened, we're interested to see what happens.'

'We're not looking for the gold, only who murdered Ethan Mitchell.'

'That's understood, but…'

'There are no buts. We're focussing on a murdered man, not on what he had stolen.'

'It's part of the enquiry.'

'If we find the gold, we'll let you know.'

'I'll keep in contact,' Rudd said. Tremayne realised that the man was only doing his job, but he couldn't help feeling a little peeved that the insurance company was sticking its grubby hands in. When he had made that claim, he remembered the trouble he'd had. He knew he would not be going out of his way to help Rudd, but the man was right. The missing gold did have some bearing on the murder investigation. He called Clare into his office. 'The missing gold, what do we know about it?'

'A private investor who wanted to store the money at his home, not far from Salisbury.'

'How much?'

'You were there when it was stolen,' Clare said.

'I know what it was worth then. How much in today's money?'

'Forty London Good Delivery bars, 99.5 per cent pure gold, approximate weight about four hundred ounces, or 12.5 kilogrammes in metric. Each bar is worth about three hundred and eighty thousand pounds sterling. You recovered twenty bars, there's another twenty missing. That's about seven million seven hundred and forty thousand pounds sterling not recovered.'

'How much was it when the insurance company paid out?'

'Almost one and a half million pounds.'

'If we find the gold for them, they're in profit by six million pounds.'

'That's correct,' Clare said.

'And my lousy claim was for four hundred pounds, and they knocked it back. Parasites, the lot of them.'

'Regardless of the value, it doesn't answer why Ethan Mitchell was shot. It can't have been for the missing gold.'

'Yarwood, I don't follow your logic.'

'Ethan's supposed to be the only one who knew where it was, and he's dead. Either the person who shot him knows where it is, or he's not interested.'

'Everyone's interested. I'd even break the law for it,' Tremayne said.

'You wouldn't, nor would I.'

'Two complete idiots, that's us.'

'Honest and poor,' Clare said.

'What do we know about the man the gold was being delivered to?'

'Selwyn Cosford. You interviewed him.'

'He's in his eighties. If you're thinking insurance fraud, you've left it a bit late,' Tremayne said.

'You must have checked if there was any connection back then,' Clare said.

'Not as fully as we should. We had a murder to deal with. Ethan had killed Martin in a drunken rage, that was our primary consideration. The missing gold was circumstantial. Others looked for it, not Homicide.'

***

Gerry Mitchell, Betty and Ethan's son, had had a troubled upbringing. It wasn't easy, Tremayne knew, to be the butt of schoolyard jokes about your father. However, it didn't excuse the young man's truculent attitude, his only defence when younger. Tremayne and Clare met up with him. He was in a combative mood. 'I heard about him,' Gerry said.

He was a tough-looking individual, sporting an unkempt beard and shoulder-length hair, unwashed for some time from what Clare could see.

'What did you reckon to your father's death?' Tremayne said.

'Who's the woman?'

'The woman is Detective Sergeant Yarwood,' Clare said. 'And I'm not some bit of fluff for you to casually disrespect.'

'No offence intended,' Gerry said. 'It's not much fun locked up waiting for the judge to send me down for a couple of years.'

'You were caught red-handed. What did you expect?'

'Nothing more. What possessed my father to be in that church?'

'We don't know. Do you have any ideas?'

'That's where the twins used to go as children.'

'The twins?'

'That's what they've always been called in our family. Most people couldn't tell them apart.'

'Why did you break into the jeweller's?' Tremayne asked.

'Just bored and it seemed easy.'

Tremayne looked at Clare. 'Gerry's a habitual criminal.'

'Tremayne, you don't change. I've been straight for the last year, apart from the jeweller's, and you're bad-mouthing me to your sergeant.'

Clare could see the young Mitchell fancied himself as a ladies' man, judging by the wink in her direction. The last thing she needed in her life was a criminal who was not even good at his chosen career.

'Why break into somewhere knowing you were going to be caught?' Tremayne said.

'I wasn't thinking.'

'Your mother could do with you by her side, but I can't get you out on bail.'

'She'll be fine. She's got Bob.'

'Your sister believes he's a good man.'

'He is. Mind you, we used to have some fierce arguments, but he was right, I'm my father's son.'

'So why follow him, if you know he's in jail for murder?'

'It's not one of those things you can control,' Gerry Mitchell said.

Clare thought him a weak excuse for a man, always blaming his lot in life on others.

'You don't seem concerned that your father is dead,' Tremayne said.

'I'm not. I used to visit him in prison occasionally. Marcia, she was keener than me on seeing him.'

'You visited him, but you're not upset?' Clare said.

'I don't have the luxury of being sad, do I? I'm locked up here, going down for two. My father knew it was poison to come back to Salisbury, but what did he do?'

'Why was it poisonous?'

'He's still got all that gold stashed somewhere. There's no way he was going to be left alone.'

'But someone killed him,' Tremayne said.

'Maybe someone didn't want questions being asked.'

'What do you know?'

'Nothing more than I've told you.'

'Gerry, whoever killed your father wasn't interested in the gold.'

'Why?'

'The person didn't have time to communicate anything. We've checked with the vicar. He left the church thirty minutes before your father's death, and returned three minutes after he was shot.'

'None of us have it. If we did, I wouldn't be breaking into a jeweller's, would I?'

'You would. It's in your nature.'

***

Tremayne remembered Selwyn Cosford as an eccentric man in his sixties at the time of the gold heist. Back then, he had sported a ponytail with a balding pate and an attractive wife of his age. Now he was in his eighties, and the ponytail was gone.

'Tremayne, good to see you,' Cosford said as he warmly shook the inspector's hand.

'This is Sergeant Yarwood.'

'Pleased to meet you. Tragic about Mitchell. I saw it on the television.'

'The man took off with your gold.'

'It was insured, no point taking a risk.'

'There were some who thought it may have been insurance fraud.'

'The gutter press mainly. You're the police, and you never found anything. And why would I bother? Money's not my problem, never was.'

Tremayne knew it wasn't, so did Clare. After all, who hadn't heard of Selwyn Cosford, the maverick financier. Not only was he making a fortune buying and selling stocks and shares, but he was also hosting a weekly programme on the television advising the average person how to invest their money, how to structure their funds for a financially secure retirement.

'You're looking fit,' Tremayne said.

'Every day, one-hour workout. I've got myself a personal trainer. She puts me through hell.'

'Your wife?'

'No longer here. We were married for a long time, but she wanted a quieter life. She's back in London with her friends, I'm down here.'

'Divorced.'

'No way. We were together through thick and thin. She's getting on a bit now, I'm not.'

'You're on your own?'

'Not me. A man has got to keep chasing the women or else he gets rusty. How about you, Tremayne? Still on your own?'

'My wife's back on a semi-permanent basis.'

'You'll need to bring Jean up here in the next month, a party I'm organising. You as well, Sergeant Yarwood. Bring someone with you.'

'I've no one, not at the present time.'

'Come anyway. There'll be lots of eligible bachelors, plenty of money as well.'

'We'll be there,' Tremayne said.

'Don't worry about us,' Cosford said to Clare. 'We used to run into each other at the pub on an occasional basis. I've known Tremayne for nigh on twenty-five years.'

'Back then, you were living well.'

'Life's been good, and I intend to live a lot longer yet. How about you, Tremayne?'

'No fortune, just a modest house in Wilton.'

'Salt of the earth, that's what you are. While I was out there grubbing in the dirt, doing deals, staking all my money, you were making sure it was safe for us to walk the streets.'

'Mr Cosford, the missing gold?' Clare said. She could see the two men reminiscing ad infinitum. She needed focus.

'The insurance covered it, and I bore no grudge at those who had taken it.'

'Why's that?'

'Ethan and Martin Mitchell's father, I used to go to school with him. I take it you read my history before you came here?'

'The son of a train driver, born and educated in Salisbury. A financial wizard, first million at the age of twenty-five, bankrupt at twenty-six,' Clare said.

'That was a great year,' Cosford said. 'Plenty of wine, women, and song.'

'Rebuilt your fortune by the age of twenty-nine. Since then, no more bankruptcies.'

'I sailed close to the wind on a few occasions. After that, the television appearances, the wealth and this house.'

'A stately home,' Tremayne said.

'Seventeenth century. A gift from a king to one of his courtiers. I bought it cheap and fixed it up. A guided tour, Sergeant Yarwood? Or is Clare acceptable?'

'Clare's fine, and yes, I'd like to look around.'

Clare had to admit she was impressed by the man. He was, as known, in his early eighties, but he maintained the sprightliness of a man in his sixties. If Clare had not known, she would have said Tremayne was the older of the two men, although Cosford was older by more than twenty years. The house was excessively large, so much so that at the end of a twenty-minute tour Clare was exhausted.

On her return, Tremayne whispered in her ear, 'What did you find out?'

'The house was built in 1650. It has seven bedrooms, eight bathrooms, and it cost over two million pounds to renovate.'

'Apart from your poor attempt at humour, what else.'

'He's a rogue who fancies himself as a modern-day lothario.'

'Did he try it on?'

'He was the perfect gentlemen, although his conversation was peppered with innuendo.'

'Could he have been in on the theft of the gold?'

'You know him and the case from back then. What do you think?'

'We could never make the connection. We came to the conclusion that the man was not involved.'

'Although he had a dubious reputation for some shady deals.'

'That's it. The man's always pushing the envelope between right and wrong. That's recorded, something he's proud of. We never found any wrongdoing on his part, and we tried, so did the insurance company, and they don't give up easily.'

'The man doesn't need the money now, judging by this house,' Clare said.

'Appearances are deceptive with these sorts of people. A lot of it is on credit, not much owned.'

'Is that the case with Cosford?'

'Who knows? What have we gained here?' Tremayne said.

'The man's a charming rogue, old enough to be my grandfather.'

'Apart from that.'

'We can't rule him out as a possible suspect, and if he was involved in an insurance fraud that went wrong, he could have wanted to silence Ethan Mitchell.'

'The letter, the voice, the church?'

'With the money that Cosford has, it's possible. It's a damn sight more convincing than the dead brother coming back from the grave.'

Cosford, temporarily occupied on a phone call, returned. 'Have you decided if I'm the villain or just one of the idle rich?'

'You could be both,' Tremayne said. Clare was always astounded, even after four years as his sergeant, at how many people he knew, whether they were a minor criminal or a lord of the realm, or a man who had more money than Midas.'

'And I could be neither,' Cosford said.

'Your benevolence towards the Mitchells is unusual.'

'Not really. Life rolls its dice, none of us knows which side it's going to end up on. Ethan's and Martin's father was an ambitious man, although he never had much success. I did. And if my first big deal, the one that ultimately sent me bankrupt, hadn't worked, I could be living in a rented house, getting by on a meagre pension.'

'The first deal sent you bankrupt. How could that be good for you?' Clare asked.

'It showed me its flaw. The next deal I struck, I made sure to cover that oversight. I've made some great decisions over the years, some not so good, but you gain from them all. That must be the way with you, Tremayne. The same with you, Clare.'

'I've no mistakes to gain from yet,' Clare said.

'On your own at your age is one mistake.'

'What were you two talking about when you were gone?' Tremayne said.

'Life in general. I know about your sergeant's history, yours as well.'

'How?'

'The internet, a research company in London. As soon as Ethan Mitchell was killed and I read that you were back on the case, I found out all that I needed to know about Clare and Holchester.'

'It's some years since he died,' Clare said. 'The memories are still painful.' Cosford was right, she knew, and even though the love of her life had turned out to be a murderer, she still loved him. After three years, she had yet to meet another man to equal him, and her once regular visits out to his grave had reduced to no more than one every couple of months. Her conversation with Selwyn Cosford, a man with a refreshing outlook on life, had left her melancholy and a little sad.

'So was losing my first million, but you don't wait or give up. You need to get out there again.'

'Cosford, why did you want to keep so much gold here?' Tremayne said. He knew how Clare felt about Cosford's advice. He had been there when Holchester had died, pinned to a tree, one of the branches piercing his chest. He had heard his dying gasps, and whereas, for Clare's sake, as much as his own, he had dismissed the night that it had occurred, it still occupied his dreams occasionally. He assumed that with Clare it was almost a nightly occurrence. It was a subject they rarely discussed, but Cosford, it was apparent, did not believe in bottling up the past. His weekly programme on the television about life, about wealth, about a positive attitude, never regretting, only learning, was watched by millions.

The man's advice to Clare, Tremayne knew, was correct. He had seen her daydreaming sometimes. If her fiancé hadn't died, she would have been married by now, a child in her arms, instead of a cottage in the Woodford valley and a cat.

'I was pushing hard, another deal, and the banks were wanting to tie up my assets, have access to my bank accounts. I knew I could hide some of them, and there was no way I was going to let them have this house as security.'

'I can understand,' Clare said.

'I was certain of the deal I was working on, yet, there are always the unknowns.'

'Unknowns?' Tremayne said.

'A financial downturn in America, talk of a recession, a banking crisis. These happen all too often, more so these days. As I said, if the worst happened, and I'm never a believer in accepting that possibility, then I would have had this house and enough money in gold to survive and to rebuild my empire. Gold never loses its value, and I'd built a vault underground for it. The insurance company had checked it out, given it the all clear.'

'If the insurance company is so pedantic, how could a security van be stopped, the driver and the guard overpowered?'

'We've been through this before,' Cosford said. 'Eighteen years ago to be precise.'

'I'm just bringing Yarwood up to date.'

'It was my gold, my choice of a security company. I had used them before, not for gold, but for antiques, valuable paintings, and they had been fine.'

'But they were not.'

'That's painfully clear. Another of life's lessons learnt.'

'If it was a second-rate security company, how were you able to arrange insurance for the gold?' Clare said.

'Their security rating was high enough. The insurance was not a problem.'

'The company now?'

'They're still operating.'

Tremayne and Clare prepared to leave. Cosford took hold of Clare's arm. 'Tremayne's right to be suspicious of me, but he's wrong. I'm innocent of all crimes levelled against me. I hope you believe me,' Cosford said with an obsequious smile.

Outside the house. 'What do you reckon to him?' Tremayne said.

'A charming man.'

'Innocent?'

'Who would know? One thing's for certain, we'll be at his get-together.'

'Don't go for any more walks around the house with him.'

'I can look after myself.'

'He's a reputation to maintain. A police officer would be another notch on his belt.'

'Then maybe you should go for a walk with him,' Clare said. 'You're more his age bracket.'

'Don't get smart, Yarwood. I could have you up on a disciplinary.'

Clare looked at her DI and smiled. He replied with a grin. They both knew it was the harmless banter of two people who respected each other.

Chapter 5

Bob Galton had worked hard to achieve the position of production manager at the small engineering company where he worked. He knew he was no high-flyer, not as his brother had become, but he was a good man, his beliefs tempered in those that his parents had instilled in him. They had warned him about marrying Betty Mitchell, the lady who worked in Accounts. Not because they did not like her, they did, but because she came with baggage: two young children, a dead brother-in-law, and a recently-divorced husband who was in prison for his murder.

Bob knew one thing, it was love, and no amount of opposition from his parents would stop him. He remembered the day they married, Betty's two children as page boy and page girl. Ethan, Betty's first husband, was in prison and pleased that his children and his wife were in safe hands. Bob had visited him a couple of times in the first months of the marriage. The meetings between a murderer and an honest man had gone well. But Bob, an unadventurous man, in that he had never travelled far from Salisbury, had known that the return of his wife's first husband would present difficulties. He had spoken at length to her about what they would do if he appeared at their door one day. Could they slam the door in his face, or would they have to do what was charitable and to invite him in, offer him a bed until he could find his way? Neither had been able to come up with a satisfactory solution to the dilemma, but now it was moot as the man had died in the church, apparently at the hands of his dead brother.

'I'm sorry he's dead,' Betty said in the kitchen of the small house she occupied with Bob and Gerry. Marcia had moved out some months previously, found herself a place with her boyfriend of two years.

'If he had come here, he would never have left, you know that,' Bob said. He looked across at his wife, as lovely as the day he had met her. To him, she was the world, yet life had dealt her two cruel blows, Ethan and Gerry. Bob knew he had tried with Gerry, even attempted to engage with him on sport and outdoor activities. Gerry, he knew, wore a chip on his shoulder, no doubt a genetic trait, although it had been tough for him after his father had been sentenced for murder, and it wasn't unusual for the young Mitchell to enter the family home with a bloodied nose and a black eye.

'What about the other boy?' Bob would say.

'He's worse than me. You'll need to square it with the headmaster. I've been suspended again.'

And that was how it was for most of the young man's schooldays: periods of study, periods of suspension. The end result was that Gerry had become a competent street brawler with no qualifications and a disjointed education. Marcia, on the other hand, had breezed through school and had left with a rounded education and an academic record of achievement.

Bob wondered why the bullying, the targeting, had been levelled at Gerry and not Marcia, but Marcia had summed it up: 'They feel they need to protect me at school. With Gerry, his attitude doesn't help. They're children, they don't understand what they're doing to him.'

Marcia had only been thirteen when she had so profoundly stated the reasons, but Bob knew she was an attractive child, and then an attractive adult, the same as her mother, whereas Gerry was tall and he had the Mitchell forehead and nose, the receding chin. Marcia was beautiful, Gerry was not handsome.

Bob had known one thing in the lead-up to Ethan Mitchell's release, the life that he had led with Betty would be irrevocably changed, and he could not allow it. He was the protector of his wife and her children. The man of no action, of limited ambition and curiosity about what lies around the next corner, would need to act and decisively, but he did not know what or how. And then Ethan Mitchell was back in Salisbury, and he was dead.

***

The Reverend Trevor Jameson walked through his church. He was sad. A church to him was a place of sanctity, a place to worship the Lord, but in one foul instant it had become a place of murder. And he knew why: the Mitchells. He knew that in another few months he was to retire from preaching and would spend his time tending his garden at the back of a house he had purchased in a small village. There he would spend his remaining years in solitude and peace, but his life had been disturbed; his church had experienced violent death.

He had feared the return of Ethan Mitchell as much as others had. The man had been one of his parishioners, a man who rarely missed Sunday service. Jameson had not disliked Ethan, only felt uneasy in his presence, and then three days after he had last spoken with him, he had killed his brother. The Mitchell's lawyer had asked the reverend to be a character witness at

Ethan's trial. He had agreed, but his speech had been monosyllabic and predictable. Words such as reliable, a believer in the good book, a loving husband and father were tantamount to a negative. He knew he should have enthused more about the man on trial for murder, used words such as a credit to his family, a man with excellent prospects, a friend, but he had not, and the jury had sensed his reluctance.

'Reverend Jameson.' A voice disturbed his thoughts. Was it the Lord? Had he come to ease the pain he felt after a murder had been committed in his church?

'Reverend Jameson, Detective Inspector Tremayne.'

Slowly the vicar looked around and focussed on the two people standing in front of him. 'I'm sorry, a million miles away,' he said.

'Detective Inspector Tremayne, Sergeant Yarwood,' Tremayne said.

'Yes, of course. What can I do for you?'

'Ethan Mitchell.'

'Tragic, and here in this church. How could anyone commit such a sin in the house of the Lord?' Jameson said.

'People commit a crime anywhere,' Clare said.

'We can't hold any more services here, not until it's been re-consecrated.'

'It's still a crime scene,' Tremayne said.

'I understand, but why would someone kill Ethan Mitchell and in here?'

'According to the letter we found in one of the man's pockets, it was his brother.'

'Gavin?'

'No, Martin.'

'That's not possible. I conducted his funeral. You were here.'

'Reverend Jameson, someone was in this church with Ethan Mitchell. Where were you?'

'In the rectory. I always have an afternoon nap from two in the afternoon, up until four.'

'Who would know this?'

'Everyone. It's not a secret.'

'The church is open during that time?'

'Always. Your crime scene investigators said there were two people in here. Martin, I remember him from when he was young up until he died. It was him in that coffin.'

'We know that,' Tremayne said. 'The issue is who else could it have been, and how did they get so close to Ethan?'

'I've no idea. Ethan and Martin were a strange pair, so alike, yet not close.'

'Inseparable, even when they wanted to be.'

'One would say something, the other would finish the sentence. It's as if they were telepathic.'

'They weren't. Why did someone lure Ethan to this church? He could have been seen.'

'Ethan was the more religious. He believed in the afterlife, heaven and hell. He might not have believed in Martin coming back from the dead, but he would have been unable to stay away,' Jameson said.

'And you, Reverend Jameson, what do you believe?'

'I'll accept the possibility of Martin wanting revenge, but in this church, it was a man.'

'Your proof?'

'He was down behind the altar when Ethan came in. Your crime scene team found the evidence.'

'We've seen the preliminary report,' Tremayne said.

'It's the missing gold that everyone's thinking about,' Jameson said.

'Mitchell was shot within minutes of entering the church. There wasn't time to tell whoever where it was.'

'Why? What if Ethan was frightened enough to tell Martin?'

'Why tell Martin?' Clare said. 'He already knew, and if he's dead, what use is it to him?'

'If it wasn't Martin, then who was it?' Jameson said.

'We thought you might be able to help.'

'Not really. The Mitchell family used to come here, Betty without fail. Ethan most times.'

'How about Gavin?'

'He rarely came. He's more cynical than his brothers. He's not a believer in our saviour, not much interested in anything from what I've been told.'

'What does that mean?' Tremayne said. The three of them were sitting in the front row of the church pews.

'I've been here for many years, and I know the Mitchells very well. Maybe it's because Gavin was the older brother, but I think he was jealous of Ethan and Martin.'

'Why be jealous?'

'It's the same with sisters, one pretty, the other plain.'

'One gets all the compliments, the other gets the platitudes about their good nature, and how they'll find themselves a good man,' Clare said.

'That's it,' Jameson said, 'but with Gavin and his brothers, it was always the focus on how alike the two were and what a shame that their elder brother didn't have a twin, or how the two had a unique bond.'

'I've not seen that in Gavin,' Tremayne said.

'Not now, the man's grown up, but when he was younger, he was looking for attention and not receiving it. Whether it's had any bearing on his subsequent life, I wouldn't know.'

'Could the missing gold have been buried in here?' Clare said. 'That would explain the significance of this place.'

'It's not that,' Jameson said.

'Do you know?'

'Ethan and Martin were married at the same time, Ethan to Betty, Martin to her sister, Julie.'

'Were they twins?' Clare said.

'Betty was one year older than Julie, although they look similar. Ethan and Martin were good-hearted in their own ways, but not attractive to women. They were eighteen years old, and both still attending the church on a regular basis. Betty and her sister, they had come to Salisbury with their parents, were here for the first time. Betty's eighteen, Julie's seventeen, and the two of them act like twins, similar clothes, similar hairstyles. They see Ethan and Martin are instantly drawn to them. The two young women reciprocate.'

'A love match?' Clare said.

'One week later, the men are hand-in-hand with the women. Ten days later, it's a Wednesday, 3 p.m. and the two couples are in the church.'

'What for?'

'It's raining outside. They've nowhere to go. For some reason, I come back to the church early. The front door's bolted, but I've a key to the vestry and into the church. I come in to look around, maybe put the prayer books in their places, and there are Ethan and Betty on one side of the church, Martin and Julie on the other.'

'What were they doing?'

'They weren't holding hands.'

'Making love?'

'Yes. They see me and hurriedly attempt to get out of the church, but they've locked the front door. It's not so easy to open, and I manage to sit them down and give them a stern lecture.'

'What happened?' Tremayne said.

'They're embarrassed, especially the two women. Ethan and Martin are excited. They were probably virgins up until then, and there they are with two attractive females. Ethan and Betty, they tell me they are serious about each other. Martin and Julie tell me the same. I tell them they need to give it six months to be sure, and they agree.'

'And no more lovemaking in the church,' Clare said.

'They knew my displeasure. Anyway, six months go by, and all four are still eager to marry. Their parents agree, and they are married in this church. In time, Gerry and Marcia are born. Martin and Julie had no children. I believe it was medical, something to do with Julie, but I never enquired. Ethan and Betty seemed to be the better marriage, although Martin and Julie kept together for a few years before separating and going their own ways.'

'Martin's ex-wife?'

'She's still around. I see her from time to time.'

'We now know why 3 p.m. on a Wednesday afternoon is significant,' Clare said. 'Nobody forgets the first place they made love.'

Chapter 6

Julie, Betty's sister and the former wife of Martin Mitchell, was not pleased to see two police officers on her doorstep. 'I'm just going out. Is this important?'

'I'm Detective Inspector Tremayne,' Tremayne said as he held up his warrant card.

'And you are?' the lady of the house said, looking at Clare.

'I'm Sergeant Clare Yarwood.'

'Why are you here? If this is about Ethan, I separated from his brother over twenty years ago.'

Clare looked at the house where the woman lived. It was large and in an affluent neighbourhood. In comparison to her sister's house, Julie was living the good life.

'May we come in?' Tremayne said.

'Make sure to wipe your shoes on the mat first.'

Inside the house, the two police officers sat on chairs in the kitchen, although kitchen denigrated the splendour of the room with the latest appliances, the marble-top work areas.

'We've worked hard for this,' Julie said.

'We?' Clare said.

'Eric and me. I met my husband around the time Martin died. He's a builder, done well for himself.'

'Your sister's not doing so well,' Tremayne said.

'That's Betty's choice. She chose to marry Bob, not that he's a bad man, but he's got no ambition. Eric's an achiever, so am I. Martin held me back.'

'Children?' Clare asked.

'One boy, he's fifteen. The doctors always said it was me when Martin and I tried to have a baby. It just goes to show how wrong they can be.'

'Ethan's dead.'

'I know. Betty phoned me, so did Gavin.'

'You're not upset?'

'Should I be? Martin died eighteen years ago, and the last time I saw him was two weeks before Ethan shot him. I've not seen Ethan since.'

'Where did you see Martin?'

'At Betty's.'

'Martin spent a lot of time at her house.'

'I always checked with Betty first, and besides, if I ran into him, we'd be polite to each other.'

'When did you last see your sister?' Tremayne said.

'We met in the city, had a bite to eat and a chat. We're still close, but Betty lives a different life to me, and Eric has no time for people who have no drive.'

'Do you?'

'I can forgive Betty for being the way she is, but not Bob, and certainly not Ethan. He was a low achiever, the same as Martin. I'm not surprised that their lives turned out the way they did.'

'Ethan was in St Mark's church after receiving a letter from Martin,' Clare said.

'Betty mumbled something about it, but it made no sense to me.'

'Are you glad he's dead?'

'Not because of Martin, but what was he going to do around here? We all knew Ethan, even you, Tremayne. The man was going to cause trouble. His death is a blessing in disguise.'

'That seems to be the general view,' Tremayne said.

'What do you expect? Betty's moved on, so have I. None of us wanted to be reminded of what happened, and none of us wanted to see Ethan. He was a leper to us, but somehow he expected a warm welcome.'

'We've seen no reason to believe that is what he expected. All we know is that he was in that church on Wednesday at 3 p.m. because of a letter that was purportedly written by his dead brother.'

'It couldn't be him. We all know he's dead.'

'We all know, and Ethan wasn't likely to believe it either, but why?'

'I know the significance of the day and the time,' Julie said.

'So do we. The Reverend Jameson told us.'

'We were all young and silly back then.'

'The missing gold, what do you know about it?' Tremayne said.

'Nothing, you know that,' Julie said. 'The police and the insurance company looked for long enough, and no doubt half of the villains in Salisbury, but nobody ever found it. It's not as if any of us prospered from it.'

'You're living well,' Clare said.

'I didn't for some years, not until I met Eric. What we have is due to hard work, nothing else.'

Tremayne and Clare knew it to be true. Eric Wilson was well known throughout Salisbury and the area as a builder of quality houses.

***

Tremayne, not a person to sit in the office and type up reports, headed over to Forensics on his and Clare's return to the police station.

'You've come at the right time,' Louise Regan said. She was sitting down, having removed her glasses.

'Don't I always?' Tremayne said.

'The writing is a forgery, almost perfect. The heavy hand used shows concentration, an effort to copy Martin Mitchell's writing.'

'Professional?'

'A gifted amateur could have managed. Mitchell's writing style was not complex. A professional wouldn't have made a mistake with the ink.'

'What do you mean?'

'There's been an attempt at ageing the letter, but the ink's recent, the last two months. That can't be hidden.'

'Was the forgery done in Salisbury?'

'Impossible to tell. It could have been done in prison, even by the dead man.'

'Someone met him in that church, shot him,' Tremayne reminded Regan.

'It doesn't stop the murdered man writing the letter, and another person being in the church, does it?'

'It doesn't, but it complicates it.'

'That's up to you, Tremayne. The letter's a forgery, the writing is recent. I'll put it into an official report, but there's nothing much that is going to help you with your enquiry.'

'My money is on one of the man's family being guilty.'

'Gambling's not one of your strong skills from what I've heard,' Regan said.

'I do alright.' Tremayne knew that his lack of success with betting on the horses was well known. He'd prefer not to be reminded of it, but he had no intention of stopping. To him, it was no costlier than a hobby, and it gave him pleasure, even if at the bemusement of others who should mind their own business.

Tremayne returned to Homicide, but not before standing outside the building for a smoke. He had started to cough more of a morning in the last couple of months than he had previously. He was concerned that it was a sign of illness to come. His father had smoked, more than he did, and he had lived until his late eighties, but then he had never experienced stress, never investigated a murder.

Inside the office Clare was hard at work, typing on her laptop. 'Anything interesting?' she said as he walked past her desk.

'It's a forgery,' Tremayne said. Clare could smell the cigarette on his clothes. It was offensive, and she could have complained, but that wasn't how their relationship worked. She put up with his smoking; he put up with her occasional melancholy.

'I need forty-five minutes,' Clare said.

Tremayne could see the moistness in her eyes. 'Do you want me to go with you?' he said.

'Today, I would. It's three years this week since Harry died.'

The two left the police station, Clare driving. The village of Avon Hill, once so sinister, was almost pleasant as they drove through it.

At the churchyard, they walked over to where Clare's long-dead fiancé was buried. 'Not much has changed since you were last here,' Tremayne said.

'After today, I'll only come on special occasions. I've been in mourning for too long,' Clare said.

Tremayne knew that was what she wanted to do, but he knew she was a sensitive woman, and she would continue to visit the man's grave for a long time into the future, or until she met someone else. The vicar came over. 'Tremayne, Clare, how are you both?'

'We're fine,' Tremayne said. He thought the vicar's comment to be insensitive. How could his sergeant be expected to be fine? She was standing next to the grave of a man she had loved.

Tremayne moved away with the man. 'Avon Hill, what's it like?' he asked.

'Those that are still here are overly religious. It's as if they're atoning for their sins.'

'Their only crime was that they allowed the paganists to hold sway over the village for so long.'

After Clare had finished placing some flowers and had said a few words, she walked over to Tremayne and the vicar. 'I could do with a drink,' she said.

'The local pub is under new management. It even won an award for its cuisine,' the vicar said.

'Anywhere except there,' Clare said. Tremayne could only agree. It was from there that the paganists had commenced their death march down to the church, intent on mass murder.

'We'll find somewhere on the way,' Tremayne said.

In the car, as they were leaving the village, Clare turned to Tremayne. 'No more sitting at home with only a cat for comfort. From now on, I intend to enjoy myself, find someone else.'

The two police officers found another pub. The publican was jovial – it seemed to be a quality that all publicans had. 'A pint of beer and a glass of wine,' he said. 'How about something to eat?'

'A steak for me,' Tremayne said.

'I'll have a salad,' Clare said.

'You'll waste away, not eating.'

'You're making up for me.'

'Ethan and Martin have a sister,' Tremayne said in an attempt to stop Clare thinking about her late fiancé.

'What about her?'

'Poor as a church mouse. She lives in a council flat, barely makes enough to feed herself. She may give us an insight, she may even know who the murderer could be.'

'She may even have the gold.'

'She could not have removed it from wherever it was.'

'Why?'

'You'll see.'

Chapter 7

Tremayne was correct in telling Clare to wait and meet Sandra Mitchell before passing judgement on the woman. The block of flats where she lived, no more than a two-minute walk from the police station on Bemerton Road, was not an impressive building. It had been built in the early sixties when the demand for public housing was at its peak, and the government of the day was willing to embrace the less fortunate. Six stories, two lifts, a graffitied entrance to the building, with all the flats fronting onto an outside walkway. Tremayne remembered checking out a flat in the building when he had first arrived in the city. He and his colleagues had rejected the flat, as they were into partying, and the flats were not conducive to a few drinks, a few sing-alongs, and too much noise.

Even back then, the building had been depressing. But now, although it had been freshly painted and some maintenance had been done, the lift up to the third floor rattled as it slowly made its way up to Sandra Mitchell's flat.

'Next time, I'll take the stairs,' Clare said.

'Next time, I'll join you,' Tremayne said.

The lift came to a jarring halt, the doors slowly opened. 'I need a cigarette,' Tremayne said.

Clare looked over at her senior. She did not like the look of him. It had only been in the last few weeks that she had noticed a deterioration in his condition. The man, of a morning, coughed until he had drunk a mug of coffee and had smoked his first cigarette. The weather was not suitable for being outside, even at ground level, but in that open passageway on the third floor the cold wind was biting.

'Don't take long,' Clare said. 'We've got to interview this woman, and then there's plenty else we can be doing.' She knew she should have mentioned his cough, and the fact that he wasn't looking well, but she decided against it for the moment. She realised she would have to at some stage, and why hadn't Jean said something to him? With Tremayne savouring his cigarette, Clare moved away and walked to the other end of the outside walkway. She made a phone call.

'Hello,' the voice at the other end said on answering.

'Jean, it's Clare. Just a quick call. Tremayne, he's coughing, not looking too good.'

'I've noticed, but you know how sensitive he is about criticism.'

'I do,' Clare said.

'It's up to us to look after him, although he mustn't know we're in collusion.'

'Agreed, let's meet soon and discuss what to do.'

'He's a cantankerous man, but you can't help loving him, can you?'

'I suppose not.' Clare ended the call.

'Who was that you were talking to?' Tremayne said as he wandered up the walkway to Clare.

'No one important. What number is the flat?'

'315.'

Tremayne knocked on the door of the flat. It opened.

'Tremayne, it's been some years,' Sandra Mitchell said.

Clare could see why the woman could not have picked up the missing gold. She used a wheelchair, and she looked very frail.

'Can we come in?' Tremayne said.

'Please do, and who's the pretty young woman with you?'

'Don't tell her she's pretty. She's hard enough to deal with as it is.'

'Detective Sergeant Clare Yarwood,' Clare said as she put her hand forward to shake Sandra Mitchell's hand.

'Tremayne, he doesn't mean what he says, you know that?' Sandra said.

'I know he's sparing with his compliments.'

'And besides, you are pretty, regardless of what Tremayne may say.'

'If you two have finished criticising me, can we come in?'

The small one-bedroom flat was spotless, with not one item out of place.

'The place is a credit to you,' Clare said.

'I like it tidy, and I'm always here.'

'You used to get out and about,' Tremayne said.

'If Betty comes over, she'll take me out, but she's been worried for a few weeks about Ethan, and now he's dead.'

'Why are you in the wheelchair, if you don't mind me asking?' Clare said.

'A foolish accident. I was sixteen, the love of my life was seventeen, and he had just bought himself a motorbike. He thought he was invincible. I'm on the back, and we're hurtling around the corners, leaning this way and that, until the front wheel gave way on an oily patch. He ended up in the hospital for a couple of weeks, I ended up in the wheelchair.'

Death by a Dead Man's Hand

'Sorry about that.'

'Nothing to be sorry about. There's nothing I can't do, and if I need, I can hobble around on crutches for a short distance.'

'The love of your life?'

'I sometimes see him around. I don't know what was so special about him then, and it's certainly no longer love, more like pity.'

'Why's that?'

'His life hasn't turned out so good. From what I'm told, he's been married a couple of times, the second wife taking the house and the children. Nowadays, you'll find him propping up the bar in a pub somewhere.'

'And you?'

'I married a good man. We had twelve years together, Norman and me, but he died a few years ago.'

'I'm sorry,' Clare said.

'No need to be. We never had much in the way of money, but we were content. It was cancer that got him in the end. Anyway, you're not here to talk about me, are you?'

'No,' Tremayne said.

'Ethan's coming back here was always going to raise anger, reawaken memories that should have been long forgotten.'

'If he had knocked on your door, would you have let him in?' Clare asked.

'After so many years, I would have.'

'At the time of Martin's murder?'

'We were all confused. Ethan and Martin, they were always trouble, but they were family. And both of them were kind to me. When Martin died, we had the double problem of his murder and Ethan being the murderer. It sapped the spirit out of our parents. They did not live long after that. Our mother became obsessive around the house, and she wouldn't even go out, except on infrequent occasions, and our father, he was remote, always shaking his head and mumbling to himself as to why.'

'And you?'

'For some time, I was emotional, but then Norman came along, and we were married within a few months. The last time my mother left the house was when she came to our wedding.'

'Ethan was in St Mark's church because he had received a letter from Martin,' Tremayne said. 'Did you know this?'

'Betty phoned.'

'Julie?'

'She hasn't phoned yet.'

'Is she the same as Betty?'

'She's married well, considers us all a little beneath her, but she's good to me.'

'Betty told you about the letter and Ethan being in the church. Can you understand why?'

'Ethan and Martin, two men who thought alike. When they were young, they loved the attention, but when they got older, it annoyed them.'

'But they were always together.'

'They couldn't help themselves. If one was thinking of going to the pub or wherever, the other would be thinking the same. It's eerie, but that's how it was.'

'Ethan's in that church. He's waiting for Martin, knowing it can't be him,' Clare said. 'What do you think was going through Ethan's mind?'

'Ethan's confused. He's been in prison for seventeen years for killing his counterpart, his nemesis, himself. He's in Salisbury because he has nowhere else to go. He couldn't have resisted the invitation.'

'Could he have believed it was his long-dead brother?'

'I'd not seen him for over ten years. Back then, he wouldn't have, but prison changes people.'

'It does and not always for the best,' Tremayne said.

'No one in our family wanted to see Ethan, but no one would have turned him away. If we were not sure what to do, how about Ethan? Maybe he was glad to be free, maybe he wasn't. He's had all those years of the prison looking after him. It would have been his support mechanism, and now, he's on the outside, and he's looking to us to take over from the prison authorities, but we can't. We're not a bad family, no worse than most others, but we can't show compassion regardless of how much we want to.'

'And how about you, Sandra? Are you pleased Ethan's dead?'

'I'm pleased for everyone involved, even Ethan. Now, we can get on with our lives.'

'The missing gold?'

'It's just an inert metal. Of what use is it to me?'

'To the others in your family?'

'They would appreciate it, who wouldn't?'

'But you wouldn't.'

'What use is the money to me? I've no interest in expensive cars, trips to the continent, or a mansion. This place serves my needs.'

As Tremayne and Clare walked the short distance back to the police station, they discussed the visit with Sandra.

'She seems fine,' Clare said.

'She probably is, but it doesn't mean she told us the whole truth, does it?' Tremayne said.

'How do we find out?'

'We interview others who know the story.'

'Such as?'

'The two security guards on the night the gold was stolen.'

'Do you know where they are?'

'I did eighteen years ago.'

'Which means I'll be searching on the internet for updated contact details,' Clare said.

'It's either you or me,' Tremayne said.

'We don't have that long. I'll find them for you.'

'I knew you would.'

***

As Tremayne left Bemerton Road Police Station that night, it was past nine in the evening. A lone man approached him. 'Inspector Tremayne,' he said.

Tremayne, not used to being accosted outside the station, looked at the man; an instant judgement was needed. Was the man dangerous? Was he aggressive? Was he a threat?

Tremayne decided that none of the three applied.

'I'm Bob Galton, Betty's husband,' the tall, thin man said. Tremayne could see he was not the sort of person to cause trouble. He wore a suit, the tie undone. In one hand he carried a newspaper, in the other a small bag. 'Can we talk?'

'In the police station?'

'I'd prefer a pub,' Galton said.

'A man after my own heart,' Tremayne said.

The two men strolled across from the station and entered a pub. It was not Tremayne's favourite, as the publican was unique in that he was not jovial or agreeable, and his beer was not the best.

'What is it? Tremayne said after he had bought himself and Galton a pint each.

'I'm worried for Betty.'

'Why?'

'She failed to tell you the truth.'

'Ethan had contacted her?'

'No. It's more serious than that. I need your word that you'll not act against Betty for what I need to tell you.'

'If it's a criminal offence, then I can't give you that promise.'

'I need to trust you. Betty's a good woman, law-abiding, the glue that unites our family. If she's arrested, then I have judged you wrong.'

'Why are you risking her freedom?'

'Betty knows where the gold bars are hidden.'

Tremayne, shocked by the revelation, picked up his pint of beer and drank it down in one gulp. He then looked in the direction of the publican and lifted the empty glass.

'How long has she known this?'

'Two days after Martin died.'

'How?' Tremayne said as he picked up his replenished glass of beer.

'Betty visited Ethan at the Police Station. He slipped her a piece of fabric ripped from the bottom of his shirt. On it was written the instructions as to where to find it.'

'Why would he do that?'

'He loved and trusted Betty, the same as I do. That's why I'm telling you.'

'Does Betty know you're here?'

'She suspects that I will do anything to protect her. We haven't spoken about my meeting you tonight.'

'And meeting with me is protection?'

'Before, when Ethan was in prison, everyone thought he knew where the gold was. No one suspected that someone else might know, but now, it's all changed.'

'Do you know who killed Ethan?'

'Not me, nor Betty. I'm what you see, middle management. I don't get involved in crime or loutish behaviour. I do my job, go home to my wife, look after her children, although with Gerry that was difficult.'

'He speaks highly of you, so does Marcia.'

'A lovely woman, and in many ways, Gerry's a good man. He's respectful to me, kind to his mother. Unfortunately, the Ethan Mitchell blood runs through his veins.'

'You met Ethan,' Tremayne said.

'A couple of times when he was in prison. We got on fine, and he understood Betty divorcing him and marrying me.'

'What has Betty done with the knowledge of where the gold is?'

'Nothing. She's kept the secret all these years.'

'Did you know?'

'Not until after Ethan died. Betty told me then.'

'And now you're telling me. Why?'

'Isn't it obvious? Whoever killed Ethan knew something. Either it was the location of the gold or the name of somebody who knew. Betty's in danger, I'm sure of it.'

'We need this gold in our possession,' Tremayne said. 'Do you have the details?'

'Not me. What about Betty? Is she in trouble with the police?'

'Why did she keep it secret?'

'I don't know, but she never told anyone, nor did she want the gold. As she told me, crime only leads to violence and death and sadness. She is quite possibly the most honest person you'll ever meet.'

'You were right to tell me. We'll need to talk to her tonight.'

'The sooner, the better. If you have the gold, then whoever killed Ethan has no reason to kill Betty.'

'Or you,' Tremayne said. 'You've seen the instructions. I'm right, aren't I?'

'Yes,' Bob Galton replied meekly.

Chapter 8

By the time Tremayne arrived at Betty and Bob's house, it was nearly eleven in the evening. It had started to rain, a slight drizzle, which reflected the downcast mood the detective inspector felt. He knew that he did not want to arrest Betty, wasn't sure if he could avoid it. She had concealed vital evidence for eighteen years; evidence that could have possibly helped at her first husband's trial. And if the gold were not found after the woman handed over the information she had, then it would reflect poorly on her. Although judging by the way that she lived, she had not benefited from the money.

Bob Galton waited in his car, as did Tremayne. After a few minutes, Clare drove up. She parked her car and walked over to Tremayne's. 'New evidence?'

'I wanted you here. This changes everything.'

The three, Tremayne, Clare, and Bob, walked up the short pathway to the house. Once inside, Bob showed the two police officers to the sitting room and put on the electric fire. He then left them and went upstairs.

After a few minutes, Betty entered the sitting room. 'Bob's told me,' She was wearing a dressing gown with slippers on her feet. 'I've not been near it.'

'You've concealed vital information. It's a criminal offence, I could have you arrested,' Tremayne said.

'You agreed to protect her,' Bob Galton said, leaping to his wife's defence.

'Mr Galton, we did not discuss that. You came to me out of concern for your wife. No doubt commendable, but there are other realities here.'

'You'll not arrest Betty?'

'It depends on what she tells us.'

Betty looked over at her husband. 'You did the right thing, whatever happens,' she said.

Clare could see genuine love between the two people.

'Betty, where's this information that Ethan gave you?'

The woman reached into her dressing gown pocket and pulled out a piece of white fabric. Clare took hold of it and held it up to a light in one corner of the room. 'I can just about make it out,' she said. 'We should ask Forensics if they can enhance the writing.'

'Not tonight,' Tremayne said. He took out his phone from his pocket and called Louise Regan. 'We've got a rush job,' he said.

'Don't you ever go to bed?' Regan said.

'It's an important lead. What time will you be in the office?'

'What time do you want me?'

'Five.'

'Hell, Tremayne. Some of us are mortal, some of us need our beauty sleep.'

'I'm beyond worrying,' Tremayne said. Clare wanted to offer a comment but did not.

'Make it six,' Louise Regan said. She then ended the phone call.

'Yarwood, 6 a.m. with Forensics.'

Tremayne turned to Betty. The man was on a high, Clare could see that. She knew she wouldn't be getting much sleep that night. 'Betty, this is serious. Your husband is right. You couldn't have kept this concealed any longer, and your life is in danger if anyone suspects you know where the gold is.'

'I've told you what I know. My life isn't threatened now, is it?'

'If the gold's there, it's not.'

'I've not been near it. Ethan told me in confidence. He wasn't sure what to do, and he loved his family. He always wanted our lives to be better, but all I wanted was for him to be here with us. This place is not palatial, but we survive. But Ethan, he was always there looking for the big chance.'

'And the big chance killed Martin, and ultimately killed Ethan. What did Ethan expect you to do with the gold?'

'I don't know what Ethan thought. Maybe he thought I'd find a way to dispose of it, and that way, our lives would be better. But I've no idea, and I had no intention of asking anyone for advice.'

'Gavin, your brother-in-law, said that he would have known how to dispose of it.'

'Knowing and doing are two separate things. Gavin's an honest man. He'd not jeopardise his freedom for the gold.'

'He could have sold the information to someone, the same as you could have.'

'There were a few who accosted me in the months after Ethan's arrest, one of them was very threatening. Even said that he would grab Marcia and that I'd never see her again.'

'What did you do?'

'I did nothing, only made sure to protect my children the best I could.'

'You could have told us, shown us the location,' Clare said.

'I had made a promise to Ethan that I would never reveal what I knew.'

'But why?'

'A promise is a promise. I did what I thought was right, what I still think is right.'

'Betty, we'll locate this gold tomorrow. In the meantime, I'll consider what you've done.'

'Will you take action against Betty?' Galton asked.

'Your wife's got enough to deal with at the present time.'

Outside, it was raining more heavily than before. Tremayne lit up a cigarette.

'Will we arrest Betty Mitchell?' Clare said.

'It's unlikely, but she was foolish holding onto the directions for so long.'

'The man she loved had asked her to keep it secret. She had no option.'

'Yarwood, your notion of right and wrong is clouded by romantic notions. You don't sit at home reading Mills and Boon novels every night, do you? This is the real world. If Betty Mitchell has committed a criminal offence, it'll make no difference that her first husband has been murdered, her son has been remanded for the break-in at a jeweller's shop.'

***

Louise Regan was in her office at six in the morning, as agreed with Tremayne. Clare apologised on entering ten minutes later. 'I didn't get to bed until after two this morning.'

'That's what you get when you work with Tremayne.'

Clare took the piece of fabric from the evidence bag and handed it over to Regan. 'It's in reasonable condition,' the forensic expert said.

'We could just about make it out last night, but one or two of the directions are faded.'

'Give me thirty minutes, help yourself to a coffee,' Regan said. Clare could see why Tremayne respected the woman. She was professional, direct, and she knew what she was doing. She was also in the office at six in the morning, when others in the building would have told Tremayne eight. Clare sat down, still tired. She closed her eyes, only to be woken up with a start.

'Here's a printout,' Louise Regan said.

Clare studied what it said and then phoned Tremayne. She realised he had taken the luxury of sleeping in for a bit longer than her. 'We need a team this morning,' she said.

'In my office, thirty minutes. Grab a few constables from the station, make sure they're kitted out,' Tremayne said.

'The crime scene investigators?'

'Let Jim Hughes know. After so many years, there may not be much to find, but if someone's been there since it was hidden, then who knows.'

Clare phoned Hughes. 'I'll be there,' his reply.

Clare knew it was not necessary for him to come and he could have delegated his responsibility, but the lure of buried treasure intrigued everyone.

After a briefing in Tremayne's office with Clare and three uniforms seconded to assist, the police convoy headed off in the direction of Emberley, a small village not far from the hijacking site of eighteen years previously. Following the instructions given, the team turned left after entering the village and headed to the intersection leading up to Longmore House.

As the police vehicles stopped alongside the gatehouse at the entrance to Longmore Park, a few of the locals appeared. 'They won't like it, your parking there,' one of them said.

'Who won't?' Tremayne said.

'Lord and Lady Linden, they're up at Longmore House. You should let them know you're here.'

Tremayne looked over at Clare. 'Go up there and let them know.'

Clare left, taking one of the locals with her. She returned within ten minutes.

'That was quick,' Tremayne said.

'They were very polite. I explained the reason, and they said to carry on. It's a magnificent house, they've offered to show me around when I'm free. It's not often I get to meet with the aristocracy.'

'They put their trousers on one leg at a time, the same as us,' Tremayne said.

Clare knew what he meant, but she also knew why he had sent her. She had been educated in an exclusive school, spoke with a refined accent. Tremayne, she knew, still had a Cornish accent, endearing in its way, but explaining to the landed gentry was more for her than for him.

'According to the directions, there's a ruined outhouse, ten feet from the back of the gatehouse,' Tremayne said.

The uniforms slowly moved forward, removing the undergrowth as needed. Jim Hughes and his team stayed close, making sure that no vital evidence was disturbed.

'I've found it,' one of the uniforms shouted.

'Stay where you are,' Hughes said. 'We'll take it from here.'

'At the left of the outhouse, there's a small pit with a metal grille. It's about five feet from where you are.'

'Found it,' Hughes said. 'It's overgrown. It'll take us some time to clear it away and check inside. What was it for?'

'No idea. Something to do with the outhouse, I suppose,' Tremayne said.

Clare and Tremayne kept their distance. The locals were curious about what was going on. Tremayne gave them enough information to satisfy them.

'The grille's off,' Hughes shouted. 'There's space down here.'

'I'll be up,' Tremayne said. He had already kitted up in coveralls with overshoes and gloves.

'I'll go down first,' Hughes said. 'I don't want you destroying the evidence.'

Two minutes later. 'Yarwood, we need you up here. Hughes is packing a few pounds, and I'm creaking in the knees. You're the only one slim enough.'

Clare was surprised by her senior's admission that he was not one hundred per cent fit. She was glad that Superintendent Moulton wasn't around to hear it.

At the entrance to the hole in the ground, Clare could see the problem. A tree root which had probably been smaller eighteen years previously had expanded and was impeding an easy entry.

'We've lowered a light for you, and there seems to be something down there. If you confirm it's the gold, we'll cut the root away.'

Clare lowered herself into the hole, Hughes and Tremayne assisting; more hindering if she had been truthful. She knew from her childhood that dark and confined spaces did not excite her, and the area under the ground was restricted, although not dark with the light that the crime scene team had placed in the hole.

'It's full of spiders,' Clare said from inside.

Death by a Dead Man's Hand

'They're harmless,' Tremayne shouted back, his voice echoing around the chamber.

'Harmless they may be, but they're crawling over me.'

'Any gold?' Hughes shouted.

'It's here,' Clare said. 'I can see ten, maybe twelve, bars.'

'There's twenty, or there should be,' Tremayne said.

'You can cut that branch and get someone else down here. They're too heavy for me to lift and I'm not staying down here indefinitely.'

'Okay, up you come. The gold solves one problem, opens up more questions.'

'You can tell me over a cup of coffee. Do they have a coffee shop in the village?'

'We'll find one soon enough,' Tremayne said.

Chapter 9

The Plough Inn in Emberley, as with pubs up and down the country, was no longer serving just beer and snacks. Now a full gourmet meal was available, or in the case of Clare and Tremayne, a coffee each.

'The most excitement we've seen for a while,' the publican said. He was a weathered man on the wrong side of seventy, with a red nose and a ruddy complexion.

'Looks like he's his own best customer,' Tremayne said to Clare, who was looking the worse for wear after being in the hole in the ground. 'What was the hole for?' he said.

'I'd say it was something to do with the outhouse.'

'Outhouse being a polite word for a toilet?'

'I suppose so. The smell wasn't too good down there either, although it must be a long time since anyone used it.'

Tremayne remembered back to his childhood and the walk down the garden to the outside toilet in the middle of winter. Back then, it was cold baths, and not too often, toilets that were none too hygienic, and insects. He had to admit he appreciated the modern facilities at his house, and with Jean in semi-residence, the smell of lavender, and clean towels.

'Is all the gold there?'

'I didn't stay down to count. I saw ten, maybe twelve, and someone had thrown down some old clothes to cover them.'

'Clothes, that makes little sense,' Tremayne said. He was glad it had been his sergeant in the hole, not him.

Death by a Dead Man's Hand

He would not admit it, but he had a lingering fear of confined spaces, as a result of a childish prank of climbing down a well at home when he was a child. He and his brother had dared each other, Tremayne being the bravest. He had entered the well, eased himself down for three feet, fallen another ten. It had been his father who had pulled him out, and it was him who had administered the belt to the bare backside of both the young boys.

'Clothes, rags? I couldn't see that well, and I wasn't picking them up to check.'

'Why?'

'There wasn't enough room to swing a cat in there.'

'We'll leave it up to Jim Hughes and his people to check it out. How does this impact the murder investigation?'

'It might prevent further murders.'

'Or create more tension.'

'It would need someone small enough to get down that hole.'

'Ethan wouldn't have been able to, nor would anyone in his family. Selwyn Cosford, a likely candidate for swindling an insurance company, isn't particularly small either.'

'Then why that hole, and who knew it was there? Even eighteen years ago it was remote, and not the sort of thing anyone would stumble on easily.'

'It has to be someone with local knowledge,' Tremayne said. He called over the publican.

'Another coffee?' the publican said.

'One for yourself, as well. We've a few questions.'

'Coffee, that's for the visitors. I'll have a pint. Are you sure you don't want one, Inspector? You look to be a drinking man.'

'It's alright, guv,' Clare said. 'I could do with a glass of wine.'

It was still not midday, yet the three in that pub were content to indulge themselves: the publican because he was alcoholic, Tremayne because he appreciated a good quality beer and the pub sold his favourite, and Clare because she was feeling less than her best after spending time in the bowels of the earth. She was also not willing to admit that she had felt scared in that hole as if its surrounds were pressing in on her.

'What do you want to know?' the publican said as he sat down next to Clare.

'Has the local gossip filtered up to here yet?' Tremayne said.

'The gold you've found.'

'That's it.'

'I received a phone call not so long ago. Is it from that van that was hijacked?'

'Almost certainly. What do you know about it?'

'Nothing really. The van was stopped not far from here. I remember one of the hijackers was killed.'

'Martin Mitchell.'

'There's a Tony Mitchell in the village.'

'Where do we find him?'

Two doors down. A small bungalow, white picket fence. He's getting on a bit, and he doesn't go far. He's here every lunchtime. You could set your clock by him.'

'Where we found the gold, what can you tell us about it?'

'Not a lot. They don't like people on their land, not that I can blame them. I've been up to Longmore house once, a special invite. They wanted to bring their wealthy friends down here to sample a traditional English pub. They wanted to check me out before they came. To make sure the pub and our food were up to their standard.'

'Was it? Were you?'

'They changed the menu, improved it actually. Apart from that, I was traditional enough. They came down here a few days later, a few famous faces. Everyone had a great night, and we all got to meet a few celebrities. Apart from then, they keep to themselves, and they like Longmore Park to be left alone.'

'Tell us about Mitchell?'

'Nothing to tell really. The man's retired, minds his business. He comes in here, has a couple of pints, a chat with everyone, and then goes back to his place. He's a keen gardener, often wins a couple of prizes at the annual fete.'

***

'If it's about what they found at the gatehouse, you're wasting your time,' Tony Mitchell, a sprightly man dressed in a white shirt and a pair of navy trousers said.

'DI Tremayne, and this is Sergeant Yarwood, we'd appreciate a few words with you.'

'Very well, come in, and don't mind the dog. His bark is worse than his bite.' Clare looked at the dog on the other side of the gate leading to the front garden. All she could see was a tired terrier-like animal of indeterminate breeding.

Outside the small bungalow, the garden was immaculate, the borders of the small lawn precise. The flowers, not blooming due to the season, were all in a line, as were the vegetables in the rear garden. It was clear that a guided tour around the garden was the price for some of the man's time. Tremayne wasn't into gardening, Clare was.

'It's important to talk to them,' Mitchell said as he discussed with Clare how to grow prize-winning vegetable marrows.

In the bungalow, small and quaint, the three sat down. Mitchell chose an old wooden chair, the two police officers made themselves comfortable on a sofa.

'I don't have much to do with the family,' Mitchell said.

'You know why we're here?' Tremayne said. The man was familiar, although he couldn't place him. Over the years, he had got to know all of the Mitchells, good and bad, but this man was proving difficult. He had the look of a Mitchell, the thin nose, the drooping shoulders, the weak chin, but he didn't seem the same. 'Have we met before?' Tremayne said, unable to rack his brain further.

'Martin's funeral, that's the only time I can remember. Mind you, you were a few years younger then, so was I.'

'Why did you mention the gatehouse when we arrived?'

'Two and two make four. In my book it does.'

'Which means?' Tremayne struggled when people made oblique remarks as if they knew something that he should know as well.

'I saw the police cars up at the gatehouse, figured you were looking for the gold.'

'Did you know it was there?'

'Not me. And as I told you, I don't have much to do with the rest of the family.'

'Why's that?'

'Martin and Ethan, they're nephews of mine. Their father was a second cousin. I suppose that makes them third cousins, but that sounds wishy-washy. Best just to call them nephews, and they always called me uncle. When they were younger, their mother used to bring them out here. She had this idea that the country air would do them good, help to control their errant ways.'

'How old were they?'

'The twins, maybe ten or eleven. They came a few times, and then they didn't.'

'Any reason?'

'They thought riding a bicycle over my vegetables was fun, I didn't. I put them on the bus within half an hour, and that was that. I've not seen them since, apart from funerals.'

'Again, why did you mention the gatehouse when we arrived?'

'Missing gold, Ethan and Martin, police cars. Did you find it?'

'We did, but why did you make the association?'

'I'd never thought about it before, but the twins were into all sorts of mischief. I know they had been into Longmore Park on a couple of occasions. The estate manager brought them back once, gave me an ear bashing about irresponsible children and it was up to the parent to discipline them.'

'You weren't the parent,' Clare said. The dog, unattractive as it was, was sitting close to her. She didn't know why it was that wherever she went with Tremayne, the animals gravitated towards her, and not him.

'Not that the estate manager cared. He had to answer to those up at the main house, and the one thing they didn't like were unwelcome visitors, especially children bent on mischief, on their land.'

'What did you do?'

'Apologised the best I could and gave the twins a good talking to.'

'Any point?' Tremayne said.

'In one ear, out the other, although after that they kept out of the park. The next day they're on a bus to Salisbury, and I'm glad of it.'

'Their mother?'

'What could she say? She knew what they were. Mind you, Gavin, their brother, used to come out, and sometimes Marcia, Ethan's daughter, drops in for a few minutes. Apart from that, I keep my distance.'

Tremayne realised that certain aspects of what the man was saying didn't ring true. For one thing, why the gatehouse, and why now? And why hadn't the man figured it out when the gold went missing.

Tremayne looked around the room, noticed no photos of a family. It reminded him of his home before Jean had returned into his life, although Mitchell's was a lot tidier than his had ever been, and his attempts at gardening had been few and far between; more of the far if he thought about it.

'When you first heard about Martin's death, what did you think?'

'I didn't hear for a day. I'm not one for watching the television, and I wasn't in contact with my relatives. The day after, I'm in the pub, and someone mentions about Martin.'

'Who was it?'

'The estate manager, a gruff Welshman. Everyone called him Taff. He'd seen it on the news, thought I'd be interested.'

'The same man who returned the twins?'

'The same one. He's dead now, so you can't go questioning him. His wife's still around, not that she'd be able to help you much.'

'What did he say?'

'Nothing much, just some snide comment about how he had known that the two of them would come to no good, not that he can talk.'

'What do you mean?'

'His son ended up in jail a few years later, dealing in drugs. The shame of it killed the man.'

'Did you go into Salisbury to offer your condolences to Martin's family?'

'I did my duty.'

'Which means you had to agree with the estate manager.'

'And why not? I could see, even when they were young, that they were destined for a life of crime. Neither of them was too bright, and both thought the world owed them a living, not the other way around. I've always worked hard, never asked for charity, and there they are, the family asking me to help with paying for the funeral.'

'What did you do?'

'I told them what I thought of them, and then I stuck my hand in my pocket, gave them what I could afford.'

'Why?'

'Guilt, I suppose. I could see them getting into trouble, and I was the one who put them on that bus. If they had kept coming out here, who knows? My influence may have helped, maybe it wouldn't.'

'You've not explained why you didn't figure out the gatehouse as the hiding place for the gold all those years before.'

'No reason to. I've not got a criminal mind, and I don't go looking for hiding places. Hindsight is a wonderful thing, but don't go trying to pin anything on me. Martin got what he deserved, so did Ethan.'

'You're a hard man,' Clare said.

'I was brought up to believe that a man is what he makes of himself. Ethan and Martin certainly did that, and from what I hear, so has Ethan's son. Marcia, now there's a bright young woman, out there working hard, and Gavin, Ethan's brother, he's more like me. Not too sociable, not making much money, but he's honest.'

'Ethan's and Martin's wives?'

'Betty, Ethan's wife, a good person, tried her best, but with Ethan and then her son, she's had more than a few crosses to bear. Julie, Martin's widow, she always saw herself as better than the rest. She married that Eric Wilson, and good luck to her.'

'Why do you say that?' Clare said.

'I know him. Before I retired, I was a roofer. I did a few jobs for the man, always had problems with him when it came to payment.'

'Apart from that?'

'He's just tough, that's all. I'm a pay on the spot type of person, and I don't like owing, but Wilson, he thrived on credit. Successful though.'

'Honest?'

'No doubt he cheats on his taxes, claims his wife's car as a business expense when all she does is swan around the place with her rich friends.'

'Betty never had much money.'

'She married a decent man after Ethan, but he's a dreamer. Works hard, no doubt, and he tried. If it had been me, Gerry would have felt the belt from me, may have done him some good, but from what I heard, Betty and what's-his-name didn't believe in corporal punishment.'

'It's archaic,' Clare said.

'Maybe it is, but it's what made this country. That and compulsory military training.'

'Conscription?'

'Why not? I did my bit for Queen and country.'

Tremayne and Clare could see that the conversation had drifted away from the present and had entered the realm of nostalgia. It was time to leave; there was still plenty to do that day.

Chapter 10

Eric Wilson could not admit to liking all of the Mitchell family, even though he had married one of them, his wife, Julie. It was his wife's house, as well as his, and if she wanted her family to be there, so be it. He only hoped they'd not scratch the marble floor in the hallway or stub their cigarettes out on the carpet.

Wilson looked around the room. There was Julie, putting the best china on display. She had arranged for a caterer to prepare food, and Wilson could see Gavin, the only remaining brother, helping himself. He had little time for the man, having found him to be singularly lacking in ambition, and then there was Betty, Julie's sister. A pleasant looking woman, he had to agree, although her life had taken its toll. Not for her the benefit of holidays overseas or health farms every few months. He knew how much they cost, but Julie made an effort to look her best. He knew about her first husband, even before they had become serious. There had been occasional words between husband and wife in the early years of their marriage when she had become sad on Martin's birthday, or the anniversary of the first wedding.

He had told her enough times that the past was the past, and it was no use feeling upset over a man who had been a waster, but she had been firm in that he had been a good man when they had first met.

In time, her looking back to the past had lessened, but seeing the entire Mitchell family in that one room, he knew they would start reflecting on what had happened, and why Ethan was in that church, and who amongst them had killed him. He knew his wife would not be in a good mood that night and for a few nights after. Wilson left them to it and went to his office on the other side of the house. He settled down, switched on the laptop, and randomly surfed the internet.

'They found the missing gold,' Gavin Mitchell said. He was not pleased to be away from his shop and the small flat above. No amount of flaunting of money with the fancy furniture and the silver tray, and the designer clothes that Julie was wearing, was going to distract him. He knew why the family was assembled. Not to discuss Ethan's funeral, and certainly not to go over a life well spent, and what a tragedy it was that he had been taken from them at such a young age.

We're here to reflect on Ethan,' Betty said. Gavin could see that she had not bought Bob Galton, her current husband with her. *Wet fish that he is*, he thought.

'Ethan's dead, killed by one of us.'

'One of the men,' Betty said.

'Not according to the police. It could have been a woman,' Gavin said.

'He was my father, and I loved him, faults and all,' Marcia said.

'But you didn't want him in our lives again, did you?' Julie said.

'I'm not sure what I feel. He had been in prison for so many years, it was hard to know what I would have done. And now we've got Gerry heading down the same road.'

'At least he hasn't got a brother he could kill, and not enough ambition to hijack a security van,' Gavin said.

'As long as he's alive, that's all I care about,' Betty said.

'He tried to rob a jeweller's, didn't even notice the security cameras, the alarms. Not very smart, if you ask me.'

'We're not asking you, Gavin. Please keep your offensive comments to yourself. She can't be expected to desert Gerry just because he's wild. Maybe with time he'll settle down,' Julie said.

'He won't,' Betty said.

'Then what are we here for?' Gavin said.

'To ensure that when the police come knocking on our doors, we're prepared.'

'Prepared for what? I've done nothing wrong.'

'Do you think they'll believe you when they find some of the bars missing?'

'Are they?' Gavin said. The woman's statement had caused everyone in the room to sit upright and to take notice.

'What do you mean?'

'Three of the bars are not there.' Betty Galton, the wife of Bob, widow of Ethan, mother of Gerry and Marcia, stood and moved over to near the window. She aimlessly looked out at the garden, not sure what to say, or how.

'Mother, what is it?' Marcia said.

Even Sandra, Ethan's and Martin's sister, attempted to lift herself out of her wheelchair. 'Are you guilty of a crime?'

'I knew where the gold was. I even took some.'

'But you live so poorly. Why?'

'I don't know. Maybe I wanted security for the future, but once I had the bars, I didn't know what to do with them.'

'Where are they now?' Gavin asked. All those years he had struggled, and there was this silly woman with close to a million pounds, and if melted down, it was untraceable.

'I've hidden them well. If I've committed a crime, then I will pay for it, but Gerry needs a competent defence lawyer, and our family, barring Julie, need help.'

'Are you willing to tell us where it is?' Gavin said, almost salivating at the thought of it. He knew why he had been honest all his life: not out of an idealistic notion of right over wrong, not because he believed in the law as opposed to crime, but because he had always feared being caught. He remembered back to a childhood indiscretion when he had stolen some chocolate from a shop, only to be apprehended and locked in a back room until a local constable had come along and given him a kick up the backside, and told him to get along, and not to err again.

'I want no part of this,' Julie said.

'That's because you don't need it,' Betty said. 'I only want it for Gerry.'

'You can't protect him, mother,' Marcia said. 'He committed the crime. He needs to be punished.'

'I know, but he will only learn from hardened criminals in prison. He will only make the mistakes that his father and uncle did.'

'I cannot be a part of this,' Sandra said.

'You need to tell the police,' Marcia said.

'I will give you forty-eight hours to decide,' Betty said. 'After that, I will throw myself on the mercy of the law, and tell them where the three bars are.'

'There'll not be much mercy,' Gavin said. 'And how long have you had this gold?'

'For sixteen years. I went out there, it was dusk, and I was frightened, but I persisted.'

'And you found it and climbed down into that hole?'

'I did. It was awful, and I couldn't use a light. I took what I could and left. I've never been back.'

'Why did you tell the police about where the gold was?'

'I felt guilty for Ethan's death. It was all because of the gold, and now he's dead. He wasn't a bad man, just unlucky, the same as Martin.'

From behind a door to the rear of the room, Eric Wilson listened. He was intrigued, and he was determined to use what he had heard to his advantage. It was true that he had worked hard to earn what he had, but there had been shortcuts, the occasional bribe, the occasional theft of building materials from another construction site in the early days. He knew what the gold could do for him. He also knew where he could dispose of it.

***

Selwyn Cosford was ebullient. Tremayne did not like it. It was him and Cosford at the man's stately home. 'It's a rare bit of luck,' Cosford said as he handed Tremayne a glass of brandy. 'It's the very best.'

'I'm still at work,' Tremayne said as he savoured the drink. He had to admit it was smooth, and if it wasn't for the circumstances, and why he was there at the behest of Cosford, and without Clare, he would have drunk more.

'It's the gold. It belongs to me, all of it.'

'I thought the insurance company paid you out,' Tremayne said. 'And why did you ask only me to come?'

The two men were sitting down in a couple of leather chairs. He had to admit the house was magnificent and Cosford certainly had good taste, but something didn't ring true, and it was niggling him. So much so, that he put down his brandy and focussed on the man opposite.

'They paid me out, sure enough, all twenty bars worth. Do you know how much it's gone up in value since then?'

'You're about to tell me.'

'Nearly five hundred per cent. It's better than money in the bank.'

'It will be evidence for a while, and doesn't it belong to the insurance company?'

'Not if I pay back what they gave me plus interest. I'll still be ahead by four hundred per cent.'

'That doesn't sound right to me,' Tremayne said. 'I thought that after they paid you out, whatever was stolen belongs to them.'

'The insurance company confuses everyone with long-winded policies full of verbiage. No one ever reads the fine print.'

'Which means you do.'

'Damn right, I do. I might have to take them to court, incur some costs, but ultimately, I'm going to make a bundle out of this.'

'Why didn't you want Yarwood here?'

'Tremayne, you've played fair by me. I want to play fair by you.'

'Are you about to offer me one of the gold bars?'

'Nothing as crass as that. Life must be tough for you. I wanted to know if there was anything I could do for you.'

'Are you trying to bribe me?'

'Not at all. You must have some worries.'

'Apart from knees that creak, and a body that fails to defy age, I've nothing to worry about.'

'But your house, your retirement?'

'I suggest we stop here,' Tremayne said, 'before you incriminate yourself and I'm forced to act.'

'I'm a man who looks after those who help him, that's all.'

'And I'm a policeman who does his job. I can envy you your success, even this house, but quite frankly, I don't want them. I want whoever killed Ethan Mitchell, nothing more.'

'You're retiring at some time. Some casual work would come in handy.'

'Selwyn, seeing that we've known each other for some years, I'll forget this conversation. I suggest you do as well.'

As Tremayne drove away from the house, he glanced in his rear-view mirror. 'All that money and he wants to bribe me,' he said out loud to himself.

***

Gavin Mitchell was a confused man. He had first opened the door to his electrical repair shop fifteen years previously, after being made redundant from the local council maintenance department. At the time, the idea of a small shop fixing electrical goods had seemed ideal for him, a man who liked to tinker. He remembered the hiding he had received after he had attempted to fix the timekeeping of the clock that sat on the mantelpiece in the main room at home when he was young – it ran slow.

In the end, after Gavin's backside had been tanned, the clock was put back where it had come from. 'It'll always remind us of Gavin,' his father had joked. The rest of the family thought it was hilarious, Gavin did not, as it was only correct twice a day, and the hands of the clock never moved again.

But now, as he surveyed his domain, Gavin, the eldest of the Mitchell brothers, realised that the business was dead. It had been three months since he had turned a profit, and that had only been marginal. He knew he was going slowly broke, and it was beyond his control. He had looked for an alternative career, but opportunities for a middle-aged man who was good at fixing things were not promising. It was the age of computers and programming, and he couldn't understand either. Sure, he could send emails, had even mastered Word and Excel, but apart from that, the complexities of the machine left him baffled.

There was unemployment, but he had never taken the dole, or he could go overseas, try his luck on an oil rig. Even if that were possible, he didn't want to go, but these were desperate times, and now, to add confusion, there was a solution. Betty Galton, his former sister-in-law, had in her possession a million pounds in gold. He opened his laptop and switched it on. *How does one melt gold? How does one dispose of it?* he thought.

He entered the search terms, fingering one key at a time, and pressed enter. If a criminal act was committed during the planning stage, then he was guilty as charged. And for once, he did not care. He hummed a tune to himself. It had been some time since he had been contented. For that night, he would forget what would be required and envisage what his life could be like with money in his pocket. Maybe a small place in the country, a dog, possibly a woman. How long had it been since he had enjoyed the closeness of another's skin?

He picked up his phone and made a call. It was a special treat for himself and for once the budget was going to be blown. He knew she'd look after him, the way she looked after so many others.

Chapter 11

Clare woke early the next day; her phone was ringing. She leant over and picked it up. 'Yarwood, I'm at the hospital,' Tremayne said.

She could tell by his voice that something was amiss. 'I'll be there in fifteen.'

'Thanks, and don't tell anyone.'

A quick shower, some food for her cat, and Clare was out of her cottage. A murder enquiry was serious; her boss being ill, more so.

Parking at the hospital, she soon found her way to outpatients, meeting someone she knew. 'It's Tremayne, he's not well,' Clare said. 'And please, not a word to anyone.'

The woman, a friend, understood. Inside, behind some screens, Tremayne was lying flat on his back. His shoes had been removed, and his tie had been loosened.

'How long have you been here?' Clare said. She knew Tremayne would not appreciate lashings of sympathy, although he looked dreadful.

'Since last night. I'd had a few drinks, a few cigarettes, and all of a sudden I'm in the back of an ambulance.'

'Does Jean know?'

'Not yet. Maybe you can phone her. She went to see her son for a few days, left me on my own.'

'Off the leash and into trouble, that's you, guv.'

'Not today, Yarwood. Maybe Moulton's right about me retiring.'

'Having you feeling sorry for yourself isn't going to help, is it?'

The nurse, standing on the other side of the bed, looked over at Clare disapprovingly. 'It's how we work,' Clare said.

'That may be the case, but Mr Tremayne has had a bit of a scare. He needs to be here for a few days while we conduct a few checks.'

'What's the problem?'

'It's not for me to say. That's for the doctor.'

'He told me to cut down on the beer, quit smoking, and take it easy.'

'Retire, is that it?' Clare said.

'They don't get it, do they?' Tremayne looked over at the nurse who was monitoring his condition. 'Sorry. We've got a murder to deal with, nothing personal.'

'Don't worry about me. We get our fair share of people, men mainly, who think they're invincible. You're not the first, not the last, who thinks they know more than the experts.'

'Call the doctor,' Tremayne said.

'You should stay, follow medical advice,' Clare said.

'And leave you on your own, now that it's getting interesting.'

'Is it worth your health?'

'I'll cut back on the cigarettes, moderate my drinking.'

'That will definitely kill you. You thrive on your bad habits.'

The doctor appeared from behind her. 'You're right. Tremayne is an old warhorse, but old horses end up in the knacker's yard eventually.'

'Yarwood, this is Doctor Warner. He's been looking after me.'

'And not getting very far. It's not the first time you've been in here, is it, Tremayne?'

'I didn't tell Yarwood last time.'

'Your boss is a stubborn and less than ideal patient,' the doctor said. Clare smiled back at the man. She immediately liked him.

'Hard work never hurt anyone,' Tremayne said.

'I would agree with you there, but beer and cigarettes will. It's either you give some of them up, or you'll be singing at the pearly gates, hoping they'll let you in.'

'Not me, sounds too boring. I reckon the other place would be more interesting, that's where all the villains go.'

'And police officers who don't follow qualified medical advice. And I don't intend to inflict you on all those sinners just yet. You'll have them all arrested within a week, hanging from the gallows in two.'

'And take that smug look off your face, Yarwood,' Tremayne said.

'Tremayne, I'm discharging you into the care of Sergeant Yarwood. If you come in here one more time in this condition, I'll make it official and report it to Superintendent Moulton,' the doctor said.

'You and Yarwood should get together, a right pair of killjoys.'

Clare smiled and looked at the doctor; he looked at her, saw she was not wearing a ring.

Tremayne sat up, eased himself around. Clare took his shoes and put them on his feet, even tying the laces for him. 'We have to look after you, doctor's orders.'

'God help me. I was better off lying on that bed.'

'It's still here if you need it,' the doctor said.

'Get me out of here, Yarwood. You and the doctor can discuss my case some other time and without me. We've got a murder to solve.'

***

Tremayne looked down at the plate in front of him. It was dinner time at the Tremayne residence. 'What's this?' he said.

'You may want to eat and drink yourself into an early grave, but as long as I'm in this house, that's what you're going to eat,' Jean said.

After Clare had phoned her, Jean, the only woman the detective inspector had loved, had returned to the house in Wilton. He had known the moment he got home that night; the place was tidy.

'How you can live the way you do, I'll never know,' Jean said.

Tremayne had looked at her standing in his hallway, pleased that she was there, not wanting to admit it.

'I can look after myself.'

'And there's Clare, worried sick about you. Why, I'll never know.'

For a moment he felt a tenderness that he had not felt in a long time. He had wanted to grab hold of her in the hallway and kiss her, but he had just finished another day at work, and he was not feeling well. He settled with, 'Glad you're here.'

'A good meal and off to bed. Tonight, you're going to sleep, and there'll be no return visits to the pub where you collapsed. I've had your superintendent on the phone wondering where you are, how you are. Supposedly, he hasn't been able to contact you.'

'Damn right. I switched off my phone to him. The man will only use my visit to the hospital to pension me off.'

'And not a bad idea. That way, I'll get to make sure you eat properly, and it's two pints of a night time now, not six or seven, the occasional eight.'

'I've gone to hell, I know it.'

'You haven't. A couple of weeks and I'll have you running around the block. Clare, she says…'

'It's you and Yarwood, my jailers.'

'Nothing of the sort. I need a husband, and she needs a detective inspector. We're both concerned, the same as you should be.'

Tremayne sat down in his favourite chair and turned on the television, before turning it off again. He turned to Jean. 'I thought my number was up.'

'Don't fight me on this, Tremayne,' Jean said. 'You can't fight nature. You're getting older, the same as I am. If you keep on abusing your body, you'll be dead within six months.'

'Did Yarwood put you up to this? I've a good mind to…'

'You've a good mind to thank her, that's what you'll do. Clare cares about you, the same as I do.'

After Jean had left to fetch him a hot drink, Tremayne switched on the television again. It was a tedious documentary, not that he took any notice of it. He'd not admit to it, but he appreciated the attention, the fact that Jean cared, the fact that Yarwood cared, though neither would receive any thanks from him.

Death by a Dead Man's Hand

A knock at the door. Jean answered it. 'A bit of a scare from what I hear,' Superintendent Moulton said as he sat down.

'I've just been overdoing it, that's all.'

'No chance to charge your phone, either.'

'Sorry about that. I wasn't in the mood to fight you over my retirement today.'

'I wasn't phoning about that. I was enquiring after your health. I was worried.'

'Not you as well.'

'What do you mean?'

'It's Jean and Yarwood, they're trying to make me change my habits.'

'They're wasting their time, but you've got to take it easy. I'll make a deal with you. If you lose a few pounds, look after your health, I'll put the retirement plan to one side.'

'Indefinitely?'

'Six months.'

'It's a deal. You won't have anything to do down at the station.'

'Contrary to your opinion of me, I do have other responsibilities.'

Jean entered the room. 'A cup of tea, Superintendent?'

'No, thanks. I should be off. Our man Tremayne needs his beauty sleep.'

'Bit late for that,' Tremayne said.

'Maybe, but rest tonight. Let Sergeant Yarwood take more of the workload.'

'She does her fair share.'

After Moulton had left, Tremayne turned to Jean. 'Every cloud has a silver lining,' he said.

'What does that mean?'

'He's given me six months to get myself fit, and no talk of retirement.'

'Retirement, you. You'd drive me mad.'

'That's not what you said before.'

'Before, I was worried that you were going to die. Now, I'm scared of you retiring.'

'I'll never retire, you know that.'

'I know it, although Bemerton Road Police Station doesn't.'

Chapter 12

The next day, it was ten in the morning before Tremayne walked through the door at Bemerton Road, the all-conquering hero. He had never known so many people pleased to see him. Everyone he passed stopped and shook his hand, wished him well. Even the woman in Accounts, who always gave Tremayne hell about his poor attempt at filling in an expense form, gave him a hug, shed a tear. 'It wouldn't be the same without you,' she said.

'Life would be simpler for you,' Tremayne said. He had felt slightly embarrassed by the woman's attention. Clare had seen the exchange between the Account's lady and Tremayne. She had smiled to herself. She had to admit he looked better, and she was glad she had phoned up Jean, her efforts clearly visible. For once, Tremayne wore a freshly-pressed suit, a white shirt, a tie that did not skew to one side.

'Don't look at me like that, Yarwood,' Tremayne said as he entered Homicide. 'I've got you and Jean fussing, and now I've got Moulton eating out of my hand. What else can go wrong?'

'We've got a visitor,' Clare said.

'I'm not eating out of your hand,' Moulton said. He was sitting on a chair not more than six feet from where Tremayne had made his disparaging comment.

'Sorry about that,' Tremayne said.

'What's this about the missing bars? Any impact on the investigation?'

'I'd say so. We've not mentioned it to any of the potential murderers yet.'

'Any reason why?'

'Cosford's excited at taking on the insurance company, the Mitchells are coming to terms with Ethan's death. I'll bring it up when the time is right, although I'm interested to see if anyone mentions it to us. Cosford should know through the insurance company, but the Mitchells won't have been told. If one of them mentions it, we'll need to ask how they knew.'

'Are you certain there were twenty missing?'

'According to the company that Cosford bought them from, and we've seen the manifest document for the transportation. Forty bars left London, we recovered twenty from the boot of the car, and now seventeen from out at Emberley. That leaves three missing. And besides, Hughes has been on the phone as I was driving in. They found a hair clip in the hole.'

'A woman took the gold?' Moulton said.

'That seems a possibility. Forensics is trying, but it's unlikely they'll find much.'

'You have your suspicions?'

'Betty, Ethan's widow, had the treasure map.'

'Primary suspect?'

'It's not normally that simple.'

Moulton left. Tremayne and Clare sat down in Tremayne's office.

'Your new best friend,' Clare said.

Tremayne chose to ignore Clare's attempt at humour. He wasn't feeling the best, even though he had put on a show on entering the police station. Clare looked at him, saw through the mask. 'I'll drive today,' she said.

'You always do. And what do you and Jean want me to do? Lie down on the back seat and take a nap.'

'If you want.'

'Not me. We've got work to do. What do you reckon to the three bars of gold that are missing?'

'Betty Galton?'

'We need to see her. I was out with Cosford the other day. Apart from some excellent brandy, he tried to bribe me.'

'Why?'

'Confidentially, and I don't want this on the record, not just yet, he's taking on the insurance company, wanting to pay the original insurance payment back and reclaim the gold.'

'Can he?'

'I've known him a long time. He's bound to bring in the smartest lawyers to take them on. He's got my vote if he wins. I've not much time for insurance companies and banks, bloodsuckers, the lot of them.'

'The bribe?'

'Intimated. He wasn't specific. I assume he wants me to corroborate his story.'

'Will you?'

'I can only give the facts.'

'It depends how you phrase it.'

'Maybe, but I'm not into corruption, and I'm certainly not going to take a bribe.'

'I know that,' Clare said. 'However, it makes him suspect.'

'He always was. He flies close to the wind, takes chances. Although I've never seen him as a criminal.'

'What's the plan for today?'

'The security van drivers, do we know where they are?'

'One of them, we do.'

'What about the other one?'

'No idea. I've an address for the first one. It's close to London. It's been checked out; the man is there.'

'Certain?'

'He has been warned by the local police not to take any holidays.'

'Criminal record?'

'Petty crime.'

'And he was entrusted with forty bars of gold.'

'He wasn't a criminal then.'

'You'd better phone your accomplice,' Tremayne said. 'Tell her I'm in your care, and I won't be home for lunch, or what constitutes a lunch.'

'It's because we love you, guv.'

'Don't give me any of that gooey nonsense. Bring the car around, I need a cigarette.'

'How many today?'

'It's my first, and yes, I'll keep it to less than five for the day. And no nagging on the way, Jean's giving me enough of that.'

Clare picked up her laptop, her handbag, and left the office. She smiled to herself as she walked down the corridor, not only on account of Tremayne but because his doctor from the previous day had phoned her up. She was going out on a date, and this time she wanted to.

***

'Another one with a fortune in his van and he lives like this,' Tremayne said. The drive up from Salisbury had taken close to two hours on account of the fog, and his need to stop every twenty minutes to stretch his legs.

Clare could see a man who should be taking it easy, a man who would work himself into an early grave. Not that she could criticise. She knew that the pressure of work had been taking its toll, and she had put on some weight, and now she was going out on Saturday evening for a meal, a bottle of wine, and whatever else. It was the first time for a long time that she had wanted to be with someone since Harry's death, and all that time with only a cat in her bed. She had tried a couple of times to enter the dating game; both had been unmitigated disasters. One of the dates, a boring man, had the personality of a prune, the other expected to sleep with her, even after he had spent the evening talking about himself, and then expected her to go halves on the bill. She had given him short shrift, almost told him where to go. But she had desisted. He worked in the same police station, and now she purposely avoided him at every opportunity, not that it stopped him sending her the occasional email, asking her when she was free. She had always deleted them. The next time, she would not. She would send him a curt reply to not contact her again or else. The prune had found himself a wife in the interim, a mousy blonde with large prescription glasses, who obviously liked dull men with no charm.

Clare parked in the street, not sure if it was safe to leave the vehicle unattended. A row of red-brick terrace houses stretched from where they were parked up the road for at least a hundred yards; behind them, it ran for another two hundred yards. Judging by the people in the street, this was low rental, low socio-economic, high crime.

'We've got a job to do,' Tremayne said. He was feeling better on account of a sleep on the way up, although he needed a cigarette. He knew what Yarwood would say if he took out a packet.

'It's the black door, number 248,' Clare said.

'Tremayne, you've aged,' the man of the house said as he opened the door.

'Vince Harding, it's been seventeen years,' Tremayne said. 'You're not looking so good either.'

'You'd better come in. I can't have you making the street look untidy. And who's the lady?'

'Sergeant Yarwood. I'm an inspector now.'

'Good for you, not so good for me. Do you want a beer?'

'We're fine,' Clare said.

Clare could see that Vince Harding had aged worse than Tremayne, and he wasn't looking so sharp. Harding, known to be fifty-three, wore an old tee shirt and a pair of shorts two sizes too small, judging by his extended belly. It was clear that he had not shaved for two or three days, and his breath stank.

'Suit yourself. I'll get myself one. No doubt you're here to ask me about the missing bars.'

'We are,' Tremayne said. 'What's the story?'

'Are you guilty, Mr Harding?' Clare said. She thought the direct approach, seeing she had not met the man before, would give notice that they weren't there for a day out.

'Call me Vince. No, I'm not guilty of any crime other than stupidity. Aidan, my offsider, he had this girlfriend. It was on the way, and he thought we could pop in. We were ahead of schedule, the van was unmarked, and it was well secured.'

'You agreed?'

'I couldn't see any harm. We'd been together as a team on and off for eighteen months, and I trusted him, the same as he trusted me. I know we've got all this gold in the back, but it seemed safe enough to agree with him.'

'And there was a promise of someone for you,' Tremayne said. 'Not much use to you now, judging by the look of you.'

'I do alright, and yes, Aidan, he said that his girlfriend would see me right, make sure there was someone for me. He was a ladies' man, was Aidan. Always had a woman on his arm, almost like a sailor with a girl in every port, but we never saw the sea, only one destination to another.

'I'd just broken up with my girlfriend, and I did love her. It came as a shock when I came home early one night, a delivery of paintings to Birmingham, if I remember. It's two in the morning, and we'd been planning to spend the night away, Aidan and me. A few drinks, find ourselves some away from home entertainment, but Aidan, he's got himself a sure bet, and he's all for driving back. Anyway, it's two in the morning, and I creep up the stairs. You know the rest.'

'She's in bed with another man.'

'Not only that, he's my brother.'

'What did you do?'

'Not much. I made sure my brother didn't look so good for a few days and slapped her across the face. The both of them looked stupid standing out in the street naked.'

'After that?' Clare said.

'I'm feeling lonely, not to say a little frustrated. It's the next day, and we've got the gold in the van. Aidan suggests the diversion. I know it's wrong, but he's keen for the woman, and I'm still…'

'Horny?' Tremayne said.

'I was trying to think of a polite word for the lady,' Vince said.

'You fancied a screw. Is that polite enough?' Clare said.

'It'll do. Anyway, I agree, not knowing that we're being followed.'

'Did Aidan?'

'Not him. He was an honest man, the same as I was.'

'You're not now.'

'Not that we stole any of the gold, but we had proved ourselves to be untrustworthy.'

'You were. What happened?'

'We're on suspended leave for a while, and then we're out on our ear. Aidan, he sets himself up as a handyman, manages to survive. For me, I'm unemployable. I find a few jobs, some half-decent, most not. Eventually, I'm at rock bottom, the bills are piling up. I see this car. Its engine is running. I get in and drive off. It's a BMW, and it's fast, too fast for me, and I wrap it around a lamppost. That time, I avoided a prison sentence, but after that, petty crime, steal this, fence that. You know the routine.'

'We do,' Clare said. 'You've headed down the slippery slope, and there's no way to come back. Why are you telling us this?'

Harding didn't answer.

Tremayne didn't fall for the hard luck story, no matter how convincingly it was told. He'd heard enough in his time. 'Was Aidan in on the hijack?'

'Neither of us was, and that's the honest truth.'

'Then how did they know what was in the van? How did they break into the driver's compartment?'

'That was Aidan. We were close to his girlfriend's place. He wasn't sure of the road to take, so he stops to wait for her to show us the way. That's when the car came up alongside. We didn't see it, only saw what was going on when one of the hijackers smashed the side window and coshed Aidan, pointed a gun at me.'

Tremayne turned to Clare. 'The van wasn't armoured. It was licensed for carrying antiques, expensive paintings, not gold.'

'Then why the gold?'

'That was the company's fault. Two of the other vehicles in the fleet had broken down. We would have taken one of those, but we couldn't, so we took the only remaining serviceable van.'

'That would negate the insurance,' Clare said.

'We checked with the boss. He phoned Cosford, who phoned the insurance company. In the end, we got all the sign-offs, and we were on our way. We had no idea how much the gold was worth, came as a surprise when we found out. On the occasions afterwards when we met up, Aidan and me, we'd joke about how easy it would have been to take one of those bars and melt it down. Even planned where we would live, the life we would have, the …'

'The women,' Clare said.

'We were young, silly, full of nonsense.'

'You were thirty-five,' Tremayne said. 'Old enough to have done your job.'

'You're right,' Harding said.

'And the girlfriend and her friend?'

'We never got there.'

'You've been feeding my sergeant with this hard luck story for long enough. What's the truth? How did the Mitchells know where you would stop? Who told them about the gold?'

'I don't know. We'd only changed the vehicle at the last moment, and the plan to visit Aidan's girlfriend had come about as we were travelling.'

'That's the problem, Yarwood,' Tremayne said. 'We were never able to understand how two minor villains were able to know what was in the van, how easy it was to break in. Now, Vince here, he's not involved. We're certain of that, but Aidan, he was a possibility.'

'We shouldn't have lost our jobs, but they needed a scapegoat.'

'Enough of the bleeding heart. You'll have me in tears,' Tremayne said.

Clare could see the old Tremayne returning. She was pleased.

'I'm right, you know I am. Up until the hijack we'd followed instructions,' Harding said. 'We were still on the correct road, although about to turn off. And we had followed all the procedures.'

'If it wasn't you, and I don't believe it was, then who? We checked with your boss, checked with Cosford, even grilled Ethan Mitchell, but he wasn't talking.'

'You were both restrained,' Clare said. 'What then?'

'Aidan had been coshed. He couldn't remember much afterwards. The two hijackers had on balaclavas. Afterwards, we were told that they were twins, not that we could tell. We were thrown into a ditch, stripped down to our underwear, and it was cold that night.'

'Not like the snug bed you were hoping for,' Tremayne said.

'Do you want me to tell your sergeant the story or don't you?'

'Carry on. I always like a bit of fiction before my bedtime.'

'One of the two gets in the van and drives off. The other one followed in their car. After that, we never saw them again. We got out of the ditch, somehow managed to untie ourselves, and eventually flagged down a vehicle. Aidan nearly got run over after he had given up on trying to get a lift for two men in their underwear.'

'Understandable,' Clare said.

'It turned out to be an off-duty policeman on his way home at the end of his shift. Once we'd warmed up with his heater, we gave him the story. He phoned his station, and the rest you know.'

'You didn't see the gold bars put into the boot of the car?'

'No. That's all there is,' Vince said.

'You're missing something,' Tremayne said.

'It was eighteen years ago. You don't expect me to remember everything in detail, do you?'

'You missed out where they offered you a bar each.'

'I wish I'd taken it. How much is it worth now?'

'More than three hundred thousand pounds.'

'And I ended up stacking shelves in a supermarket for fifty pounds a week.'

'Life isn't fair, you know that. I should be chief inspector now, but I'm not bellyaching about it.'

'And I should be worth a fortune. You were a difficult man back then, Tremayne. You still are.'

'You're right, Vince. I believed your story back then. I still do.'

'Was Aidan in on it?' Clare said.

'It's unlikely,' Tremayne said. 'He was a smart arse with a loud mouth, I remember that.'

'He was the last time I saw him,' Vince said, 'but he wasn't involved.'

'It's an inside job,' Clare said. 'It has to be.'

'We know that, but we could never make the connection, and besides, we had a murder. The theft of forty gold bars, unfortunate as it was, was secondary.'

'Those gold bars destroyed my life,' Harding said.

'Don't give me the bleeding-heart routine again and give me one of your beers.'

'Guv, you promised,' Clare said.

'It'll give you and Jean something to talk about tonight. No doubt you and her will be comparing notes.'

'What's up, Tremayne?' Vince said.

'Getting old, the same as you. Only I've got Yarwood and my ex-wife checking on me.'

'You're two up on me. It would be nice to have someone worry about me, but there's not much hope of that now.'

'I'll take a beer, as well,' Clare said.

Chapter 13

On the drive back to Salisbury, Tremayne dozed, only to wake when Clare drove over a bump in the road. It was late afternoon, and she was taking him home whether he liked it or not. He still needed rest, and she could conduct the next interview on her own.

At the front door of Tremayne's house, Jean said, 'Home early, dear. You can help me with the washing up.' She winked at Clare.

'Get me out of here quick, Yarwood. Find me some villains to deal with.'

'Don't worry, Tremayne,' Jean said. 'It's an early night for you.'

'The warder and her accomplice, both together.'

'I'll see you tomorrow. I'll go and have a little chat with Betty Galton,' Clare said.

'Ethan's widow.'

'No one else could have taken those three bars.'

'I don't want to arrest her, not just yet. This case pivots around her, and if they know she's got the gold, then you know what happens.'

'The culprits are flushed out of the woodwork.'

'Not only that. The local villains still aiming for a chance at the main game will become visible, and those three bars are worth close to a million pounds.'

'A quiet chat, nothing heavy. That's the best way with her,' Clare said.

'Give me a call when you're through.'

'She'll call you in the morning,' Jean said.

Clare got into her car and drove off. A quick detour to her cottage to feed her cat, and then over to visit Ethan Mitchell's widow. She found her alone in the house. 'Bob's gone out for an hour, and Gerry's trial is soon.'

'What are his chances?'

'His lawyer reckons he's got a good chance of a suspended sentence. Do you think Tremayne would say a word on his behalf?'

'We can only ask. He probably will, if it's allowed.'

'Any reason why not?'

'I'll talk to Tremayne. You've got enough to deal with, what with Gerry, and then Ethan, and the three gold bars. Where are they, by the way?'

'Has anyone been talking?'

'Not to us. I suggest you put on the kettle, and you and I will have a chat about why you broke the law.'

'Are you going to arrest me?'

'Not today. We need to find Ethan's killer, and you're the focus. You always have been, gold or no gold.'

'How do you know?'

'They found a hair clip in the hole, and it wasn't mine. It could only be you, but why?'

'I don't know. I could see that our lives had always been difficult, and there, in a hole, was all that wealth. Selwyn Cosford was covered by his insurance, and all we had was a dead relative and Ethan in jail for his murder. I knew where the gatehouse was, and I went up there one afternoon, just as it was getting dark. No one saw me, and I could just about get down to the gold. I didn't know what to do. In the end, I managed to lift out three of them. After that, I moved them to another location.'

'Does anyone else know about this?'

'I told the family yesterday. I gave them forty-eight hours to decide.'

'Decide what?'

'Whether I hand it over to you or them.'

'Their reaction?'

'Nothing. It's a lot of money. Gavin would know what to do.'

'I could arrest you for what you've just told me.'

'I worry about Gerry. He needs guidance, and without me, he'll only commit another crime.'

'You forgot the tea,' Clare said.

'I'll make it right now.'

'Not now. We're going for a drive.'

'Emberley?'

'Yes. It's near to the gatehouse. The bars were heavy, and you didn't move them far.'

'Have you got some old clothes?' Betty said.

'Coveralls in the back of the car. A set for you as well.'

***

Clare knew she should have called Tremayne but decided against it. She had played a hunch, and it had worked out. If Tremayne had been one hundred per cent, he would have come to the same conclusion.

Clare knew that if Betty retrieved the three bars, then she was guilty of another offence, and neither she nor Tremayne was keen on seeing Gerry's mother in prison at the same time as him.

Emberley, a pleasant enough village most times, did not look so welcoming as they drove up to the gatehouse. For one thing, the estate manager was nearby when they stopped the vehicle. 'Stay here,' Clare said to Betty.

'What are you doing here?' the manager said. 'We've had enough excitement up here as it is.'

'Sergeant Yarwood.'

'My apologies. We've had a few of the local hooligans looking around, causing a nuisance.'

Clare could tell that the man didn't broker any dissent at Longmore Park. In the past, she could imagine him taking a shot at a poacher who was after the pheasants that were known to be in the area. Clare could not like the man, but then, maybe it was because he reminded her of her father, unsociable and unforgiving. She remembered that he had not spoken to her for two weeks after she had told him and her mother that she was going to join the police force.

'We're just here to have a look around. See if it stirs any memories.'

'You've got a woman in the car.'

'We're here without the crowds. If you could leave us, we would appreciate it.'

'Fine by me. I'll station myself down the road. That way you'll not be disturbed. If you find anything, just remember who's helping.'

Returning to her car, Clare went around to the back and took out two sets of coveralls as well as gloves and overshoes. 'Put these on,' she said to Betty.

The two women then climbed over the crime scene tape and made their way back to where the seventeen gold bars had been recovered. Standing at the side of the hole and shining a torch down, Clare could see that the tree root which had impeded entry for everyone except her had been cut.

'You climbed down there in the dark?' Clare said.

'I was scared witless. My grandmother was keen on telling us ghost stories when we were young, not that I believed them, but you know…'

'I do,' Clare said. She had had an older friend who liked to tell them as well. Although that was when they were children, standing there as the darkness enveloped the area, an owl hooting in the distance, the lights of the main house just visible through the trees, was enough to scare anyone. It reminded Clare of that night at Avon Hill, up in Cuthbert's Wood, when she had nearly died and Harry, her fiancé, had. Clare shed a tear, the first for a long time.

'Bad memories?' Betty said, who could see Clare's face in the torchlight.

'A long time ago.'

'We've all got them. I still think back to when Ethan shot Martin, and now to when someone shot Ethan. I can feel the bullet, imagine the agony.'

'It doesn't help being here, does it? We'd best focus, find this gold, and get out of here.'

'I was going to let the family have it,' Betty said.

'We don't want to charge you, but you're making it difficult.'

'All that money and Selwyn Cosford doesn't care either way. To him, it's pocket money. And if he cheats on his taxes, or defrauds the insurance company, no one puts him in jail. But for us, the Mitchells, we're the battlers, and we get slammed down every time.'

'Betty, a deal,' Clare said. 'You tell me where these three bars are, and we'll get out of here, have a quiet drink and a talk.'

'Done. I carried the bars, one at a time, up further into the trees. Not far, maybe fifty feet. It wasn't so overgrown then, and there was a full moon.'

The two women, comical if it wasn't so serious, ventured forth, Clare in front, guided by Betty. Clare would brush a branch to one side, only for it to return and strike Betty in the face. Intrepid explorers they were not, and it was not deepest Africa, but it was harder going than they had imagined. After some distance, Betty said, 'It's near here.'

'Where? All I can see are trees and undergrowth.'

'It's changed, but I know it's here.'

Clare shone her torch around the area. 'Any help?'

'Over there. You can see those two trees, one with a broken branch.'

'I can?'

'I found a hole there, badger's probably. I put the three bars there.'

'There's no hole now.'

'We'll need to dig. I can tell you exactly where it is now. It's been a long time, but my memory's coming back.'

Clare took hold of the small spade she had brought with her. The two women were down on their hands and knees. One was holding the torch, the other digging. After twenty minutes, neither woman was conscious of the exact time spent and both of them were exhausted and perspiring. 'There's something here,' Clare said.

'It's got to be it,' Betty replied.

The first bar came out of the ground nice and easy. The second took a little longer, and the third took another five minutes before it was free from the earth.

'It's not every day you dig up a million pounds, is it?' Clare said.

'And we're going to do the right thing?'

'You are, Betty. Tremayne and I, we'll back you up. We'll say that you assisted us with our enquiries.'

'I had promised to give the family forty-eight hours to consider my offer.'

'And what would they have done? We would have caught whoever took you up on the offer, and they'd be doing time, the same as you. This is the best way.'

'I know, but…'

'There are no buts. Let's get out of here before anyone sees us.'

'The man on the way in, he saw us.'

'He's not seen the gold, and besides, he'll not count for much.'

'He's a miserable bastard,' Betty said. 'I've met him before.'

'When?'

'I used to come out with Marcia sometimes to see Ethan's uncle.'

'Which way back?' Clare said.

'I don't know. It's this way, I think.'

The return trip was not as tricky as the outward journey, but now the two were carrying buried treasure. Clare had hold of two of the bars, Betty had one and the torch.

'I can see the gatehouse over there,' Clare said. 'And there's something propped up against it.'

Betty shone the torch at the propped-up shape. 'It's a man,' she said. The two women, still holding the bars, hurried forward.

'Oh my God!' Betty said. 'It's Gavin. He's dead.'

Clare took one look, checked for a pulse. She then took out her phone. 'Jean, you'll need to wake Tremayne. Organise a car for him if it's necessary. He's needed out at Emberley, the same place.' She then phoned Jim Hughes.

***

'A knife in the back,' Hughes said. The crime scene team were scouring the area looking for additional clues, not confident they would find any more. After all, it had only been a few days since they had been through the area.

'We retrieved the three missing bars,' Clare said.

'It's a crime scene. What were you doing here without us?'

'It was important.'

'Maybe it was, but you could have destroyed vital evidence.'

'We didn't. And regardless, I've got to look after Betty.'

'The pub was open when we came through. It may be best if you wait down there. Tremayne, is he on his way? Now there's someone who breaks the rules. He's taught you well.'

Marcia, Betty's daughter, was at the pub on their arrival. 'Why, Mother?'

'I wanted to help, and now Gavin's dead. Who next?'

Clare went to the bar and ordered two brandies. One for her, one for the woman she had brought out to the village. She knew there would be flak for entering a crime scene without prior approval. Even Tremayne, in the brief phone conversation she had had with him, had expressed his concern. He had not been critical, she knew him better than that.

'I never told anyone where it was,' Betty said. Her daughter had her arm around her.

'Gavin figured it out, the same as I did.'

'He could have asked. I would have told him.'

'You said forty-eight hours,' Marcia reminded her. 'Maybe he didn't want the others to know what he was up to.'

'Someone did,' Clare said.

'Who would do that?' Betty said.

'Could it be the same person who killed Ethan at St Mark's?' Marcia said.

'We'll let Forensics check the area,' Clare said. 'We'll know more then. Marcia, can you look after your mother?'

'I will.'

Clare drove the short distance back to the gatehouse. Tremayne was there on her arrival. 'I hope you got someone to drive,' Clare said.

'Jean brought me here. I'll get a ride back with you when we leave.'

'You're looking better.'

'I feel better, no thanks to you and Jean, cutting me back on my cigarettes. A man has got to have his vices, you must know that.'

'We do.'

'This is not good, Yarwood. You shouldn't have been up here on your own with a possible suspect.'

'It's what you would have done.'

'I know, but I'm longer in the tooth than you. The most they can do is pension me off. You're bright and young, your future is ahead of you.'

Clare walked over to Jean's car. 'Is he okay?'

'He's Tremayne. Indestructible, that man.'

'They said that about the Titanic, or was it unsinkable?'

'You were right to phone me up,' Jean said. 'If he had missed the action, he'd have been angry. Are you in trouble?'

'Probably, but I'll survive. There's another body.'

Jean left, and Clare walked back to where Tremayne and Hughes were discussing the latest death. 'Comparing notes?' Tremayne said.

'I was just attempting to be sociable,' Clare said. 'What do we know about Gavin Mitchell's death?'

'A knife in the back, messy,' Hughes said.

'How long ago?'

'Sometime during the day. We found Mitchell's car down a lane to the rear of the village. The man must have been anxious for those three bars.'

'You've got them?'

'We have. What made you come out here?'

'A hunch. It had to be Betty after you found that hair clip.'

'We went over the area with a metal detector, surprised we didn't find them.'

'You've seen where they were. Nobody looked over there.'

'That's a mark against us. It looks as if you're not the only one in trouble,' Hughes said.

'If we could focus,' Tremayne said. 'What's the situation with Gavin Mitchell?'

'We're checking the area, but the man was looking for the gold.'

'It doesn't take an Einstein to figure that out.' Tremayne said.

'Maybe you should be back in your bed, Tremayne. If you hold on, I'll give you the details,' Hughes said.

'Okay.'

'The man had a powerful torch with him, as well as some implements for digging. He also had a metal detector. No idea why he thought the bars were here.'

'I did,' Clare said.

'You're trained to think, he wasn't.'

'Anyway, someone else must have had the same idea.'

'His family?'

'We had not advertised the fact that three bars were missing,' Tremayne said.

'Maybe you didn't, but the word gets around. It's a wonder the place wasn't crawling with fortune seekers.'

'I thought there was a watch on the area.'

'There was, but they had been called away. The place has had no one here for the last eight hours.'

'The blade entered the man in his back, and he would have died within minutes,' Hughes said. 'There's more than one stab wound. Apart from that, there's not much more to tell. We're checking the area, but no fingerprints, no footprints that we can pick up. The place had plenty of people here not so long ago when we were checking, and Mitchell and whoever killed him kept to where we have been. Mitchell could have made it to the road in front and called for help. He would still have died, but he wouldn't have remained around the back of the gatehouse.'

'Why didn't he?' Tremayne asked.

'Yarwood knows why,' Hughes said.

'He had caught his clothes on a protruding bolt at the back of the gatehouse. In his weakened state, he couldn't break free.'

'Where to, Yarwood?' Tremayne said.

'His family, and then Selwyn Cosford.'

'Playing your hunches again?'

'That man's full of greed.'

'He seems more obvious than the family.'

'Could it have been someone unknown?'

'It's possible, but murder, that's something else.'

'So is a million pounds in gold. I'd kill for that,' Tremayne said.

'No, you wouldn't, and neither would I.'

'If you two are going to stand here and talk, I'm off,' Hughes said. 'There's a crime scene team in need of leadership. We'll hand the gold bars over as evidence during the day.'

'Don't leave them at reception, will you?'

'At least you've got your humour back,' Hughes said. 'Not that it's any good.'

Chapter 14

Social media picked up on the death of Gavin Mitchell within an hour. The fact that the gold had been retrieved, and there was nothing to be found or seen, did not deter the curious, the greedy, and the plain stupid from visiting Emberley. Extra uniforms had to be brought in from Salisbury to ensure that no one could get near the crime scene.

'There are a lot of bored people out there,' Superintendent Moulton said. Tremayne and Clare were in his office. Both were standing up.

'What am I going to do with you two,' Moulton said. 'And sit down. You make the place look untidy.'

It was the first dressing down for Clare, one of many for her senior. She looked over at him, noticed the sheepish and contrite look, knew that he was neither.

'Tremayne, can't you control your people?'

'Sergeant Yarwood used her initiative. I can only commend her.'

'If there hadn't been another body, then maybe we could have brushed this over. What were you thinking, Yarwood?' Moulton said.

'Betty Galton, Ethan Mitchell's former wife, had to be the person with the three bars of gold. I decided to confront her. She admitted to hiding the bars.'

'But why didn't you take someone from the crime scene team? What if there was evidence out there?'

'I acted on the spur of the moment. No one knew where to look, and there was always the risk of someone else coming along to look for it. I wasn't aware she had told her family, not immediately.'

'Gavin Mitchell, what do we know about him?'

'I've known him a long time,' Tremayne said. 'A solitary man. Sometimes he would go to the pub for a pint. Not much to tell. He kept to himself, had no criminal record, and he wasn't close to Ethan. He showed no emotion when I spoke to him about his dead brother.'

'Tremayne, what's your health like? Don't give me any of that "I'm fine, couldn't be better".'

'It's the truth,' Tremayne said.

'No, it's not. I've got eyes, the same as Yarwood. She's covering for you. Commendable in itself, but this is a police station, not an old dog's home. Either you're up to the task, or you're not. I've got enough to put you out of your misery.'

'But you're not going to, sir.'

'I've a fondness for old dogs.'

Clare felt the need to speak. 'DI Tremayne is conscious of his health, and he has voluntarily committed himself to a four-week detox. His cigarette smoking has been reduced, and he will be limiting his consumption of alcohol.'

'He's trained you well, I'll grant him that,' Moulton said. 'Tremayne and a four-week detox. He wouldn't even know the word. It's you and Jean, you've ganged up on him. It's amazing. I've spent years trying to pin him down, and then two women come along and succeed. Write up your report, solve these murders and get out of my office, will you.'

'Is that it?' Tremayne said.

'Yarwood made an error, but no harm's been done. You, Tremayne, are on your last legs and don't pretend, but I'm not going to make martyrs out of either of you.'

Outside Moulton's office, Tremayne let out a sigh of relief. He turned to Clare. 'What's a four-week detox?' he said.

'Something you're not going to like.'
'That's what I thought.'

***

Tremayne and Clare were sitting in his office. 'That went better than I expected,' Tremayne said.

'For you. I've got a black mark against me now.'

'Not with Moulton. You did find the missing gold, but what about Betty? She's guilty of a few crimes.'

'We need to look after her.'

'Yarwood, don't get emotional with these people. Betty may be a decent person, but her family has got a history, and it's not too good.'

'Hers or the Mitchells?'

'She married into the family. She must have known what Ethan was like.'

'You're not going to arrest her, are you?'

'My life's bad enough as it is with you and Jean. I don't want to add to my burden by arresting the woman.'

Clare made a phone call. Betty was out at her sister's place – a family gathering.

'I'm sorry about Gavin,' Tremayne said to Sandra, the only surviving sibling, on his and Clare's arrival at Julie and Eric Wilson's house.

'Why did he have to die?'

'Why do people do a lot of things?' Tremayne said. 'Often it is the most innocent who suffer.'

Clare noticed that Tremayne's blunt approach at consolation did not work. She went over and put her arm around the woman. 'We'll find out who did it,' she said.

'One of those in here,' Sandra's reply.

It seemed logical, Clare had to admit. On the sofa sat Betty, Marcia, and Julie. Standing in the far corner, Eric, Julie's husband. Bob, Betty's husband, sat on a chair close to the fireplace.

'It wasn't any of us. I refuse to believe it,' Betty said. Tremayne thought she was only saying the words out of a need for them to be heard, not because she believed them.

'We can't rule out the possibility,' Tremayne said.

'We've no need of the money,' Eric Wilson said.

'A million pounds? Everyone has need of that sort of money, even you. I'm not here to point the finger. Gavin has died, and we need to find his killer. If he's not here, then it must be someone who knew about the missing bars.'

'It's known by us. One of the others must have talked,' Wilson said.

'Have you?'

'Not me.'

'How about the others? Has anyone else felt the need to gossip,' Tremayne said, looking over at Eric Wilson who was receiving disapproving glances from his wife.

There's a man who won't be getting his dinner at home tonight, Tremayne thought.

'Assume the others haven't told anyone,' Bob Galton said.

'I'm sorry about this, Betty, but we'll need to question everyone in turn,' Tremayne said.

'If it finds Gavin's killer, Ethan's as well.'

'Yarwood worked on a hunch. You, Betty, were willing to give the bars to anyone in this room.'

'It seemed the right thing to do. So much has happened because of the gold. I thought that somehow some good would have come from the three bars. I was wrong.'

'Why would Gavin go out there? He was not an ambitious man, more laidback than most.'

'His business is broke. Maybe he was desperate,' Wilson said.

Tremayne instinctively did not like the man. His success was well known, but he had a smugness about him.

'Betty, did you tell anyone here that the gold was near to where the others had been found?'

'No. Only Marcia.'

'Marcia, what have you to say?'

'I told no one, not even my boyfriend.' Tremayne wanted to believe the woman. Her brother's trial was in a week, and Tremayne knew he was down as a character witness. He hoped his statement would not be diluted by an errant sister, another murdering relative.

Chapter 15

It was a Friday, four days after Gavin Mitchell had died. The village fete was scheduled for that Saturday, and the preparations were well under way. There were some who had wanted to cancel it that year, on account of the murder up at the gatehouse, but the majority consensus had been to carry on regardless.

One of those busy setting up the bunting in the field across from Tony Mitchell's cottage decided to check why the man's dog was barking. Inside the house, he could see the animal. He opened the front door; it came flying out and around to the back of the house.

The neighbour followed it. In the middle of the immaculate garden, in a bed of Tony Mitchell's prize-winning vegetables, was the body of a man. It could be no one else. The neighbour, panicking, hurried as best he could around to the front of the house, and out on to the road. 'Help! Help!' he shouted. Bert Clasby was an old man who should have been taking it easy. He shouted once again and collapsed to the ground.

A vehicle stopped, looked at him and called for an ambulance. Bert Clasby was pronounced dead outside Tony Mitchell's house. The ambulance would have two to transport.

'Too late for him. You'd better call the police,' the medic said as he examined the body in the vegetables.

Tremayne could see the pattern yet again. One person dies, and then it's a succession, some obviously related, others more obscure. He knew Superintendent Moulton would want answers, and a four-week detox did

Death by a Dead Man's Hand

not help the body, any more than it helped the brain. He was starving, and neither Jean nor Yarwood were sympathetic. He was sure they were secretly meeting late at night in some hidden glade to plot the next abomination to put on his plate. He had suffered the diet shakes – supposed to satisfy the hunger but they didn't. He had endured the broccoli, and the cauliflower, even the cabbage. What next, he wondered. He had to admit that he felt better, but seeing another Mitchell dead and surrounded by vegetable marrows did not help. He moved back to a seat near to the house.

'Don't sit there. This is a crime scene,' Jim Hughes said. A crime scene tent was over Mitchell's body. Out on the street, Betty had arrived with Marcia. Both wanted answers, answers neither Tremayne nor Clare could give.

'We're flying blind on this one,' Tremayne admitted. All four had relocated to the Plough Inn and had found a table with four chairs outside.

'Tony, he wasn't like us,' Marcia said. 'He thought we were not up to his standard.'

'Tony liked the quiet life. Why would anyone kill him?' Betty said.

'Why would anyone kill Gavin?'

'Gavin was after the gold, so was someone else, but Tony had lived in the village for years. As long as he had his garden, he didn't want any more.'

'He wasn't killed for his vegetables,' Tremayne said. He knew why Tony Mitchell had been killed. It was greed, and it was consuming everyone who came into contact with the gold, directly or indirectly. If anyone knew anything, no matter how insignificant, that person had leverage. But against who, Tremayne pondered. He looked over at Clare. He had trained her well, and he could see that she was also running the possibilities through her mind.

'Would Tony have known about the gold at the gatehouse, Betty? It's important,' Tremayne said.

'Not that I know, but then Ethan never had time to explain to me the full story. He just gave me the directions. Maybe Tony knew something. He always seemed to know what was going on in the village. He was a strange man in many ways, decent, though. That's why I let Gerry and Marcia come out here.'

'What do you mean?'

'You know, stories.'

'You'll need to be specific,' Tremayne said. Clare knew what Betty was staying. She realised that Tremayne was being obtuse, attempting to bring out information that may or may not be relevant.

'Tony and young children.'

'Did he have any history?'

'No, but he's here alone, and I never saw him with a girlfriend, not even when he was younger. Not that he was a bad-looking man, but he was always a bit odd.'

'Odd? You'd better tell us all you know,' Tremayne said.

Betty took a deep breath. 'There were some in the family that thought he was gay, not that I ever saw any evidence.'

'Did it matter?'

'Not to me, but there were others who disapproved.'

'Such as?'

'Gavin didn't like it much, the reason he never came out here very often.'

'Do you suspect that Ethan and Martin were interfered with?'

'Ethan would have told me. Gavin never had a girlfriend, either. I read about it once in a magazine, or maybe it was a documentary on the television. The young child scarred for life, unable to show his emotions, afraid of rejection, afraid of intimacy.'

'Mother, Gavin wasn't like that,' Marcia said. 'He used to look me up and down when I was in my teens. He wasn't gay, maybe just not interested in being with anyone, and besides, I thought he used to go around to that woman who lived not far from us.'

'Which woman?' Clare asked.

'Grace Bethany,' Betty said.

'A prostitute?'

'Not that you'd know.'

'Are you certain about her?'

'It's a few years since we've seen her, but yes, she was on the game. And Gavin, he used to go around there, so did Ethan sometimes. What with Martin, they probably got a family concession.'

'Mother!'

'What do you want me to say, Marcia? There are four Mitchells dead now, and you want me to protect the good name of your father, and don't pretend you didn't know.'

'I was five when my father went to prison.'

'Maybe you didn't know, but your father was no saint, thankfully. Apart from his pathetic attempts at being the master criminal, he was a good man, a good lover, too.'

Tremayne realised that the Mitchells were an open family, too open for him. Yarwood, he knew, more reserved than she'd admit to, would be embarrassed by the conversation. Even when he had teased her about

Harry Holchester, and their romantic getaways, she'd blush. Not that it had stopped him asking.

'Gavin was looking for the gold,' Clare said. 'He was nowhere near it, but someone else was there. Could it have been Tony?'

Tremayne wasn't sure where his sergeant was heading.

'Would Tony have been capable of killing someone?'

'Capable, but it couldn't have been him,' Betty said.

'Why?'

'He'd been in the army, sergeant major. You'd not know it looking at him, but he had a ferocious bark when he was younger. One of our friends remembered him from training, said he was a right bastard, having them marching cross-country if anyone didn't keep in step. But in the village, he rarely raised his voice. He had a medal for gallantry, the Military Cross. He told me once that he had killed a man in battle, not that he was proud of it. I don't think he even had a weapon in the house.'

'We've not found one.'

'What would he want with the gold? Betty said. 'His house was paid for, and he had his pension.'

'Greed and passion, the two variables that transform the most benign into raging psychopaths,' Tremayne said.

'Philosophical,' Clare said.

'It's true, I know that.'

***

Tremayne and Clare headed back to Tony Mitchell's house. Betty and Marcia had left for Salisbury, another family gathering, another death to explain. Clare felt sorry for Marcia, not sure what to make of Betty.

Back at Mitchell's house, Tremayne took a seat, pulled out a cigarette from its packet. 'Don't look at me like that, Yarwood. And don't go telling Jean. She'll have me drying the dishes as penance,' he said.

'We're keeping notes.'

'We've spoken about getting married again.'

'You've mentioned it before. And why not?'

'It seems silly at our age, and besides, people don't get married anymore.'

'When have other people worried you? If the two of you want to get married, then get married.'

'We'd want you there, in some official capacity.'

'I can't be the best man, can I?'

'We'll figure something out.'

'I'd be honoured,' Clare said.

'How about you and the doctor? Any chance of a double wedding?'

'Keith Tremayne, a romantic. Wait until I tell them back at the station. Maybe you could start up a lonely hearts column in the police gazette. Advice for those in love.'

'Yarwood, your cynicism knows no bounds. I've created a monster.'

'You've created a good police officer, and you know it,' Clare said. It was a moment of respect, even fondness, between the two police officers. Tremayne knew it could not last. It was a murder enquiry, and the stakes were high. Apart from the murder of Martin Mitchell, eighteen years previously, there was no culprit.

'Getting back to the reason we get paid, who killed Gavin Mitchell?' Tremayne said.

'If we discount Tony, then there are Eric Wilson and Bob Galton.'

'Does it have to be a man?'

'Not necessarily, but the knife was thrust deep. It would have required some force.'

'Either Wilson or Galton could have done it. Wilson's a sharp businessman, possibly in financial trouble. If he did, then did Julie know? What about their marriage? Is it solid or on the rocks?'

'I'll talk to Julie,' Clare said.

'I'll put the heat on Wilson.'

'Bob Galton?'

'Who knows with that man. He's not the most impressive, probably doesn't even cheat on his taxes,' Tremayne said.

'Do you?'

'You know what I mean. The man gives the impression of being honest, too honest for me.'

'You've spent too long with villains. Some people are naturally good and decent.'

'Nobody's that good. Everyone's got a vice, something they're not proud of. Are you saying you never once hopped off a bus without paying?'

'Never.'

'I don't believe it.'

Clare failed to say that her parents always ensured she had a pass, and the need to pay had not arisen. She also forgot to mention that at the age of eleven, she had stolen a bar of chocolate from a shop.

'Are you still here?' Jim Hughes said as he came out of the front door of Mitchell's house.

'We were waiting for you,' Clare said.

'It's a good job you're here, saves me phoning.'

'You've found something?' Tremayne said, casually throwing what remained of his cigarette over the front fence of the garden and into the road.

'I found this,' Hughes said, as he handed over a notebook. 'Check on the second page.'

Tremayne stood up from where he was sitting, holding one of his knees as he did so. Clare could tell that the cartilage in his knee joint was not as good as it used to be. She made a mental note: Jean to purchase tablets for sore knee joints.

Tremayne rested the notebook on a small garden table and opened it at page two. 'What do you make of this, Yarwood?' he said.

'It depends how old it is.'

'The calendar on the inside front cover shows it to be seventeen years.'

'Which means that Tony Mitchell knew where the gold was. All these years and he never touched it.'

'But why? It makes no sense,' Clare said.

'It's not the same handwriting as the note you had before,' Hughes said. 'We found other examples of Tony Mitchell's writing. He drew this map.'

In front of the three of them was a detailed map of where the twenty bars had been buried.

'Either he was in on it, or he had seen the twins, made the connection and found the gold,' Tremayne said.

'We'll never know,' Clare said.

'Anything else in the house?'

'Only this,' Hughes said as he handed over a piece of paper. 'We found it pinned to the refrigerator.'

'It's a phone number,' Clare said.

'Yarwood, get a check on who Tony Mitchell phoned in the last two weeks. If this number was dialled, then there's something amiss,' Tremayne said.

'Could it be the person who killed Gavin Mitchell?' Clare said.

'Unlikely, but more people knew about the buried treasure than we originally assumed.'

'But no one touched it.'

'That's another mystery.'

Chapter 16

The Mitchells met. This time not at Julie and Eric Wilson's house, but at Betty and Bob's. Eric Wilson was not present, which was as well, as there was not much room. Julie did not like being in the house; too many memories of where she had come from.

Sandra, a woman who prided herself on her housekeeping, was also present. She looked around her at the dust on the window sill, the hairs on the carpet from a dog, the newspaper thrown to one side.

'You've heard the news,' Betty said.

'If you had not hidden those three bars, Gavin would still be alive,' Sandra said.

Betty had considered it before. She knew the woman was right. 'I was wrong,' she said.

'You did it for the right reason,' Julie said, defending her sister. 'We always thought Gavin had more sense.'

'He saw his chance,' Bob said. He had been tempted to take the three bars for himself and to melt them down. He had a friend whom he could trust. Then, over time, he would slowly sell the gold in small quantities, no questions asked. That way, he could give Betty a better life without raising suspicion. He looked over at her, knew that he loved her, knew that she envied her sister with her builder husband. Galton knew he would never be a high-flyer, but he could be better than he was.

'The gold has been a curse,' Marcia said.

'The twins were always going to come to a sticky end,' Julie said.

'We're missing the point,' Betty said. 'Gavin was looking for the three bars, so was someone else. And why would any of you want to look? I had offered them to you with no conditions.'

'You never told anyone it was near to where the other bars had been hidden,' Marcia said.

'Gavin must have figured it out, or he was just fishing around, hoping he would strike lucky.'

'After the police had been over the area, not a chance.'

'They were in the wrong area,' Betty said. 'Someone in this room killed Gavin, or maybe it was Eric.'

'Don't you go accusing my husband just because he's not here,' Julie said, anxious to defend her husband, not sure of his innocence.

'I'm not accusing anyone, but don't you see it? If one of us is a murderer, then who's next? Who knows something about the gold, and how it came to be in the back of that van? And why would Ethan and Martin think about removing twenty bars and placing them into that hole in the ground? Neither would have scored ten out of ten for original thought. If they had, they would have figured out what to do with the gold before they took it. There are plenty of rogues who would have helped.'

'Are you saying they didn't know it was gold in the back of that van?' Marcia said.

'I'm not saying anything, just speculating. Someone's a murderer, and it's more than likely one of us. And if there are more secrets, secrets that we may know, may not even attach much significance to, then we're all potential targets.'

'Or potential murderers,' Sandra said. 'Count me out, I can't move enough to kill anyone.'

'If the look in your eyes could kill, I'd be stone dead by now,' Betty said.

'You killed Gavin, and what about Tony? Did you kill him, and who was in that church with Ethan? Maybe you didn't want him back. You were willing to keep three of the bars for yourself. And then what? Take off with your dopey husband, go and live in Spain. Have you considered Gerry, he's in for a stretch in prison?'

'You foul-mouthed woman, how dare you to insult my husband.'

'Mother, stop it. You as well, Sandra. We should be united, not fighting like this.'

'Marcia's right,' Bob said. 'Gavin was foolish to look for the gold, but so was someone else. Could anyone else have known?'

'Such as?'

'I don't know. Maybe someone in the village saw me that night when I moved the three bars,' Betty said. 'It's a small village, news travels. It wouldn't have been hard to make the connection.'

***

Tremayne perused Tony Mitchell's phone records. 'Here it is. Two phone calls in the last week. Yarwood, you're driving.'

Selwyn Cosford had not expected another visit from Tremayne and Clare. 'You've had some more deaths,' he said.

'It's official,' Tremayne said. 'We need to sit down and talk.'

'In the library, if that's okay.' The man was ingratiating, almost as if he had expected the visit. The three sat down on dark brown leather chairs. 'I often come in here for the peace and solitude.'

'Tony Mitchell,' Tremayne said.

'I thought you'd be here sometime about him.'

'Why?'

'We've known each other for a long time. We were friends back when neither of us had any money. I trusted the man.'

'Did you?'

'Tremayne, I've known you for a long time as well. What do you think?'

'I'm not paid to think. I'm paid to prove. We've nothing against you apart from you trying to offer me a sweetener.'

Cosford looked over at Clare.

'Don't worry about Yarwood,' Tremayne said. 'She'll not say anything. If you're guilty of a misdemeanour, even murder, it's not going to look good for me.'

'And me,' Clare said. 'I've kept quiet as well.'

'Tremayne, Clare, you misjudge me. I don't bribe, I assist. And Tony Mitchell and our friendship, it's harmless.'

'You never mentioned this friendship before.'

'Why would I? Tony was a secretive man. He's not an open book like me. Hell, I'm even in Wikipedia. Tony preferred to keep his past hidden, and he didn't go around talking about what he knew and who he knew. He could have used our friendship to his benefit, but he never did. Not once did he ask a favour, and there were times when he could have used it.'

'Such as?'

'Have you checked his military record?'

'Not yet. Betty Mitchell mentioned that he had killed a man once.'

'Amazing she knew that much. Tony Mitchell was your bona fide hero. We were in Malaya together, during the Malay Emergency. We had walked into an ambush. It was Tony who killed three of the insurgents and got us out of there. He received a medal for bravery.'

'We never found a medal at his house.'

'Tony was not proud of what he had done. As far as he was concerned, he was responding to the situation, and the fact that his life was in danger didn't cross his mind. The medal's somewhere, although knowing Tony he may just have thrown it out. Just because I kept in contact with him doesn't mean I murdered him.'

'You could always get someone to do it for you,' Tremayne said.

'No doubt I could, but what's the point. I've got plenty of money, a few gold bars here and there are not going to affect my life.'

'But you want to take on the insurance company.'

'Haven't you? Haven't they sucked the money off you for years, and then, in your hour of need, they're there with their excuses, the clauses in the contract that everyone fails to read.'

'They've cheated me,' Tremayne said.

'Tony told me about his relatives. He liked Gavin and his sister. He didn't think they had much going for them. The twins, Ethan and Martin, he thought they were wasters, although they had both married well. It goes to show, women are fickle. Now me, I chose my wives according to how they suited my station in life.'

'Not out of love?' Clare said.

'Love, yes, of course,' Cosford said, but not very convincingly.

'How many wives?' Tremayne asked.

'Check on Wikipedia. They're listed there.'

'I'm asking you.'

'Okay. Apart from my first wife, there was Cherie, and then Meg, and Bronwyn. She was the perfect woman.'

'What happened?' Clare said.

'On holiday in Greece. We were coming around a corner, she was driving. A pothole in the road and the car flipped.'

'I'm sorry about that, painful memories.'

'For a few years. And then there was Sally. I liked her, but it didn't last long. The last I heard, she had found herself someone in the Caribbean.'

'That's a few,' Tremayne said.

'You met a few of them over the years.'

'I'd agree about Bronwyn. She was also the only one close to your age. Sally wasn't.'

'She was fun though, made an old man feel young again.'

Clare had to admit that the man, old enough to be her grandfather, had an easy way about him. Most men his age would have been sitting in front of a television or hobbling around, but he was alert and full of life.

'Tony Mitchell knew where the missing gold was,' Tremayne said.

'I didn't know. Why?'

'He had known for seventeen years, possibly from the time it was stolen. We found proof. Are you saying he never mentioned this to you?'

'That's exactly what I'm saying. I owed the man a debt of gratitude, but we didn't keep in regular contact. Our lives moved in different areas. I'm gregarious, always looking for the next opportunity. Tony was self-effacing, not a party animal. I invited him out here a few times over the years, but he only came once, and then he sat down, barely talking to anyone. The reluctant hero, that's what he was. More of a Clark Kent than a Superman, but when the chips are down, he was there for you.'

'But you had phoned him a few times recently.'

'Of course. His relatives, even if he wasn't close to them, are dying. I'm not about to phone Betty or her sister, but I felt I should call Tony. He was glad to talk, more talkative than I ever remember him. We were planning to meet up in the next week, go for a meal.'

'Is that it? Did you know Betty and Julie?'

'I knew them. Not well, but Salisbury's a small place. No doubt you know everyone,' Cosford said.

'He does,' Clare said.

'Seriously, my relationship with Tony Mitchell goes back a long way. Check with the War Museum. They'll have a record of us in Malaysia. Better than that, wait a minute.'

Cosford left the room. 'What do you reckon?' Tremayne asked.

'He tells a good story. It could be true.'

'Some of it may be, but it's too coincidental.'

The door to the library opened and in came Cosford. 'Here you are,' he said, as he handed Tremayne a black and white framed photo.

'That's me, the skinny fresh-faced youth with the pimples. On my right, that's Tony.'

'I can see the resemblance,' Clare said. She was standing behind Tremayne looking over his shoulder.

'Your eyesight's better than mine. Selwyn, I'll take your word that you and Tony Mitchell were in Malaysia together. It still doesn't answer why the gold was buried no more than two hundred yards from his house, and he had a map.'

'I can't help you there. If there's nothing else you need, I've got to go up to London.'

'Are you driving?'

'Not me. I've got a chauffeur.'

'Pretty?' Clare said.

'I doubt if he would appreciate being called pretty. George has been with me for over twenty years. You might find him pretty if you like 50-year-old men with a beer gut.'

'I don't think so.'

Chapter 17

Tremayne was working on hunches. The conversation with Selwyn Cosford had left him unconvinced. It was if the man had been prepared for his and Yarwood's visit, and the affability, the ready answers, the finding of the grainy picture of a group of soldiers in the jungle, was pre-organised.

It was correct about Tony Mitchell, and his medal; Clare had checked. Also, Selwyn Cosford had been one of those who had been saved by Mitchell. A hero the man may have been, but it didn't obviate him from murder.

Tremayne knew he and Yarwood needed to dig deeper, to apply some lateral thinking to the problem. 'Yarwood, my house, tonight at 8 p.m. Jean's cooking dinner for us.'

It wasn't often that Clare was invited. 'Special occasion?' she said.

'We're going to solve these murders at the dining room table. White wine will do.'

'You're very presumptive that I'll bring a bottle.'

'You're the sort who always turns up with something, and if it's a cake, I can't eat it.'

'You're not satisfied with what Cosford said?'

'It's not only him. It's the whole case up until now. Too many people knew about the gold and where it was hidden. How can that be?'

'No one, barring a saint, could resist that much money.'

'A saint and an honest police officer,' Tremayne said.

'Saint Tremayne, it has a nice ring to it,' Clare said. 'Of the holy order of losers.'

'Jokes aside, how could it stay there that long? People must have walked across there a few times, and there was graffiti on the back of the gatehouse. The local tearaways must have got up there.'

'Not with that estate manager. What was his name?'

'Devlin O'Connor. He doesn't miss much. We should go and see him again, find out what he knows.'

'He'll know something, men like him always do. Probably got an inflated opinion of himself, imagines that because he reports to them up at Longmore House, he's more important than he is. What about this guided tour that you've been promised?'

'The invite's still there. Do you want to come?'

'Make it tomorrow morning, early.'

'It's a tour, not a chance for you to grill the owners, and definitely not a chance for you to case the joint.'

'You're making my halo slip. I promise not to notice the antiques and the paintings on the walls.'

'You won't, and who knows, they may even invite you for tea.'

'I'll need practice with lifting my pinkie finger.'

'I'll make sure they give you a mug. I don't want them changing your proletarian ways.'

'Peasant stock and proud of it. Not like you, Yarwood, with your expensive education. And remember, my house at 8 p.m.'

'I'll be there.'

'Good. I've got to go. Jean's got me on a treadmill at a local gym. All that money down the drain. I could as easily go for a walk every morning.'

'But you won't, and Jean knows it.'

***

Clare walked around the police station. Not that she didn't have work to do, but Homicide without Tremayne in his office somehow seemed incomplete.

She found Accounts, checked on her expenses, realised they always entered her bank account on the last day of the month. It was time wasting, and she knew it. On the top floor of the building, Superintendent Moulton was in his office. He was a man who believed in an open door. He saw her walking down the corridor outside. 'Sergeant Yarwood, a moment of your time, please.'

Clare, sensing trouble, kept walking. 'Yarwood, you heard me,' came the raised voice of the superintendent.

'Sorry, sir, a million miles away.'

'Rubbish. You were worried that I was going to ask you about Tremayne.'

'Some of that, I suppose.'

'Look here, Sergeant. Let's not beat around the bush. The man's getting on, and his health's not good. A great track record, better than anyone else in this building, but we can't ignore the facts.'

'I'll defend DI Tremayne, you know that.'

'Good for you, but there's going to come a time when he won't be up to it. What's the plan? Has he discussed the possibility?'

'He's aware of his own mortality, but policing is his life. What else has he got?'

'He's not on his own.'

'Jean is there most of the time.'

'At least he'll have company. Not the sort of person for an animal, is he?'

'The creature would starve. Not that DI Tremayne would be cruel, on the contrary. He's got a soft spot for animals and wayward criminals. It's just that…'

'Tremayne is Tremayne, is that what you're trying to say?' Moulton said.

'That's it. The poor animal would be at home wondering where its dinner is, and Tremayne, he'd be giving a villain the third degree.'

'I've protected him so far, I don't know how much longer. We've all got someone we report to, even me.'

'He's on a get fit regime. He's at the gym now.'

'Tremayne in a pair of shorts and a tee shirt. It doesn't bear thinking about.'

'Not the prettiest of sights, I'll grant you that,' Clare said, realising that she was enjoying her conversation with the superintendent.

'Your current murder enquiry, how's it going?'

'Three dead now, sir.'

'There's pressure for me to bring in extra help. I know that you and Tremayne work better the way you are, but what can I do to stave off the help?'

'Say an arrest is imminent.'

'Is it?'

'Not really. So far, we've retrieved all the gold, so the motive for further murders has gone.'

'Has it?'

'That's the theory, although there are still plenty of unknowns. More than one person knew where the missing gold was, but no one had taken it. Millions of pounds ready for the taking and no one took advantage. The Mitchells, none of them are flush with money, all except one of the women who remarried after Martin died. He died eighteen years ago, as you know.'

'Before my time. Tremayne was the arresting officer.'

'He was.'

'And no attempts to find the gold back then?'

'There were, but none were successful,' Clare said.

'And now it all becomes easier.'

'You're not thinking…?'

'Dereliction of duty, Tremayne not following through?'

'I can't believe that,' Clare said, perturbed by Moulton's comment.

'Neither can I. Back then he was a junior officer, just starting out. He did a great job considering his rank, and he had a DI to report to, the same as you. Not an easy man by all accounts, but he's dead and buried now.'

'Is it relevant?'

'I suppose not. But it makes you wonder if Tremayne's old DI was covering for someone. Back then, there was less accountability, less cross-checking. The reason that so many of Salisbury's finest law enforcers dabbled in taking a few backhanders. Not so easy these days, but it still goes on. Does he intend to say a good word for Gerry Mitchell, the would-be master thief?'

'He's not too keen, but he'll do it for Mitchell's mother.'

'That's his problem. He could be arresting her tomorrow.'

'He's arrested people before that he's liked. He'll not enjoy it, but he'll do it, and you know it.'

'Just make sure he doesn't make a fool of himself. And get him fit, or fitter than he is now. It'd be a shame if I had to stand him down, but like Tremayne, I'll do my duty.'

Clare left Moulton's office, a smile on her face. She had seen the human side of Superintendent Moulton, and she had liked it.

***

Tremayne, a man who enjoyed a pub lunch, usually a steak with chips, and a few pints of beer to wash it down, was not pleased with the repast placed in front of him.

'It's for your own good,' Jean said. She had dressed for the occasion, had her hair done. Clare had only had the opportunity to check her makeup at the police station. Her next-door neighbours had fed her cat.

'Not enough to feed a bird,' Tremayne said. It was the loving repartee between two people glad to be sharing each other's time.

'It looks good to me, Jean,' Clare said.

Tremayne had poured the wine, white, at his request. He was correct in specifying the colour, as Clare knew she would not turn up empty handed at anyone's house for a meal without bringing wine. To do so would have smacked of bad manners.

On the plates in front of them were roast chicken with potatoes. A bowl of salad sat to one side.

'And what did Moulton have to say?' Tremayne said.

'No talking shop tonight,' Jean said.

'What do you want me to talk about? Horse racing, the state of the nation?'

'You'll not win, Jean,' Clare said.

'The man's obsessed. I hope you're not.'
'I think I am.'
'It's time you found yourself a nice man and settled down.'
'She has,' Tremayne said.
'Please. He asked me out, I've said yes. It hardly constitutes a deep and meaningful relationship.'
'Okay, a one-night stand.'
'Tremayne, how can you talk to Clare like that?' Jean said.
'Yarwood's used to it.'
'Unfortunately, I am.'
'How's your food?' Jean said.
'It's lovely, delicious,' Clare said. Tremayne mumbled his compliments.
'What do you fancy in the 2.30 at Goodwood?' Tremayne said.
'And what's that for?' Jean said.
'You told me not to talk about the current investigation.'
'You see what I have to put up with.' Jean looked at Clare, raised her hands in a gesture of defeat.
'I need to tell Tremayne about Superintendent Moulton, anyway,' Clare said.
'Did he give you the normal routine about my retirement?'
'He was more interested to see you in your gym outfit.'
'You two had a good laugh at my expense, is that it?'
'Sort of. He still wants results.'
'Sorry, Jean,' Tremayne said. 'It can't be helped.'
'That's fine. It's nice to have Clare here, isn't it?'
'If you say so,' Tremayne said.

147

'Ignore him,' Clare said.

'The same at work as he is here?' Jean said.

'He's a pussycat here.'

'If you two are finished,' Tremayne said.

'We're finished. Talk about your murders, if you like,' Jean said.

'I'm not comfortable with Selwyn Cosford,' Tremayne said.

'Your reasons?' Clare said.

'Nothing firm, but the man's successful, highly educated. He plays the game, and he plays to win. He could have still been behind the original heist.'

'And if he was, what's it got to do with the murders.'

'That's the point. It doesn't really. Martin and Ethan had the gold in the boot of their car. But if it was intended for Cosford, one of his insurance fiddles, then why were the two brothers arguing?'

'They were arguing over the twenty bars in the boot of the car, not the forty that were taken.'

'Are you implying that Cosford may have been the intended recipient of the twenty that Betty knew about?'

'Maybe.'

'Then why put them in that hole behind the gatehouse? Why not somewhere else, a pre-arranged drop-off point.'

'Plausible deniability.'

'Cosford did not know where the gold was, and he wanted it that way. And if the Mitchells are arrested, he can still claim the insurance money. It's risk-free to him, with an added bonus if he pulls it off.'

'But Ethan Mitchell never mentioned Cosford,' Clare said.

'He never mentioned where the gold was buried either. Cosford could have set it up, so the twins didn't know it was him, and at some time in the future, when and how we don't know, Cosford would have made a one-off payment and retrieved the gold.'

'After the insurance claim has been settled.'

'He would have had to place a great deal of trust in the Mitchells.'

'Cosford's a local man. He would have known their father, even Martin and Ethan. Over a period of time, he could have quizzed them, come up with an evaluation as to whether he could trust them.'

'Tony Mitchell advising?'

'Possibly involved. He knew where the gold was. It could be that he was there when the gold was buried, the intermediary between the twins and Cosford. Now we know that Tony Mitchell was a trustworthy man, a war hero, and he had saved Cosford in battle. That sort of bond is not easy to break.'

'It's complex, but it's possible. But why was the gold in that hole for twenty years?'

'Cosford would know, but he's not going to tell us.'

'A motive for Tony Mitchell's death?'

'It's possible. War buddies aside, Cosford doesn't want anyone knowing the truth.'

'Mitchell would never have spoken.'

'An assumption. What if the man was ill, his mind starting to wander. Cosford's let him live all these years, knowing that he knew where the gold was, but now there's no gold. And Cosford's a man who likes to win. If we arrested Tony Mitchell as an accessory to the gold heist, the man might have told us all we needed to know.'

'We never suspected him.'

'In time we would have. Cosford would have known that, so he acted.'

'Gavin Mitchell?'

'That doesn't make sense. Betty was willing to tell him where it was.'

'Others in the family may have wanted some of it. Gavin's led a boring, less than successful life. He's reaching an age where he's starting to reflect on opportunities lost. He's keen to make his mark, see the world, even find himself a woman, young or old. The others in the family are debating, ready to get together with Betty and agree to share. Gavin's done the calculations, realised there'll not be enough for him.'

'He's wandering around blind up at the gatehouse.'

'What options does he have? He's smarter than Martin and Ethan. He knows that Betty is not a strong woman, and he knows how much three bars of gold weighs. He's desperate. He's ferreting around, hoping that he'll stumble across the gold. He has a torch and a metal detector. Given enough time, he would have found it.'

'Not with that estate manager, O'Connor. He wouldn't miss much.'

'If he had seen Gavin, he would have been suspicious. Anyone that goes near Longmore Park is soon picked up by him. There have been complaints about him roughing up people before. I checked. Charges were laid against him once after he stopped a couple of youths who were walking along a public footpath, a little too close to the estate for him. One of them gave O'Connor some lip, and he gave him and his friend a smack on the head with the staff that he carries. One of them was in intensive care for a few weeks, possible brain damage.'

'The outcome?'

'The youth recovered. Devlin O'Connor was held over for aggravated assault. It was a possible prison sentence, but strings were pulled.'

'He got off?'

'A five hundred pound fine, court expenses against him. He didn't pay.'

'Who did?'

'Where we're going tomorrow.'

Chapter 18

It was eight thirty in the morning when Tremayne and Clare crossed the border into Devlin O'Connor's territory. Up the road, they could see his Land Rover coming at a rapid speed to waylay those who had failed to check with him.

Clare was driving, Tremayne was nursing his sore calf muscles after a mile at slow walking pace on the treadmill, with the instructor promising to raise the speed the next time. Even after that, he had lifted weights for ten minutes, miniscule compared to what some of the others were lifting, but enough to make his arms ache. Clare had looked over at him, decided against offering a comment.

'What are you doing here?' O'Connor said.

'We're police officers,' Tremayne leaned over from his side of the vehicle and shouted over at the Land Rover.

'We don't like visitors up here.'

Tremayne got out of Clare's car and walked around to the open window of O'Connor's vehicle. 'Now look here, O'Connor, you're not the lord and master around here. There's been a murder behind your gatehouse, and your testimony that you were at home fast asleep doesn't stack up. And if we want to go and knock on the door of the main house uninvited, we have the authority, not you. Do you have any more to say, or do I have to arrest you for obstructing two police officers?'

'We get the occasional sightseer up here. Some of them don't like it when I turn them around.'

'If it's a problem, put a gate and a guard at the entrance.'

'That costs money.'

'How come you didn't know about the gold? You seem to know everything else that happens around here.'

'They never told me you were coming.'

'They, meaning the main house?'

'That's it.'

'Yarwood said they were friendly.'

'They are.'

'Then why hassle us? Do you have any guilty secrets up here, growing marijuana, a secret opium den?'

'Of course not. I do my job. Others may think it's a cushy number, but it's not. We get the occasional drunk with a gun, fancies a pheasant or a deer. I've got to deal with them, somehow not get shot, but I can't shoot back.'

'Don't worry. We'll not touch them.'

'Deer?' Clare said.

'You'll see them close to the main house,' O'Connor said.

'We'll be in touch later. We need to talk to you again,' Tremayne said.

'You've got my number.'

'We have.'

O'Connor put the Land Rover into first gear and drove off.

'An unpleasant man,' Clare said.

'A man who doesn't miss much. He must know more than he's telling us.'

***

It was remarkable, Clare thought, as she and Tremayne were shown around the Georgian mansion. She was the one with the clear voice, the one who pronounced her vowels, enunciated her words, and there they were, the owners of the house, English aristocracy, and they were wholly charmed by Tremayne.

They loved his accent, his downtrodden look, they even wanted to hear about him at the gym, and how many murders he'd solved, the villains he had put away.

'This is my great-grandfather,' his lordship said. 'He was in the military, the rank of Colonel. The one over here, the imperious-looking gentlemen, he was a rogue, hanged as a spy by the enemy during one of the colonial wars.'

Tremayne had to admit he was enjoying the guided tour. He wasn't sure why, and he had visited a few stately homes when he was younger, but here, there was no monotone guide, no ropes closing off the private quarters. This time they went everywhere, including the separate bedrooms of the lord and his lady. Even the children's bedroom, another room painted and papered in dark red velvet. 'There's a ghost in here. All our guests want to try it out, most don't last the night.'

'I don't believe in the unknown,' Tremayne said. 'There's always an explanation.'

'Neither do we, but no one stays in the room.'

'Maybe you've tricked it out.'

'Not us, but it's a good idea. Do you reckon you could spend the night in that room?'

'I reckon so.'

Clare was staggered when Tremayne received an invite to come for dinner within the next month and to sleep in the room. She was even more staggered when he accepted.

Tremayne didn't need to worry about his pinkie finger or the etiquette of how to drink a cup of tea. The four of them sat in the kitchen, each with an old mug.

'Apart from the title and the estate, we're regular people,' her ladyship said. 'It's just that people expect more from us.'

'Jealous, I suppose,' Tremayne said.

'It's a lot of work looking after a place like this.'

'Devlin O'Connor seems to have his finger on the pulse.'

'O'Connor's a rough man, but there are some who see plenty, believe it's theirs to take.'

'Is that why you tolerate him?' Clare said.

'He's a decent man, and we trust him.'

'We need your take on what's happened down at the gatehouse,' Tremayne said.

'We've followed it with interest, not that we can add much to what you already know. The gatehouse has not been used for a long time, and neither of us has walked around the back of it,' his lordship said.

'Did you know Tony Mitchell?'

'We knew him through the village fete. He often won a prize for his vegetables. Apart from that, we didn't see him often. We're not here a lot of the time, either. Business in London, trips overseas.'

'Were you surprised when the gold was discovered?'

'Shocked would be a more appropriate word. We knew about the gold being stolen from the van, not far from here, but not that it was on our land.'

'Devlin O'Connor?' Tremayne said.

'I know he looks a likely character to be involved, but we've always found him to be honest,' Lord Linden said.

'Several million pounds of gold would tempt anyone.'

'There's plenty in this house that's worth that sort of money.'

'Not so easy to melt down,' Tremayne said.

'Not that difficult either, and small items here and there add up. Some of them would be worth good money.'

'Is this place alarmed?'

'Yes, but there are a dozen people on the estate who come in here when we're away.'

'Coming back to the murders,' Tremayne said. 'Gavin Mitchell, did you know him?'

'No. We read that he was a relative of Tony Mitchell.'

'He was, although they were not close. Tony Mitchell had known that the gold was on your land for eighteen years, and he never touched it. So did Ethan Mitchell's ex-wife. He was murdered in St Mark's in Salisbury.'

'We know the church,' her ladyship said.

'I don't think there's much more we can add, do you?' his lordship said.

'Not for now,' Tremayne said.

Both he and Clare stood up and made for the back door of the house. 'That mug you were drinking from,' his lordship said. 'Antique, worth several hundred pounds.'

'And I was going to take it as a souvenir,' Tremayne said without smiling.

'No, you weren't, Detective Inspector. And remember, Saturday fortnight, informal, just the family and a few friends, and bring your wife. Sergeant Yarwood, Clare, you as well. And make sure to bring someone.'

Death by a Dead Man's Hand

'I'm single.'

'A pretty woman like you,' her ladyship said. 'I don't believe it.'

***

Selwyn Cosford looked at the man standing in front of him. He looked young enough to be a grandson, but he wasn't, and he was not agreeable.

'Mr Cosford, I don't see how we can process your claim,' Paul Rudd of Gainsford Insurance said.

The two men were at Cosford's mansion. Both were seated in the library, both were hostile. Cosford recognised the degree-educated, process-driven pen pusher. Rudd knew the ugly face of aggressive capitalism. Even Rudd had heard of Cosford before driving down the long sweeping road that was Cosford's driveway. He had parked his Ford Fiesta behind a Jaguar. He knew it was Cosford's by the personalised number plates.

A uniformed butler had opened the door for him. After that, the walk to the library past the artworks, past a statue which he was sure he'd seen in a museum in London. Rudd laid claim to being a bibliophile, reading at least two books a week, but in that room, there were thousands. He walked around as he waited, saw titles he had read, others that did not interest him, and others that he wanted to read but were not readily available.

'A great collection,' Rudd said on Cosford entering. The two men had exchanged the usual pleasantries, discussed literature and favourite authors, before directing their conversation to money, namely Selwyn Cosford's recovered gold bars, and why he was entitled to them. It was then that the two men realised that a common interest did not cross the divide that separated them.

'Eighteen years ago, when you settled on my claim, you paid the cash equivalent. Today it's worth over five times that.'

'I'll concede the point,' Rudd said, who knew the reason why he was dealing with Cosford. He was the man who had knocked back more claims, some legit, most fraudulent, in the four years he had been with Gainsford Insurance. He knew that Cosford was a chancer, assuming his reputation, his weekly television programmes, would somehow save the day.

'Then what are you going to do about it?'

'What do you want me to do? We paid out the claim amount, as agreed. You signed a declaration that all was in order, end of the matter.'

'For you, but here we are. The gold's been recovered. It's got a substantial premium on what you paid me, and inflation has only gone up sixty-three per cent. I'm out of pocket, and the insurance company has made a killing.'

'On the contrary, Gainsford Insurance has covered the deficit for those eighteen years and has not earned any interest on the money. If I did the calculations, it could well be that you owe us money.'

'How dare you come in here and threaten me.'

'I'm not threatening. I'm here because you are a valued customer. It was you who requested that we use a different transport company.'

'I had written approval from your company.'

'You had an authorised letter from an employee who no longer works for us.'

'A competent man,' Cosford said.

'Is that why you, Mr Cosford, subsequently employed him? Believe me, if I had been in the company back then, you would not have been given insurance. Mr Cosford, quite frankly, you represent a poor risk. There have been several claims over the years, some suspicious.'

Cosford studied the young man, a schoolboy when the gold initially went missing. He liked what he saw, a fighter. A man similar to him at that age: brash, determined, aggressive.

'Paul, I can call you Paul, can't I?'

Rudd recognised the smarm offensive. 'Yes, that would be fine.'

'And you must call me Selwyn.'

'Sorry, I can't do that. My upbringing, your age.'

'Very well,' Cosford said. He wasn't sure if Rudd was honest, or whether he was trying to maintain a distance.

'We paid out on a painting that was damaged in the house. Was it repaired?'

'It was. It cost me more than your pay-out.'

'And its value?'

'The market for a Turner is not good.'

'Mr Cosford, our estimate is one million pounds. You have it insured with us for one million one hundred thousand, am I correct?'

'Probably. I leave the incidentals to others to deal with.'

'In that case, I can deal with your people, not you.'

'I have a special interest in the gold.'

'Mr Cosford, you have a special interest in the money, or is this another of your games. You're notorious for reading the small print on any legal contract, bending it to your interpretation, bringing in experts to debate the intricacies. It was how you managed to claim six hundred and fifty thousand for a Ferrari, even when it was being driven by your granddaughter?'

'She was insured, and you said she was not.'

'She was insured to drive it between certain hours, and in certain weather conditions. I wouldn't have paid. If you have such disregard for vehicles of that calibre, then you are a …'

'Philistine?'

'That's not a word I would use, but yes.'

'I've another one in the garage. Several in fact. Do you want to see them?'

'Personally, yes. Professionally, no. Mr Cosford, your claim is null and void. We at Gainsford Insurance will not be compensating you for any financial loss that you may feel you have incurred with these twenty bars. They will remain the property of my company and will be credited to the account of Gainsford Insurance once they have been sold.'

'Congratulations,' Cosford said.

'For what?'

'The way you handled yourself. It's not often I meet someone who can stand up to me.'

'I'm sure it isn't.'

'The cars. Are you ready now?'

'Are you willing to sign a document that you will not make any further claim on Gainsford Insurance?'

'I'll bring in the lawyers, see what they can do.'

'You'll not win.'

'Maybe I won't, but it'll be fun trying.'

'Mr Cosford, you are a devious man who plays with people. It's no wonder that you've been so successful.'

'The cars are in the garage. Let's go.'

While Rudd checked out the vehicles – Ferraris, Jaguars, Rolls Royces – Cosford made a phone call.

'Maggie, you know you're always joking that you'd marry a man like your grandfather?'

'There's no one like you, Granddad.'

'There is. He's at my place. Get over here and take him for a ride in one of the cars.'

'Ten minutes.'

Selwyn Cosford could see that he could kill two birds with the one stone. Someone for his favourite granddaughter, and a chance to still win with the insurance company. Rudd was right, he knew that, but then Paul Rudd was of the same ilk as him. He could even be the man to take over from him when his time came. His son, Maggie's father, the spoilt child of a wealthy man, wasn't.

Chapter 19

'I don't like it,' Tremayne said. He was sitting in his office and leaning back with his arms behind his head.

'What do you mean?' Clare said.

'Martin and Ethan, not the smartest two men, strike lucky with a van carrying gold bullion.'

'Hardly lucky, both are dead.'

'You know what I mean.'

'I do. But you conducted the investigation eighteen years ago.'

'I was still wet behind the ears, then. A bit like you, Yarwood, and I didn't have a mentor, only a boss.'

'What about him?'

'The man was competent, but he was taking it easy. No ulcers for him, plenty for me.'

'You've no ulcers,' Clare said.

'I will with the way you and Jean feed me.'

'Apart from that.'

'The twins steal the gold. They've got twenty bars of gold in the boot of a car, another twenty hidden. They don't know what to do, and they argue.'

'It wasn't out of character.'

'No. But why hide twenty bars?'

'They only had a car. Each of those bars weighed over twelve kilos, that's twenty-five pounds each. Maybe it would have been too heavy for the car. A thousand pounds, that's close to half a ton.'

'I don't buy it. They had some arrangement with someone, and for whatever reason, it didn't work out.'

Death by a Dead Man's Hand

'There were plenty of places where two vehicles could have met, transferred the gold across.'

'I can still see the hand of Selwyn Cosford behind this,' Tremayne said. 'He could have said to the twins to hide half, keep half, and then he'd contact them afterwards.'

'But it all went wrong, and Martin was killed by Ethan. The end result was that Cosford had no gold, only the insurance money. If he had played it right, he could have had the insurance as well as the gold, and he'd have no difficulty moving it out of the country. The Middle East, India, no questions asked.'

'Tony Mitchell's a friend of Cosford's, and he had a map. Why didn't he tell Cosford?'

'Unknowns, yet again. Mitchell and Cosford were men who had a shared history. That doesn't make them friends. You investigated this thoroughly eighteen years ago,' Clare said.

'I know, but we couldn't get anywhere. In the end, a conviction for Ethan Mitchell, a promotion for me,' Tremayne said.

'For the investigation?'

'In part, but I was due.'

Tremayne took out a packet of cigarettes, put it back in his pocket again.

'You're allowed five a day,' Clare said.

'You two are driving me crazy, you know that.'

'We know it, but Moulton will have you out of here if you don't look after yourself.'

'He'll have us both out if we don't find a murderer.'

'What about the drivers of the van? How come the twins were able to get into the driver's compartment?

Even if it were not full security, they wouldn't have left the doors unlocked.'

'The vehicle was checked. No fault found, and Ethan had smashed the driver's window with a mallet.'

'But why was the vehicle stopped, and how did the twins know?'

'Yet again, you're going over old history,' Tremayne said.

'I'm not suggesting any negligence, but the twins had struck lucky, they've got the gold, the hiding place, yet they argue over what to do next.'

'They weren't planners, more spur of the moment.'

'Who told them to place the gold in that hole? Was it Tony Mitchell? He had a good map, Ethan only had a sketch.'

'Maybe Cosford had something on Tony. We've only Cosford's statement that Tony had been out to his place, and there's no knowledge of Cosford visiting Tony.'

'The publican at the Plough Inn seems to know most of what's going on.'

'Vince Harding, the driver, couldn't stop giving you the eye. We'll talk to him first' Tremayne said.

***

Vince Harding was entertaining when Tremayne and Clare knocked on his door. Inside the house, the sound of a woman squealing, the voice of a man in hot pursuit.

'Not the best time,' Clare said.

'He'll be angry when we break up his night of romance,' Tremayne said.

'It doesn't sound much like romance to me,' Clare said. She was more of a candlelit dinner person. The curtains were not closed fully, and she had seen two overweight people running around half-naked, the woman still with a bra on, feigning modesty, and Harding down to his Y-fronts. To her, it was carnal lust, not romance.

'Harding, it's Tremayne and Yarwood.' Tremayne banged on the window with his fist, a mischievous smile on his face. Clare thought him cruel.

'Go away. I'm busy,' Harding shouted back.

'Murder waits for no man. It's either you open this door, or we'll break it down.'

'With what?' Clare said.

'I want him angry, livid would be better.'

The woman inside could be seen putting on her clothes and picking up her handbag. Vince Harding pulled on his trousers, wrestled with his tee shirt and opened the door.

'What right have you to disturb me? I've broken no law.'

'Waking the neighbours could be an offence.'

'Around here? Are you joking? Her, two doors down, she's screaming all night, and up the road, a couple of druggies who sing all night, and then screw all day.'

'We know you were in on the gold heist,' Tremayne said.

Clare knew Tremayne was trying to break the man's story. The woman that Harding had been entertaining with his manly ardour brushed past the three standing at the front door. 'See you later,' she said.

'Sorry about tonight,' Harding said.

'Don't worry. I'll add it to your account.'

'Local girl?' Tremayne said.

'Hardly a girl, but she's the best I can afford.' Clare thought the man disgusting.

'Harding, you and Aidan Farrell were in on the heist. We know that now. What do you have to say?'

'It destroyed my life, you know that.'

'It didn't. You destroyed it yourself with your negative attitude, your slovenly appearance,' Clare said.

'Tremayne, we've been through this how many times? It was eighteen years ago. It was late at night, and we were looking for Aidan's girlfriend. How were we to know that Martin and Ethan Mitchell were going to come up behind us?'

'How did you know their names?' Clare said.

'We gave evidence at the trial of one of them. Do you think we were meeting up with them, devising a plan?'

'Why not?'

'And why would we? We had a good number with the company. Each week we'd take something here, something there. On a few occasions, we brought back a vehicle from the continent.'

'Where on the continent?'

'This is all on record. Nothing was found to be illegal, and Tremayne knows this. I've a good mind to write to my Member of Parliament, or maybe there's an ombudsman that deals with police brutality.'

'I'll give you the phone numbers before we leave,' Tremayne said. 'It doesn't alter the fact that something was overlooked in the original investigation. Something that Yarwood and I intend to rectify. Vince, it's eighteen years, long enough for the gold heist to be a distant memory to most people. And Martin and Ethan Mitchell are both dead, as are their brother and their uncle. No one's going to pin you down, sentence you to time in prison.'

'Rubbish, and you know it. You would arrest me within five minutes if I gave you anything.'

'Do you have something? It would be best to talk,' Clare said.

'I wasn't driving, Aidan was.'

'Are you saying he was in on the heist?'

'I'm not saying anything. I'm just trying to get you out of my house.'

'I'm trying to help you,' Tremayne said.

Clare could see Harding wavering. He had to be involved somehow.

'Now, we know that Ethan Mitchell could keep a secret, so could his wife and his uncle. How about you? Have you kept it secret as to how you stopped at a pre-arranged spot and let the Mitchells cosh your offsider, truss you both up and drive off?' Tremayne said.

'It wasn't like that. Aidan was keen for this woman. Back then, you had to get out a map and look for the address. You must remember it, Tremayne.'

'I do. That doesn't explain why two men with a good track record would risk it all for a couple of women.'

'How old are you, Tremayne? Two young men, full of energy. What was more important? A piece of tail or following company procedures?'

'Where's Aidan Farrell?'

'I've not seen him for a few years, probably thirteen or fourteen.'

'Any idea where he is now?'

'The last I heard, he was back in Ireland. Married, by all accounts.'

'The girl he was meeting that night?'

'It may be her, but I wasn't invited to the wedding, wouldn't have gone anyway.'

'Why not?'

'After the trial, and with us unemployed, we went our separate ways. Apart from the job at the security company, we didn't have a lot in common.'

'Vince, I'm going to arrest you, take you back to Salisbury. You've fed us nonsense. You know something, and we need it.'

'On what charge?'

'Perverting the course of justice.'

Clare realised that Tremayne could not arrest the man for not telling him what he wanted to hear. She hoped her senior knew what he was doing.

'Aidan received this phone call. It was his girlfriend. She was telling him where to stop, and she'd come out and meet us, bring her friend as well.'

'Why didn't this come out at the trial?'

'We were in enough trouble as it was. We kept quiet, hoped we could keep our jobs, but you and your colleagues had done your job well. We weren't found to be involved, but the mud stuck.'

'Mud now proved,' Tremayne said.

'It's the truth. If we hadn't had our tongues hanging out, we wouldn't have stopped.'

'Are you saying that you're innocent of the crime, even Aidan Farrell?'

'Guilty of stupidity, that's all.'

'Guilty of withholding information at a trial for murder. That's a criminal offence.'

'There must be a statute of limitations.'

'It doesn't apply, but I'll not arrest you. Where can we find Aidan? Where can we find this girlfriend?'

'Aidan's in Ireland. I'll give you his phone number. You can trace it to an address.'

'The girlfriend?'

'I never met her.'
'Don't phone Aidan Farrell.'
'I won't,' Vince Harding said.

Chapter 20

Betty Galton was preparing to travel to Gerry's trial. She did not expect two police officers on her doorstep.

'Tony Mitchell knew where the gold was,' Tremayne said.

'Not from me, he didn't.'

'We believe he knew even before you.'

'How? Why?'

'We hoped you could tell us.'

'The man kept his cards close to his chest. We never even knew about him and Selwyn Cosford,' Betty said.

'When did you find out?'

'I saw them talking to each other in Salisbury. Tony told me some of the story. How do you know?'

'Cosford told us. We believe that Tony was keeping the gold for someone, but we're short on ideas. Maybe you could fill us in.'

'Not now. I've got Gerry to consider.'

'Do you know something?'

'No. Ethan gave me what I gave you. If Tony was involved, can't you leave it alone?'

Tremayne gave his character statement in defence of Gerry Mitchell later that day. It was to be a short trial. Tremayne knew the judge to be a stickler for stiff sentences. The prosecution was excellent; the defence, by and large, incompetent.

There had been a plea in the summing up by the defence, a small ineffectual man with a whining voice, of how the man on trial had suffered the ignominy of his father being found guilty of murder and spending seventeen years in prison, only to be killed soon after his release. The usual broken home routine did not work, as the prosecution showed that Betty, his mother, had married a man of good repute, and the family home had been stable and loving through the accused's formative years. In the end, a three-year sentence, out in less for good behaviour.

Tremayne had to agree with the judge, the accused's mother did not.

'He's just a child,' Betty said outside the courtroom.

'We'll appeal,' the defence lawyer said.

'Don't bother, Betty,' Tremayne said. 'He'll be out soon enough with good behaviour. There's no point in wasting your time. You've still got Bob and Marcia.'

'Somehow it doesn't seem enough.'

Tremayne took Betty by the arm and marched her next door to a pub. A stiff brandy would not go amiss.

After Betty had revived, Tremayne said, 'Gerry will be fine. But we've got to find Ethan's murderer. Tony's involved, I know it.'

'Instinct?'

'Too many years in the police force. Nothing is a simple as it looks until we solve it, and then it's only too obvious. Martin and Ethan weren't smart enough for the job, but Tony was.'

'He never committed a criminal act in his life.'

'Selwyn Cosford's a suspect. Could he and Tony be working together?'

'Tony was a loner, never trusted anyone, not even Selwyn. Tony told me once that he didn't like the man very much.'

'When?'

'I can't remember, but it was a long time ago.'

***

Tremayne and Clare spent more time waiting for the plane at Southampton airport than they did in the air. The weather in Southampton had been blustery. On arrival in Dublin, it was raining, almost sleeting.

'My first time here,' Tremayne said.

'I've been once before,' Clare said.

Tremayne did not hear her answer. He was focussed on a man in the crowd outside the terminal. 'Tremayne, you're getting old,' the man said.

'You're not looking so good yourself,' Tremayne said. 'This is Sergeant Yarwood.'

'Inspector Murphy. Call me Paddy, everyone else does.'

Clare shook the man's hand. He had a strong Irish accent and a firm voice. He was older than Tremayne, not showing it as much as her senior.

'We've worked together a few times in the past,' Tremayne said.

'It's my countrymen. They want to get over to England and cause trouble. It's on account of your warm weather.'

'Compared to here, it probably is,' Clare said.

'Anyway, we've found Aidan Farrell for you. We've nothing against him, so don't go in there with the heavy boots. The man's made something of himself, somewhat of a celebrity.'

'How?'

'He set up a transport company here in Ireland. He's often on the television.'

'Why did we have so much trouble finding him?'

'Aidan Farrell changed his name to Garrity, his mother's maiden name.'

'Any reason why?'

'You'd better ask him. I've told him you're here and why. I can't say he was too pleased, but he's agreed. We're off to his office. It's not far from here, about twenty minutes.'

The last time Tremayne had seen Aidan Farrell, it had been at Ethan Mitchell's trial. Back then, he had had long hair with a Mexican bandit moustache. Now, before the three police officers stood a well-dressed man in a suit. His attempt at Pancho Villa was no longer present; his long hair had been cut short, with greying at the temples.

'Detective Inspector Tremayne, I don't wish to be reminded of what happened that night.'

Outside the office, a fleet of trucks.

'You've done well,' Tremayne said.

'I've worked hard, so has my wife.'

'What caused you to change. Eighteen years ago you were a cocky individual, full of yourself.'

'People change, you've changed.'

'Not for the better,' Tremayne said. 'Whereas you have, for the better.'

'Good living, a good wife, a good family.'

'You're married?'

'Let's not beat around the bush, Tremayne. You know all about me. Inspector Murphy has obviously given you a profile of me and my life.'

'Ethan Mitchell's been murdered,' Tremayne said.

'I read about it,' Farrell said.

'We need to go over the heist. We know that you and Harding stopped the van that night after a phone call from your girlfriend.'

'She wasn't my girlfriend, just a casual acquaintance.'

'You were sleeping with her?'

'If she was available.'

'Why did you arrange to meet her that night? Why not another night?'

'She phoned, I responded. A man has got to take every opportunity he can.'

'Even if he's carrying gold bullion?'

'Even. Do you know how many times a security van gets hijacked in England?'

'Not the exact figure, but single digits.'

'That's about it. If we were on a long-distance trip, Harding and me, we'd sometimes take a detour, try to break up the monotony. Okay, not strictly according to the book, but nothing ever went wrong. She phones me up, tells me she's at home, not far away, and she's got a friend for Harding. He's not in a good mood, just found his wife with another man. He's up for it, so am I. It's only an hour, maybe less, and then we'd be on our way.'

'And?'

'We're travelling out from Andover. She gives me directions and to pull in at a layby, which I did. And then, there's a mallet coming through my window, a gun pointing at me. Fifteen minutes later, after I had been coshed, I wake up in a ditch with Harding, minus my uniform.'

'The woman?'

'I never saw her again. After a few years scratching around in England, I came back to Ireland.'

'But you've seen Vince Harding a few times since.'

'If I was in his area, I'd give him a call. But then, he became a slob, and as you can see, I wised up.'

'Your wife, does she know the story?'

'Some of it. She's a local. We met in Dublin fifteen years back. Two children now, and I prefer my past to stay where it belongs.'

'How do we find the woman you were going to meet?'

'After eighteen years?'

'Yes. We consider her suspect.'

'I did at the time, but the police were all for implicating Harding and me. I read that you had found twenty bars. A lot of money. It would come in handy.'

'Do you need it?' Clare said.

'I'm aiming to expand into England, and the opposition will attempt to undercut me, the same as they did here. The extra cash would come in handy.'

'How did you manage the competition here?'

'Hard work.'

'Why Garrity?' Clare said.

'There's a competitor, Farrell and Sons. I thought it better to use my mother's maiden name.'

'That's true,' Paddy Murphy said.

It was late afternoon by the time the conversation with Farrell had concluded. Tremayne and Clare booked into their hotel. Murphy and Tremayne had some catching up to do and a few pints of Guinness to down.

'What did you reckon?' Clare said when she joined the men later. She could see that Tremayne was not keeping to his couple of pints. Both men were almost at the standing up and singing stage of inebriation. Clare knew she was not and would never be.

'Farrell, he's straight,' Murphy said.

'I'm inclined to agree,' Tremayne said. His words were starting to slur. 'We knew about the girlfriend, could never find her.'

'We have a name, Eileen Bleakes,' Clare said.

'Did you try to find her?' Paddy said.

'We weren't complete amateurs,' Tremayne said. 'Of course we tried, but she'd gone. Not so difficult to disappear then. If she had travelled to the continent, no passport needed, she could have grabbed a flight and gone anywhere.'

'There are databases at the airlines,' Clare said.

'And some people will get you a forged passport for two thousand pounds, three if you want top notch.'

'We need to find her.'

'Easier said than done,' Tremayne said. 'She wasn't the mastermind, we know that.'

'How?'

'Her next-door neighbour to where she had been renting told us that she was a friendly woman, but disorganised. Inside the place, which she had left in a hurry, no incriminating evidence.'

Clare wanted to discuss the case. The two men wanted to drink and reminisce, the pastime of two men approaching retirement, unable to comprehend a life without a badge. Clare left and went to her room. She turned on her laptop. An email from the doctor, confirming that the date was still on. She replied in the affirmative. She then entered Garrity Trucking Company into the search engine. Apart from an impressive website, there was not much to be gained. It was as Paddy Murphy had said, as Aidan Farrell had confirmed. She expanded the image of Farrell's wife on the website and studied it: age, height, hair colour, distinguishing features. There were none that easily identified her as Eileen Bleakes. The woman's neighbour had given a detailed description of her, as had Aidan Farrell. His had been the least well regarded, as he had been a suspect at the time.

Death by a Dead Man's Hand

Regardless, Clare sent off the website image to Face Recognition to see what they could come up with. Downstairs in the bar, she could hear the melodious tones of Murphy and Tremayne, another person accompanying them on the piano.

Clare sent a message to Jean: *the man's going to suffer for his sins in the next week*. She smiled at her and Jean's little conversations, but the diet regime, the treadmill, the reduced cigarettes and alcohol had already had some beneficial effect on Tremayne.

Chapter 21

Dublin Airport and an early morning flight back to Southampton. Clare was looking forward to getting back to her cottage and her cat. Tremayne stood to her side at the check-in counter. He was not looking good after a heavy night and a few too many pints of Guinness.

'Serves you right,' Clare said as he looked over at her for sympathy.

'Don't tell Jean,' Tremayne said.

'Jean's interested in your well-being, and you go and get drunk with Paddy Murphy. No doubt he looks no better than you, but then he's got no one to care for him.'

'Good luck to him,' Tremayne said.

'You don't mean it. You love Jean being around, fussing over you. Does she fetch your slippers yet?'

'I had a dog that did once, but Jean took it with her when she moved out all those years ago. Maybe I'll have a word about my slippers to her. It only seems fair.'

'Fair to you. I suggest you don't go home until late. I sent an image of Farrell's wife over to Facial Recognition.'

'The missing girlfriend?'

'It's a long shot, but I don't think it's her.'

At Southampton, Clare paid the overnight parking fee and they headed back to Salisbury and Bemerton Road Police Station. By the time they entered the building, Tremayne was back to his usual self.

'Do we believe Farrell?' Tremayne said to Clare in his office.

'His story is plausible.'

'Setting up a business needs a lot of money, the sort Farrell never had.'

'His wife's family?'

'Some of it came from there, although he may have had another source.'

'There was no money from the gold bars. If there were a payoff, it would only have come from Cosford for a job well done.'

'And he wasn't going to pay for anything, not after the gold had gone missing or had been retrieved from the boot of the car. One thing that we can say about Cosford is that he and his money are not easily parted, and not to a truck driver just because he had a girlfriend and had been coshed on the back of his head.'

'Where did Farrell initially meet the missing girlfriend?'

'A club in London. We checked it out. Back then, it was the sort of place Farrell would go if he were on the prowl. Nowadays, it's been turned into a discount pharmacy.'

'The girlfriend's crucial,' Clare said.

'The girlfriend can't be found. We tried back then, but Farrell only knew her as Jane. He didn't even have a surname; can you believe it?'

'I can. Farrell's a hunter, only interested in whether the female is willing.'

'And this girlfriend must have been if he was willing to risk his job.'

'If Cosford's behind this, he'd know where the girlfriend is, or at least who she was.'

'Do you fancy a trip to London?' Tremayne said.

'You're offering to drive?'

'Get real, Yarwood. We need to meet up with the security van company.'

'Are you ready?'

'After I've had a cigarette, first of the day.'

***

To the west of London, close to Heathrow, was the head office of Morrison's Security.

'Did you set the business up?' Clare asked Colin Morrison, the owner of the business.

'Not me. My father did back in the forties, just after the war. Back then, it was much easier. A couple of old trucks and you were in business. Now, it's almost impossible with the upfront costs, and the competition is fierce.'

'You managed to survive, even after losing all that gold,' Tremayne said. He and Morrison had met a long time ago. Back then, the man had been evasive. Now, he looked tired.

'A dent in the company's reputation and there were a few lean years, but people forget.'

'You've kept yourself up to date on the missing gold?'

'I'd prefer to forget about it, a black mark against the company. Any attempt by you to imply that somehow we were responsible, then you'll need to be talking through my lawyer.'

'Still sensitive?' Tremayne said. Back then, Morrison had been younger, fitter, and a fighting man.

'Why not? We had built our reputation over many years, and then one incident, and we are lambasted. Our competition took every opportunity to run us down.'

'Mr Morrison, one thing I don't understand,' Clare said.

'What's that?'

'There was a problem with your vans, so you swap to a vehicle with no more than a couple of extra locks.'

'It happens from time to time.'

'But why? It was eighteen years ago. Trucks are reliable, so why were two out of service?'

'We're not talking about the family car, a hundred miles a week. Our trucks traverse the length and breadth of the United Kingdom, into Europe as well.'

'We're not here for a promotional,' Tremayne said. He could see Morrison giving the story that he had reserved for the media when Cosford's gold had been stolen. He knew that Clare was asking the same questions as he had, and he knew the answers, but there was no harm in them being asked again.

'If you'd let me finish,' Morrison said. He sat back in his chair, taking a breath, and then spoke again. 'The two vehicles that were out of service. One had just come in from Switzerland. It had a brake problem. A heavy load, a few too many steep descents.'

'Plausible,' Clare said.

'The other vehicle had just done an overnighter from Scotland. It was due for a service. The driver had reported a grinding noise in the gearbox. Do you know how much it costs for another gearbox, and the inconvenience if the vehicle breaks down and we have to send a replacement?'

'You're about to tell me.'

'A lot of money.'

'Okay, let's assume you're left with one van. It's not the ideal solution, but you decide to use it. There's still the insurance, and there are forty bars of gold worth three million pounds in the back.'

'This has all been explained before. If you had checked with Inspector Tremayne, you'd know that the insurance company had agreed to the van. All the paperwork was in place. And besides, the shipment was secret, and nobody in this company knew what Harding and Farrell were carrying.'

'Except you, the drivers, and Cosford.'

'Apart from us four and the insurance company. It was a three-hour trip down, and at the other end, Cosford would take the gold.'

'Take? Him personally?'

'Harding and Farrell would have been responsible for moving it from the van to a room at the back of his mansion. Once that had been completed, Cosford would have signed off, and the two men would have returned back here.'

'You expected them back that night?'

'We did. We didn't know that Farrell was intent on a late-night seduction. That was not agreed to.'

'Do the drivers sometimes take different routes, stop for a break?'

'It happens. Not that we know about it, and we've never had a problem, not before, not since.'

'Farrell's girlfriend knew about the gold.'

'It's eighteen years, and we went over this back then. Do you expect me to remember something else after such a long time?'

'We expect you to tell the truth,' Clare said.

'Get out of my office,' Morrison said. 'I'll not say another word without my lawyer present.'

'Guilty conscience?' Yarwood said, realising that Clare had broken through Morrison's shield of invulnerability. 'What else do you transport?' Tremayne had trained his sergeant well, he knew that. Men like Morrison don't get rattled easily, but she had come at him gently, raising the pressure, even smiling, and the man had cracked.

'There is no guilt. We are a professional organisation, staffed by motivated employees.'

'We've had the promotional, Mr Morrison,' Clare said. 'Have there been any other insurance claims for broken, destroyed, or stolen items over the years, and remember we can check?'

'Nothing, apart from a painting that was damaged, but the vehicle was in a crash.'

'Paintings are cased for transport. It must have been a serious crash.'

Keep it up, Yarwood, Tremayne thought. See how far you can push the man.

'It was, and if there's nothing else…' Morrison said.

'There is.'

'What is it? What scurrilous lies do you want to perpetuate?'

'Not lies, just the truth. An audit of this company and what it transports, would that be acceptable?'

'It would not. We have vehicles going in and out of here all the time. We're a busy company transporting all over Europe. We do not have the time or the interest for the police to enter these premises, and unless you have a warrant or charges are levelled, I would request, in fact, insist, that you do not return.'

'Any problems with illegals trying to get into your vehicles for a trip across the channel?' Tremayne said.

'It's a constant.'

'How about drugs? They must be more profitable than paintings and antiques, more profitable than gold, easier to transport, easier to distribute.'

'Are you accusing me, Tremayne?' Morrison was up on his feet, attempting to punch a phone number into his mobile, his hands shaking.'

'Do you want me to do it?' Clare said. 'Your lawyer?'

'Yes.'

'He won't be much help when we arrest you for the transportation of drugs into this country.'

'You won't find me guilty of that, nor illegals.'

'Or maybe it was trafficking women. What nationality was Farrell's girlfriend? Mr Morrison, there's something here that you're not telling us.'

'This is unacceptable,' Morrison said, having regained some of his composure.

'Lying to the police is unacceptable.,' Tremayne said. 'We hadn't considered trafficking women eighteen years ago, not such a problem, but now Yarwood may have hit the nail on the head. You've done well here, better than the competition. Maybe they play by the book, maybe you don't.'

'I met the girlfriend once, I'll not deny it.'

'How?'

'She was here with Farrell.'

'You never mentioned it during our original investigation.'

'Why would I? She wasn't the focus back then. You asked the standard questions, and your people checked the loading documents, and that was that.'

'Why did you sack Harding and Farrell?'

'I paid them off.'

'But you knew the girlfriend.'

'She was polite, attractive, and keen on Farrell.'

'He was being set up,' Clare said. 'And you, Mr Morrison, were involved.'

'Please leave. We have no more to talk about.'

The two police officers left Morrison in his office. Tremayne had seen him head over to the drinks cabinet to pour himself a whisky.

'You were tough in there,' Tremayne said to Clare once they were sitting back in her car.

'He could be innocent,' Clare said.

'It's worth checking. I don't see the angle on the gold, though. He had nothing to gain.'

'He would have if Ethan and Martin hadn't quarrelled. Forty bars of gold would have been his, or Cosford's.'

Chapter 22

Tremayne could see two major players, Colin Morrison and Selwyn Cosford, as well as a sprinkling of minors. He made a few phone calls, called in a few favours. It was a new day, and Tremayne had had the benefit of a good sleep and Jean's attention. Not that it had stopped her giving him a few sharp words for getting drunk in Ireland.

'Morrison?' Clare said. The two were in the office at Bemerton Road.

'They'll conduct random checks on his vehicles, the ones coming in from Europe mainly,' Tremayne said.

'Is he involved with the gold?'

'It's possible. And if he wasn't, we can't be sure that he's strictly legal now.'

'I can't say I trust him,' Clare said.

'What do we have on Ethan's murderer?'

'No more than we had before.'

'And Gavin Mitchell?'

'A knife, easily obtained.'

'Tony Mitchell?'

'A nine millimetre bullet. Not the same gun as Ethan.'

'Three murders, no common thread.'

'Ethan Mitchell was murdered because someone didn't want him going after the gold, Gavin because he was, and Tony because he knew where it was,' Clare said.

'Morrison can't be involved with any of the murders unless Ethan was tied in to him. Farrell's girlfriend was the conduit that connects Morrison to

Farrell, and probably to Cosford. If she knew Cosford, then how did he set it up?'

'The man's got plenty of money, why would he bother?'

'Cosford has sailed close to the wind on a couple of occasions. I can remember him driving around Salisbury in an old car.'

'No money?'

'One of his deals hadn't worked out. Not that it worried him.'

'Supreme confidence?'

'Total. Another couple of months and he was driving a Ferrari. That's how the man ticks.'

'Not a life for me,' Clare said.

'That's the difference between most people and people like Cosford. He'd go after the gold, money or no money. He needs the adrenaline rush.'

***

Clare took the phone call. 'Lord Linden here. Is Tremayne there?'

'He's just gone outside. He'll be back within a few minutes.'

'Sergeant, Clare, if I may be so bold, O'Connor took off last night. I thought you should know.'

'Thank you. Any reason?'

'None from us.'

'It could be a family emergency.'

'It's possible, but it's out of character.'

'He had a place on the estate?'

'A small cottage. We've knocked on the door, no answer.'

'You've not been in?'

'I'll leave that to you. It's doesn't look good us searching an employee's premises.'

'Begging your pardon, but do you get involved with your staff on a day-to-day basis?'

'Rarely, but we had some pheasants taken last night. O'Connor would have dealt with it, but when I phoned him, he'd gone, no answer.'

'We'll be there within the hour,' Clare said.

'Come up to the main house, park around the back.'

'Inspector Tremayne's back. We're on our way.'

'Our housekeeper will show you up.'

'Who was that?' Tremayne said as he exhaled the last remnants of his cigarette smoke over Clare.

'Devlin O'Connor's done a runner.'

'Curiouser and curiouser,' Tremayne said, remembering the line from *Alice in Wonderland*. 'Men such as O'Connor don't vanish in the night. It's not in their nature. What's the drill?'

'We're meeting his lordship at the main house. After that, we'll check O'Connor's cottage.'

Outside the police station, Clare walked towards her car. Tremayne, she could see, was dragging his heels, hoping to take a few puffs of another cigarette.

'Don't bother,' Clare said. 'Jean's got me counting, and you've had one. Midday you can have another.'

'Yarwood, you're becoming a pain.'

'If you want to die, that's up to you, but for me, I don't intend to have you polluting my car.'

After their brief verbal exchange, the two police officers drove out to Emberley. By the time they arrived, the clouds had opened, and they had to make a run for the back door.

Death by a Dead Man's Hand

'Inspector Tremayne, Sergeant Yarwood, his lordship is waiting upstairs for you,' the housekeeper, a jolly little woman with a ruddy complexion, said.

'You don't mind,' Linden said as he picked up a cigar from a box on his table. 'Tremayne?' The three were sitting in a room off the main hall. 'A smoking room in the past. The women would be in one room, embroidering, and the men would be in here discussing business and politics. Different times, if Sergeant Yarwood's formed the impression that I'm an old fossil with antiquated views. No doubt some momentous decisions were made in this room, but now it's a quiet retreat, nothing more.'

'Thank you,' Tremayne said. Clare realised she could say nothing about the cigar.

She had to admit that the smell of a Cuban cigar was not altogether unpleasant; her father treated himself to one at Christmas.

'O'Connor never said much,' Linden said. 'We can't say that we knew him very well.'

'What's his history?'

'Not much to tell. He arrived here about eighteen years ago, not long after the gold had been buried in that hole down by the gatehouse. Our former estate manager had died, and O'Connor had all the credentials.'

'Are you certain he's gone?'

'I've got a key to his cottage. It may be best if you go and look.'

Clare took the key and left the room, Tremayne following after he had finished the cigar. 'That was great,' he said.

'Take one for later.'

'Don't mind if I do. Yarwood won't like it, neither will my wife.'

'One of my few luxuries. I've got a touch of gout, cold houses, not enough exercise. Still, I'm not complaining. How about you, Tremayne?'

'Too many cigarettes, too many pints of beer. I'm on doctor's orders, or should I say wife's orders.'

'A good woman?'

'One of the best.'

Clare waited for Tremayne.

Finding their way back down through the house, they went out through the back door by the kitchen. The estate manager's cottage was not far, semi-enclosed by a brick wall. After the opulence of the main house, the cottage was small in comparison. Clare put the key in the front door lock and turned it. The door opened slowly, creaking as it went.

'I'll take upstairs,' Clare said as she climbed the narrow stairs, constructed in a time when people were smaller, and no doubt thinner. At the top of the stairs was a small passageway. At the far end, a bathroom. The cabinet was open and empty. She looked in the main bedroom, the bed clean and tidy. She looked in the wardrobe: no clothes, no shoes.

Downstairs, Tremayne was finding the same. The man had gone.

'Unusual,' Clare said as she came back downstairs.

'What do you mean?'

'Eighteen years and nothing to show for it, no personal touches in the cottage.'

'I can understand that,' Tremayne said.

Clare phoned up Jim Hughes, the station's CSE. 'We need a couple of your people to check out a cottage at Longmore Park. See if you can find any fingerprints.'

'The murderer?' Hughes asked.

'He wasn't high on our list until he took off. No forwarding address, no severance pay. Something's not right.'

'He's left the Land Rover here. Put out an APB, will you?' Tremayne said once Clare had ended her call with Hughes.

'Leave it with me,' Clare said. 'He could have killed Gavin and Tony Mitchell,' she said.

'But why? The man couldn't have been involved with the gold heist, and he's been driving past the gold for years. Why, all of a sudden, would he start murdering people, and why Gavin?'

'We'll wait for the findings from the CSIs,' Clare said. 'We've got a funeral to attend.'

***

With three of the Mitchell clan dead, it would have been logical to have a joint service. At least, that was what Julie, Martin Mitchell's widow, had suggested. 'Get all the hurt and sorrow out and over with at the same time,' she had said.

'Don't talk crazy,' Betty, her sister, had said in reply.

'It's your money, not mine. Eric knows about saving money.'

'Your husband, Eric, is a sanctimonious pig. I was married to Ethan, and he's the father of my two children. He gets a proper send-off, Mitchell style.'

The church was not St Mark's, the expected choice, but Betty had been firm that she didn't want Ethan's funeral in the same place where he had been murdered.

St Francis, at the top of Castle Road, was chosen as the most suitable. Tremayne and Clare kept to the back. At the front, Betty sat with Marcia and Gerry. The convicted felon had been given special leave from prison to attend. A prison officer stood behind him.

Also present were Julie and her husband, Eric. Bob was to the left of his wife, his arm around her. Betty was stoic, not crying, although looking very sad. Sandra, the sister of three brothers, was just to the left of Bob, her wheelchair slightly in front of the pews.

The coffin was brought in. Tremayne looked around, saw a familiar face. 'Just stay here, Yarwood. I've got someone I need to talk to.'

Tremayne slowly edged to the left along the line of pews and then slid back three, causing some at the front to look around. He knew he should not be focussing attention on himself at such a solemn time, but it was necessary.

'Selwyn, what brings you here?'

'Guilt. I've told you that before. It was my gold, and it cost the man his life.'

'That was Martin, this is Ethan.'

'I know. What about the others? That's four now.'

The vicar stood, the congregation rising as well. The service was a blur to Tremayne. Gerry got up to say a few words, did better than Tremayne expected. He could see that Yarwood had moved closer to Sandra, Ethan's sister, and had placed her arm on her shoulder. The woman seemed to respond to the gesture.

Marcia spoke, as Tremayne knew she would. She mentioned the man's many good qualities, glossed over the others. At the end, the coffin was borne by six men, Tremayne included, at a special request of the family. How many times, he thought to himself as he bore the weight on his shoulder, had he arrested someone, only to be a friend of the culprit and his family. He had to admit to some sadness as the man was placed inside the hearse for the short drive to the cemetery.

Outside the church, before the cortege left, Cosford approached Betty. 'Sorry about your loss.'

'It's not your fault, Selwyn. Martin and Ethan were always trouble. Your gold or someone else's, it wouldn't have made any difference.'

'Please give my condolences to Sandra. I don't know her well, and I barely knew Gavin.'

'Gavin was a fool, the same as his brothers.'

'Regardless, it's not a nice way to go.'

'Tony's funeral is in a couple of weeks. I'd like you to be there. Maybe you could mention what he did in Malaya.'

'He wouldn't like it known, but I'll do it. He needs credit for it. His medals?'

'I've no idea. You knew Tony, no fuss with him. He probably threw them out.'

'Maybe. I'll see if I can get replacements.'

'We'd like that,' Betty said as she climbed into the back seat of the limousine hired for the occasion.

'Nice touch,' Tremayne said to Cosford as the two men stood near the road, both knowing that what separated them was unresolved.

Chapter 23

Tremayne sat in his chair and looked at the report he had to prepare. It did not excite him, nor did the laptop. He was still a pen and paper man, and back in the early days a report did not take hours. All he had to do was to write it and then read it through once before sending it off. But now, there was the file to open, to date, to save, to insert the subject, the reference number, and that was before writing. And even then, there would be the closing of the document, the cross-checks where the computer would ask 'Have you done this?', 'Have you done that?'

Eventually, after more time than he considered worthwhile, he'd press the enter key, and the report would be sent.

As Tremayne prepared to walk out of his office, disenchanted with the report, Jim Hughes walked in. 'I thought you'd like it straight from the horse's mouth,' he said.

'If you're the horse.'

'No shortage of prints in the cottage.'

'Any of importance?'

'Devlin O'Connor was convicted of attempted murder, spent five years in prison before being released. He used a different name back then.'

'How long ago?'

Hughes pushed four pages of print across the desk. 'Read this.'

Clare came into the office. 'Anything interesting?'

'You can read it after Tremayne.'

'Five years for the attempted murder of a fellow student at university. According to this, there was a woman involved. She had been playing the field, and both of the men wanted her for himself. After a drinking bout in a Dublin pub, both men had gone outside, egged on by their friends. After ten minutes of name-calling and prancing around, O'Connor lost his temper, drew a knife and stabbed the other man in the stomach. O'Connor admitted that he was drunk and it was unintentional, so did the other man when he came out of emergency surgery. The judge sentenced our man O'Connor to prison. He had a different name then,' Tremayne said.

'How long ago?'

'Twenty-nine years, long enough for it to be forgotten.'

'Does that make him guilty of the murders of Gavin and Tony Mitchell?' Clare said.

'Not in itself,' Tremayne said.

'He took off, self-preservation. You can't blame him.'

'I'm not blaming him. I just want him back. The man knows something, and as you say, it's self-preservation. That's a good enough reason not to tell us the truth.'

Devlin O'Connor was no longer a minor player. He was now major league. Clare upgraded the APB to critical, detain at all costs, the person is deemed potentially violent, possibly armed.

'He can't have gone far,' Tremayne said, more out of hope than belief. Lord and Lady Linden were surprised when they were told.

'He used to take the children fishing,' Lady Linden said.

'He was convicted for a one-off offence a long time ago. Under normal circumstances, and after so many years, we would regard him as non-violent.'

'But now?'

'He could be our murderer, but I'm not convinced. Too many variables, and if he knew about the gold, he certainly hasn't benefited from it.'

'You'll place him under arrest when you capture him?'

'We'll remand him in custody.'

'If he's innocent, he's welcome back here,' Lord Linden said.

'That's very generous of you,' Tremayne said.

'The man has proved his worth to us. We'll not hold his past against him.'

***

Tremayne did not like people giving him orders, and especially not Selwyn Cosford. 'I need you out here at my place, no excuses,' had been the command.

'Cosford, I'm not your hired help,' Tremayne had said, but to no avail. The man on the other end of the phone was agitated. Tremayne knew Cosford to be a wily fox, not the sort of person to fall for the usual tricks, but an angry man, however induced, was likely to let something slip.

Tremayne arrived at Cosford's place at ten in the morning. Outside in the driveway was a car he had not seen before. Inside the house was a man he knew too well: Henry Barker, Cosford's lawyer and a man Tremayne had crossed swords with before.

'Tremayne, you've been talking to Colin Morrison, accusing him of being involved in the theft of my client's gold,' Barker, grey-haired and close to Cosford's age, said. He was wearing a three-piece suit, one size too small.

Tremayne recognised an attempt at intimidation. *Don't try it on with me*, he thought.

He could see Cosford standing to one side, almost as if he was the second at a boxing match. 'You're wasting your time, Barker. I'm investigating a murder, not a break-in at a kindergarten.'

'Still with the smart answers. When did we last meet?'

'Not long enough ago for me.'

Tremayne knew that it would be better to treat the man with some respect, but he had always suspected him. He operated out of a small office in Salisbury. It was neither luxurious nor efficient, files of papers stacked on top of one another, yet he numbered Selwyn Cosford amongst his clients, and one or two other entrepreneurs who sailed close to the wind.

'What were you doing with Colin Morrison?'

'Is that any of your concern?'

'It is if it throws doubt on Mr Cosford's good character.'

'Cosford's able to look after himself. Or am I getting too close to the truth? Was there fraud? We still haven't found this mysterious girlfriend. Who was she, Cosford? One of your floozies? She was the age you like. Attractive from what we've been told.'

'You can't come in here and start accusing my client.'

'Barker, I wasn't coming here at all. It was Selwyn who summoned me as if I was one of his staff. This is a setup, and you're feeding me nonsense, hoping for me to compromise myself. To give you something that you can take to Superintendent Moulton to get me off the case.'

'That wasn't the purpose,' Barker said, backing off slightly.

'What was it, another bribe? I kept quiet about the previous one.'

Barker turned to Cosford. 'Is this true?'

'Not a bribe, more an "if you scratch my back, I'll scratch yours".'

'For a smart man, you can be a bloody fool sometimes,' Barker said.

The lawyer turned to Tremayne. 'Inspector, let's be civil.' Tremayne did not like the change in Barker, suspicious to him.

Tremayne made a phone call. 'In the house,' he said.

Turning back to face Barker. 'Sergeant Yarwood is outside. I brought her just in case I need a witness, and it appears that I do.'

Clare came in and took a seat in the centre of the room. Barker came over and shook her hand, smiled at her. 'Please to meet you. Tremayne thinks we have a problem with him.'

Clare had spent enough time in Homicide, and with Tremayne, to know a deceitful man, the sort of person who couldn't lie straight in his bed of a night.

'I'm here for Detective Inspector Tremayne. I'll record the conversation if that's okay with you and Mr Cosford.'

'Of course it is. We are concerned that his visit to Colin Morrison is an attempt to cast doubt on Mr Cosford's innocence.'

'It's not, and you know it,' Tremayne said. 'You intend to try and get me to back off. And so far, I've resisted placing the blame on Cosford, but he's looking awfully suspicious, as is Morrison. Eighteen years ago,

Death by a Dead Man's Hand

Cosford and Morrison were not as financially sound as they are now. The proceeds from the gold, as well as the insurance money, would have come in handy. And why's Farrell able to set up a business in Ireland? That needs money, and the man had nothing after Morrison sacked him.'

'Farrell?' Barker said.

'Aidan Farrell,' Cosford said. 'He was the driver of the security van, took a nasty hit on the head.'

'Don't pretend with me, Barker,' Tremayne said. Clare could see that her senior was playing a dangerous game. He was not dealing with a couple of hooligans, but with smart people, influential people. People who played golf with the police hierarchy and would be on Christian name terms with a few politicians.

'Okay, Tremayne, have it your way. I've been acting for Mr Cosford for a long time. I know all about the gold, and the Mitchells, and how you acted as a character witness for one of them recently. Are you trying to protect them? Battlers, are they, like you? And my client is the big bad wolf, ready to blow their house down?'

Touché, Clare thought.

'You'll not pin that on me,' Tremayne said. Clare could tell that he was rattled. It was not often that someone could beat him at his own game. She could see that Barker was not the sort of person to have up against you in a court of law.

'What is it with Morrison? Is he a suspect?' Barker said.

'Morrison is a person of interest. And using another van to transport the gold smacks of subterfuge. There's no way that a company involved in the transportation of so much of value would have allowed it to be transported in an unsuitable vehicle, and there's no way an insurance company would agree to it unless there was collusion. What was your part in this, Barker?'

'You were invited out here to discuss this matter.'

'It was no invite. If I hadn't taken you on, you'd have attempted to knobble me, offer me something I couldn't refuse. Is that why the three Mitchells have died? Did they know something about you and Cosford and Morrison? You're about the same height as Martin, do you have a gun?'

'This is intimidation,' Barker said. The man was red in the face. He looked as if he was about to take a swing at Tremayne. Clare stood up, ready to intervene.

'Sit down, Yarwood. I want this man to take a swing at me. Then I can arrest him. It'll give us time to check him out. He's in on this, I'm sure of it. Selwyn, you'd better get yourself another lawyer. This one's not going to save you. And as for Morrison, we'll find out what he's up to. Maybe you're involved with him, and what he's transporting, apart from gold bars and paintings that get damaged.'

'It may be time for us to leave,' Clare said.

'Let's go.'

It took two cigarettes before Tremayne calmed down. She thought he was going to have a coronary.

***

Clare drove back to Bemerton Road Police Station, diverting long enough for Tremayne to have lunch with Jean.

At the station, Superintendent Moulton was waiting in his office. 'I hope you know what you're doing, Tremayne.'

'Cosford's involved. We just need to ride him. Granted, he's too old to have murdered anyone, but something's amiss. I'm not sure what it is, but I intend to find out.'

'Devlin O'Connor has been arrested.'

'Is he comfortable?'

'As comfortable as he can be.'

'How long have you known about O'Connor?'

'They picked him up in Wales ten minutes ago. Supposedly, he walked into a police station there, said who he was,' Moulton said.

'I still don't think he's our man,' Tremayne said.

'He was around the area where two people were killed.'

'He's a man who watches and listens. He knows more about the village of Emberley and Longmore Park than anyone else. Where are they holding him?'

'Cardiff.'

'Time is of the essence. Cosford is covering his tracks, so is Morrison.'

'What about the Mitchells?' Moulton said.

'They're not as smart. We'll see through them whatever they do.'

Chapter 24

'Why did you run?' Tremayne asked Devlin O'Connor. 'We had nothing on you.'

'I didn't want to leave,' O'Connor said.

The three, Tremayne, Clare, and O'Connor were sitting in the interview room at Cardiff Central Police Station on King Edward VII Avenue. Clare would have appreciated an hour to recuperate after driving the hundred miles from Salisbury, but Tremayne was keen to get to O'Connor. He had a friend from years back at the station and he had eased the two police officers through the building and into the interview room. O'Connor had declined legal representation.

'If you had stayed, then we'd have never found out who you were.'

'You would have, that's how the police work. It was a long time ago when I used that knife. I was a lot younger, hot-headed.'

It was obvious from the man's condition that O'Connor had been sleeping rough for a few nights. He had stubble on his face and scratches on his arm.

'What happened?' Clare said.

'It's nothing. I just headed into the forest. I needed time to think.'

'What for? An alibi or a confession?'

'Neither.'

'Then what?'

'After I had served my time, I drifted around for a few years, mainly in Europe. I changed my name, and it was good, but I wanted a quiet life. I knew what I had done, almost killed a man, and believe me, I'm still capable. I've got a ferocious temper, and a few pints too many, a few shots of a happy hour, and it could happen again. Up there at Longmore Park, they treated me well, no one asked questions.'

'But you left.'

'I had to.'

'Why?'

'Because I knew the gold was there.'

Tremayne sat back in his chair and looked hard at the man. He saw a contrite man, not sure what to say or do. 'Do you need legal aid?'

'I've committed no crime.'

'The gold?'

'I saw Tony Mitchell around the back of the gatehouse.'

'How long ago?'

'It must have been sixteen years ago. I could see him from a distance. I had been checking on a broken fence, and I had a pair of binoculars around my neck. I could see him in there, so I rested the binoculars on a fence post and focussed on him. He stayed about ten minutes and then he left. After he had gone, I walked around where he had been. It was early morning, a dew was on the ground, and it was not difficult to follow his tracks. I could see the metal grate. I knelt down and pulled it clear. I always carry a torch, so I shone it down.'

'What did you see?'

'At first, nothing.'

'Afterwards?'

'I pulled some old clothing to one side with an old branch, and there was the gold.'

'You didn't take it.'

'Not me. I put the grate back and got out of there in a hurry. I knew of the gold and the van that had been hijacked. It was before my time, but people in the village occasionally talked about it.'

'But you never touched it, never told anyone.'

'Inspector, believe me. I had nearly killed a man once. I'm pleased to be at Longmore Park, a dream job for me, and then there is all this gold. If I had told the police, my secret would be out. If I took some of it, I was a criminal. And I didn't need it, either. I had a good job, a rent-free cottage. What else did I want?'

'And if the job had ended, would you have taken the gold?'

'Never. I knew my weaknesses, and stolen gold would not solve them. In time, I ceased to think about the gold, and then the murders started. If I had come forward all those years ago, then none of them would have happened.'

'You can never be sure. It's not for you to blame yourself.'

'But I do. I remember that night when I drew the knife. I still have nightmares.'

'What happened to the man?'

'I've no idea, and the woman we were fighting over, I can barely remember her name. I've told you all I know. Are there any charges?'

'You've not told us everything.'

'What do you mean?'

'Gavin Mitchell.'

'Do you think I could have killed him?'

'You could have taken the twenty bars. Why would you bother with three?'

'My cover was about to be blown. I could have been desperate.'

Death by a Dead Man's Hand

'Did you see anything the night of his death?'

'I saw someone. It was a dark night, moonless, and I could see a flashing light. I moved down there, slowly. I used to stalk wild deer in my youth so I could be quiet. Mitchell's moving around, he's got a metal detector. I know what he's after, but I just watch. After some time, he looks as if he's about to give up. I was going to grab hold of him, give him a piece of my mind.'

'Threaten him?'

'Probably. He needed to know that he was not welcome on private land. I've located his car, and I'm not far away. Then another person comes up the lane.'

'Name?'

'Let me finish. He sees the car, and he moves into the wood. He's quiet, quieter than me. He disappears for twelve minutes. I checked on my watch. He then comes back out and walks down the lane.'

'Who was it?'

'Tony Mitchell.'

'Are you sure? He was an old man.'

'It was him. I don't know why, but it was him.'

'Did you check on Gavin Mitchell.'

'I intended to, but I wasn't sure what to do. I know I should have phoned you, but you'd not believe me. Tony Mitchell was well known, well liked, and I had a history of violence. I went back to my cottage, thought about what to do for a few hours. I then decided to check on the other man. It was daylight, and the sun was shining through the trees. I trained my binoculars on the area where I had seen Gavin Mitchell. I could see him standing up, motionless. I was about to go and check, but then the two women appeared. Sergeant Yarwood showed her badge, the other woman I knew was a Mitchell. There was no more I could do, except act as though I knew nothing.'

'Tony Mitchell, are you certain it was him?'

'Positive. He went into the wood. I didn't see him kill the other man, and I didn't hear anything. That's the truth.'

'It's plausible. We know that Tony Mitchell was a war hero, no doubt skilled in moving through a Malay jungle without making a noise.'

'Did you confront him afterwards?' Clare said.

'No. I was confused, not sure what to do.'

***

Selwyn Cosford had taken a chance on Tremayne, only to have it backfire. And now the man had called him into Bemerton Road Police Station.

Across from Cosford in the interview room, Tremayne. Alongside Tremayne, Clare. Facing her was Henry Barker, Cosford's lawyer, and a man not to be trusted according to Tremayne.

'Mr Cosford, you were a close friend of Tony Mitchell,' Tremayne said.

'We were acquaintances. He saved my life once. I owed him a debt of gratitude.'

'What if I told you that Tony Mitchell killed Gavin Mitchell?'

'I'd say you were in the land of make-believe.'

'Why? The man's capable of killing.'

'The Malayan Emergency. We were soldiers. That came with the job.'

'It must make it easier, though.'

'It does. I had been there shooting across at the enemy. I could have killed someone, probably did.'

'Did Tony?'

'He was like a lot of men in wartime. He did his duty and then came home. He neither spoke about it nor reminisced, and he never went to reunions.'

'What did he do? He seems to have spent his life without a woman.'

'When he was younger, he used to get about. Not everyone's obsessed with getting laid.'

'You are.'

'We were opposites, Tony and me, but we shared something that those who've not been in the heat of battle can understand.'

'What was he doing at the back of the gatehouse?'

'Why are you asking me?'

'Was Tony good with a knife?'

'He'd been trained, the same as we all had.'

'You're a similar age, similar build. It was dark, our witness could have been mistaken.'

'Are you accusing my client of murder?' Barker said. He was more circumspect, Clare noticed. He had already had one encounter with Tremayne, and the verdict was still out on who had won.

'If Tony murdered Gavin, then why? Only three bars are missing. It's hardly worth your time and effort.'

'A million pounds is worth it, but not murder. And besides, I've got an insurance claim going through.'

'Successfully?'

If my granddaughter is as good as I think she is, Cosford thought. 'Yes. I'll return the money from the original insurance claim plus agreed interest, taking into account inflation. And then the gold will be mine. It's millions to me, it could have been…' he said.

'You nearly let it slip, Cosford. You're losing your touch. Early stages of dementia, is it? Are you afraid you'll not be able to hold it together for much longer, making contingency plans for when you're dribbling, stuck in a bed, unable to say a word?'

'This is scurrilous,' Barker shouted. 'This is badgering of the worst kind. My client is an important man and should be treated with respect.'

'Your client is a man who has used civil law to his advantage for many years. The slippery road to the criminal is not that far. I suggest you advise your client to be careful in what he says. If Tony Mitchell is, as we think and Cosford states, an honourable man, he would not kill without reason. He saved Cosford's life many years ago, maybe he was attempting to save it again, but why in that wood makes no sense.'

'Unless Gavin knew something already, and the wood was the ideal opportunity,' Clare said.

'Yarwood's right,' Tremayne said. 'What is it? What is everyone hiding? Did you still have a hold over Tony Mitchell? He was a brave man in Malaya, but what else did he do? Any atrocities? Did you and he, and your fellow soldiers, kill innocent villagers? Did you enjoy it, did he?'

'It was war. Collateral damage is inevitable.'

'Cold-blooded murder is not,' Tremayne said.

Clare could tell that Tremayne had hit a raw nerve.

Selwyn Cosford was sitting back, his face downcast. 'Memories are sometimes painful.'

'An atrocity?'

'Army intelligence. We had received information that the enemy was in a village in the jungle. We helicoptered in and then trekked for a couple of days. The village was empty. Tony took one side, I took the other. We then declared it safe. The other soldiers, twelve in total, entered through the centre of the village. Once they had cleared the jungle, the place came alive. The enemy had been hiding in the roofs, under the ground in makeshift pits. We had missed it. Tony sprang into action, I cowered behind one of the houses. I was the coward, he was the hero. He knew the truth, but never once did he mention it.'

'Of the twelve?'

'Five walked out alive. Another nine villagers used as shields by the communists died as well.'

'And what did the army do?'

'They covered it up, gave Tony a medal. After that, we rarely spoke. He had the guilt that he was only doing his job. I had the guilt that I was a coward. I couldn't kill a man regardless of how much I wanted.'

'Did you know about this?' Tremayne said to Barker.

'Never.'

'Tony may have followed the man into the wood, but he couldn't have killed him,' Cosford said.

'Then who did, and did Tony see the dead body?'

'He had seen death enough times.'

***

Betty Galton made her daily pilgrimage out to Ethan Mitchell's resting place. It was next to his brother, Martin; a simple plaque for both. For anyone walking around the cemetery, the two plaques would have given no indication that one had murdered the other, and that the other had been killed too.

'Every day?' Tremayne said as he walked up behind the woman. She was kneeling down, pulling some weeds.

'Bob sees it as somehow disloyal to him, seeing that I'm married to him now.'

'It is, you know that. You may want to believe differently, but the twins were both losers.'

'Ethan was the father of my children. I can't deny him that.'

'How's Gerry?'

'I saw him last week. He's joined the gym, and he's taking a few of the courses on offer.'

Tremayne knew what the gym meant, as well as the courses. A chance to toughen up to be able to fend off others in the showers; the courses to pass the time.

'Tony was in the wood with Gavin,' Tremayne said. 'He's our prime suspect.'

'Not Tony.'

'Why not?'

'Oh, I don't know. Tony was always so mild-mannered, and he had no issues with Gavin.'

'He liked Marcia, as well. How about you?'

'I got along fine with him. I used to take Martin and Ethan's side whenever he criticised them, but he was right, the same as you. But when you're young, it's not always that clear.'

'Why would someone kill Gavin? He wasn't near the gold, and it was unlikely he would find it.'

'Neither Bob nor Eric liked him very much.'

'Why's that?'

'Bob used to think that Gavin was a dead fish, and he was in many ways. Eric didn't like him because he had no ambition.'

'Ambition is not all it's cracked up to be,' Tremayne said, knowing that as a young constable he had been keen, volunteered for any stakeout, and a chance to show his inspector what an asset he was. Not that it had done him any good. Once the inspector's superiors had started singing the praise of their new constable, the inspector's attitude towards him changed. All the unpleasant jobs had started to come his way, and the opportunity to impress had gone. Six months later, so had the inspector, lung cancer.

'Eric's got some financial difficulties; Julie confided in me.'

'He could be violent.'

'He's a tough businessman, but the economy is against him. He's overstretched, that's the term Julie used, although I don't really know what it means. I didn't want to let on that I had no idea what she was talking about.'

'He's borrowed more than he can pay back. If interest rates go up, the bank could call in its debt.'

'He would be bankrupt, is that it?'

'If not bankrupt, then their lifestyle would be at risk. He might be forced to sell the house, sell the fancy cars.'

'Julie wouldn't like that.'

'Like it or not like, the banks won't care. Is Eric a fighter?'

'He'll not give in easily.'

'Capable of murder?'

'You don't think…?'

'I don't think. I deal in facts,' Tremayne said.

'Selwyn?'

'How do you know Cosford?'

'He was a friend of my father, a friend of Tony. He's another man who'll fight.'

'He already is.'

'Do you mind, Tremayne? I would like a few minutes alone with Ethan.'

'Is he listening?'

'I'm a believer, every Sunday at church. He's there, although whether it's up or down, I'm not sure. How about you, Tremayne, do you believe?'

'Too cynical, I'm afraid.'

'I'm sorry about that. We all need something to deal with the madness of our lives, the sorrows, the disappointments.'

'And it helps?'

'It does. Otherwise, I couldn't carry on.'

All of a sudden Tremayne felt sad, an unusual state for him. He realised that he had spent a lifetime in the underbelly of society, being exposed to all the weaknesses of people's lives, the senseless deaths of too many. He walked away from Betty Galton, now on her knees, one hand resting on Ethan's plaque, the other on the ground. He could see her mouthing words in silent prayer. For a moment he wished he could forget all that he had seen in his life. He kept walking, picking up the pace as he neared his car.

Chapter 25

Colin Morrison had plenty to worry about. The second truck in two days attempting to cross the English Channel from Calais had been stopped and subjected to a rigorous search. 'Just routine, checking for illegals,' according to the customs officer in charge. Morrison knew it wasn't.

With the impact it had on his business, Morrison could only wish that it was better for those attempting to get a ride across the English Channel, than it was for him at the present time. Not that he often considered the less fortunate. He knew he was a driven man who had clawed his way from a nobody to somebody. Building up the business he had taken over from his father, a couple of old trucks that regularly broke down, to a fleet of over a hundred trucks had taken years, and he knew that if the police kept digging, they would find irregularities. It had been necessary to cut corners a few times, transport goods he shouldn't have, not that it had ever concerned him, but now…

Outside his office, another truck, fully loaded with antiques, was about to make the trip to a draughty castle at the end of a Scottish loch. One more addition to a Russian billionaire's real estate holdings. Better him than me, Morrison thought.

Morrison made a phone call. 'What are the chances of calling off the next haul from the continent?'

'Not good, unless you want to find yourself face down in a ditch somewhere.'

Morrison hung up the phone, dialled another number, Tremayne's number. A voice answered. Morrison slammed down the phone, hoping that his number had not registered.

Tremayne, fitter than he had been in a long time, called over to Clare. 'We're going for a little trip.'

Clare looked over at her boss, marvelled at the man's changed appearance. It was as if he had lost ten years. He sat straighter, no more slouching half-on, half-off his chair. His hair had even regained some colour. *Jean's work*, she thought. And the rough and heavy voice, the result of too many cigarettes, had mellowed. Even the air inside Homicide smelt better. Clare missed the old Tremayne, back when he had been the caricature of the archetypal older police detective. The man who always solved the case, when the younger, the smarter, were floundering.

'Where to?' Clare said. She could see developments.

'London.'

'The car needs fuel.'

'You can stop on the way.'

It was early morning; the traffic was in their favour. Apart from a stop at a service station on the way to fill the petrol tank, and for Tremayne to smoke a cigarette, they made good time. It was eleven in the morning when the two of them entered Colin Morrison's premises. They could see the man's car in its parking spot.

Clare parked her car next to the Bentley. Inside, at reception, was the woman from their previous visit.

'Morrison,' Tremayne said. He felt no need to refer to the man by his Christian name. Villains don't deserve that respect, and the police inspector smelt a rat, a rat so big that it was going to make a few bars of gold look small time.

Death by a Dead Man's Hand

'Mr Morrison's in a meeting. I'll let him know you're here.'

'Detective Inspector Tremayne and Sergeant Yarwood.'

'Yes, I remember you both from the last time.'

The two officers took a seat. 'She's not pleased to see us,' Tremayne said.

'Last time you almost accused her of stalling us.'

'Not me.'

'Not directly, but you were rude.'

'Me, never.'

Morrison came out from his office. He was effusive. 'Get our guests a cup of tea each,' he said to the receptionist. He gave her a wink.

'Not another one,' Tremayne mumbled to Clare.

'A wink doesn't constitute a raging love affair. If it did, I've been having it off with half a dozen men down at Bemerton Road.'

'Not a bad idea, if you don't mind me saying so.'

'I do. And focus on Morrison. I hope you know what you're doing.'

'Playing hunches. This man's worried, can't you see it?'

'He looks to be busy.'

Inside Morrison's office, utilitarian but comfortable, Tremayne and Clare sat on one side of his desk. On the other side, Morrison sat behind a large monitor. He moved it to one side.

'What is this about, Inspector Tremayne?'

'You phoned me up.'

'I dialled the wrong number. I hope you haven't come all this way for nothing.'

'You wanted to tell me something, I know that.'

'Believe me, it was a mistake. I sometimes do it, in too much of a hurry most of the time.'

The receptionist came in, another wink from her boss, a thank you from Clare, a nod of the head from Tremayne.

'Morrison, I know when someone's lying, always have. You're in trouble. It may be financial, possibly criminal, but you're weighing up the options. I'm here to make sure you make the right decision.'

Clare took a sip of tea. She looked over at Tremayne, then at Morrison. It was two men sounding off against each other. It was not swords or duelling pistols, purely the intellect and cunning of one, the years of policing with the other. This was Tremayne at his finest, she knew that.

'My dear inspector,' Morrison said. Clare knew the man had lost it when he started to become over friendly. Tremayne was nobody's 'dear'.

'I've got you and Cosford pegged for the hijacking of forty bars of gold. Your company had been up and running for a few years by then and making decent money. After the gold, not that Cosford would have paid what he owed you, seeing that he didn't have the forty bars, your business flourished. Either it was due to your business acumen or probably, as I suspect, smuggling, and I'm not talking about fake Gucci handbags out of China.'

'This is fanciful nonsense,' Morrison said. A wrong word to use with Tremayne, Clare knew.

'Let me tell you, I've known Selwyn Cosford for longer than you've had this business. The man's sharp, and he pushes the boundaries. Never criminal from what I know, but I'm leaning towards him as a major villain, and you as his lieutenant. Am I getting close?'

'I need my lawyer here.'
'How long?'
'Ten, fifteen minutes.'
'Okay, you go and phone him. We'll wait.'
Morrison left the office. Tremayne picked up his cup of tea. 'I could do with a cigarette,' he said.
'You're doing fine without it. Do we have anything on Morrison?'
'No.'
'This could backfire. A smart lawyer could ask you to put up proof.'
'He could.'
'And you don't care, do you?'
'Not today. I want an arrest. This man is as good as any.'
'He'll not admit to anything in this office.'
'I know he won't, but if I ride him enough, he'll make mistakes.'

***

It was close to twenty-five minutes before Morrison returned, long enough for the receptionist to bring Tremayne and Clare another cup of tea, as well as some biscuits. Clare did not eat the biscuits, Tremayne did.
'Sorry about that,' Morrison said. 'A problem with one of the trucks.' Tremayne knew he was lying, so did Clare.
'Your lawyer?' Clare said.
'He can't make it. You'll have to deal with me.'
'You did not check on one of your trucks,' Tremayne said. 'You went outside and made a phone call to a number in East London.'

Clare knew that Tremayne had contacts in London who'd help him, but a phone tap required more authority, and Morrison was not accused of any crime.

'A truck in East London, where's the problem in that?' Morrison said. The calmness that he had displayed on entering the room after the break was gone.

'You have three trucks in Calais, am I correct?'

'Two or three, that's possible. But how do you know this?'

'Mr Morrison, I've been a police officer for over thirty years. In that time, I've made a lot of contacts: some villains, some police officers. I have contacts with customs and border control. What do you want to tell me, or do you want your lawyer this time?'

'There's nothing to tell.'

'You made a phone call to a Terry Wright.'

'How do you know this?'

Clare was interested to know as well.

'Terry Wright is under surveillance. It was pure luck that we were here when you phoned him. His phone conversation was overheard. I've just received a message.'

'I asked him to look into the problem with the truck.'

'Wright is a major villain,' Tremayne said, 'and you have been bringing drugs into this country. You have three trucks in Calais. They will be taken down to the chassis if necessary. If there are any women in the back of them, then that will be an additional charge.'

'There are no women,' Morrison said. Clare could see that he was shaking, and there was perspiration on his forehead. She didn't know how Tremayne had done it, but it was a masterful interrogation.

'Yarwood, phone the local station, get some uniforms over here,' Tremayne said.

'I've not committed any crime. I demand to have my lawyer present.'

'I gave you the opportunity, you declined. It's on record.'

'Mr Morrison, an officer from Serious and Organised Crime Command will be here to arrest you. Once the uniforms arrive, we'll leave you to them. We will talk again about the gold bullion.'

On the way back to Salisbury, Clare asked for an explanation.

'I repaid a favour to someone in Serious and Organised Crime Command. He can take the credit for the arrest. Terry Wright was pure luck. As for the trucks, an SMS on the way up to London. They found drugs in one of the trucks at Calais, although Morrison's involvement was still unsure. His phone call to Wright sealed his guilt. Sorry I didn't let you know beforehand, but I wanted you to look surprised as well, to add to the tension.'

'You were brilliant,' Clare said, realising that for once she had broken the cardinal rule that existed between them: she had paid him a compliment.

'Pull over here. I need a cigarette.' Clare could only smile at her boss as he stood outside in the cold. She messaged Jean. *Give him a good feed tonight. He's deserved it.*

Chapter 26

Gavin Mitchell's funeral was less emotional than his brother Ethan's.

Tremayne sat in a pew at the back of the church. 'Where's Sergeant Yarwood?' Eric Wilson said as he sat down beside him. It was still early; the service had not started.

'She's coming, just wrapping up in the office.'

'Gavin was a strange bird,' Wilson said.

'What do you mean?'

'His being up at Emberley. What sort of man goes searching around with a metal detector and a spade?'

'It takes all sorts,' Tremayne said. He did not appreciate the intrusion by Wilson, a man he did not like, although there was no suspicion against him, and he had made a success of his life. *Maybe that was it*, Tremayne thought. His retirement was coming, and what did he have to show for it? A house in need of TLC, a police pension. It wasn't much – sufficient for him – but now he had Jean, and she deserved better.

'I saw O'Connor the other day. He spoke highly of you.'

'What else?'

'Nothing. I've got a job at Longmore House. The building's nearly three hundred years old, and it needs some renovations.'

'Good money?'

'The money's good, but the expenses are a nightmare. I need to be careful, or I could run into a cost overrun, and it's heritage listed. It's not a quick in and out.

This time, I've got to bring in inspectors from here and there to check that I'm renovating it correctly. The newer materials are better, but that's the way it is.'

'What do you think of the house?'

'Impressive, but not that I'd want it.'

'Why's that?'

'The maintenance. It would be a nightmare.'

'You could rent out the rooms, help to pay for the upkeep,' Tremayne said. 'We suspected O'Connor for a while.'

'He's another strange one.'

'Lord Linden trusts him.'

'Even so, all that money, and not far away.'

'The gold or the main house?'

'Both, I suppose. It would have to be a temptation, not that I got to look around the whole house, but there seemed to be plenty worth taking.'

'I've been around it. There is.'

'Who took you?'

'Lord and Lady Linden.'

'It's that innate charm of yours.'

'A big house and plenty of money doesn't make anyone better than the next person.'

'You should try telling that to Julie. She came from nothing, and you'd think she'd be glad with what we've got. The best house in the street, the latest car, and I can't tell you how much she spends on clothes. Wears them once and then they hang in the wardrobe. I'd rather see my money in assets, not throwing it away on some nonsense.'

Tremayne could not get a handle on the man. Was he trying to imply that business was tough, or that his marriage to Julie, Martin's widow, was on the rocks? Or was he just a man who complained a lot? Whatever it was,

Eric Wilson was the sort of man who would have been interested in the gold, would have known what to do with it.

'Have you found out who killed Gavin?' Wilson said.

'Not yet. What do you reckon?'

'Why would Gavin go looking on his own? It makes no sense, and he's not the adventurous type, scared of his own shadow most of the time.'

'I always saw him as decent,' Tremayne said.

'Don't get me wrong. I can't say I thought much about the man. Apart from family gatherings, all too often in the last month, he kept to himself. But out there in Emberley? The man must have been desperate or stupid.'

'He wasn't smart like you.'

'And why in the wrong area? According to Betty, it was some distance away.'

'Not that far, and our crime scene investigators missed it.'

The coffin appeared at the entrance to the church. Wilson left and scurried back to his place with the family.

'What did he want?' Clare whispered in Tremayne's ear.

Tremayne turned around to find his sergeant one row behind. She was dressed in black.

'Did you hear?'

'Some of it. The man's just fishing.'

'That's what I reckoned.'

Tremayne and Clare's conversation was cut short by the arrival of the coffin at the front of the church. Sandra made a speech, so did Marcia. Gerry was there again, a prison officer nearby. Betty clung to Gerry during the service. Eric Wilson looked at the young man with

Death by a Dead Man's Hand

sideways glances – disapproving from what Tremayne could make out. Bob Galton, Gerry's stepfather, spoke to him, although the conversation was muted and consisted of Bob saying something, Gerry nodding his head.

The relationship between stepfather and stepson was known to be cordial, although the responses from Gerry did not indicate that to be the case. Tremayne assumed it was the occasion, the hushed atmosphere.

Neither Gerry nor Bob was considered as a serious candidate for any of the crimes, Gerry having the most reliable alibi of all, he was in police custody. Bob Galton, a man who had achieved middle management but lacked the drive to go further, was similar to Gavin in many ways, although he was more communicative.

Tremayne knew that was what he was, middle management. Not a bad place to be, but the future was unclear. Another visit to the doctor, another diagnosis, less than ideal. He knew that Jean's exercise routine and healthy living were not going to do the trick. He could see an early end to his life, and it would not necessarily be pleasant. He had spent a sleepless night a few nights back. He had lain in bed, Jean at his side. There had been a movie on the television that he had watched to while away the time; an old English farce, the actors, all famous names from his youth, all long dead, and the movie a series of calamities, a love affair – no nudity back then – and weather that was always idyllic, a far distance from reality, and everyone was smoking.

And now the doctor was telling him to stop smoking.

'It's ten years if you don't, maybe twenty if you do. Emphysema, not a pretty sight, with a ventilator at your side, you lying there. And what about your wife?'

'We're not married, used to be,' Tremayne had said, the doctor checking his heartbeat, his blood pressure.

'Considering the abuse you've subjected your body to, you're in fair condition, but there are clear signs that your lungs have been affected. No doubt you drink more than you should.'

'I like a pint.'

'More than a pint, and too often. It's up to you, but I'm giving you fair warning.'

'I've got a few murders to solve. Sometimes a pub's a good place to get people to open up.'

'It's your future.'

'Thanks, doctor,' Tremayne said as he got off of the examination table and put on his shoes. 'I can't give you any more of my time.'

He walked out of the doctor's surgery feeling worse than when he had gone in.

Maybe once the current investigation is wrapped up, I'll give up the cigarettes, Tremayne thought, but he was not convinced. He had spent his career as the grumpy, cigarette smoking, beer drinking police officer. Anything else wouldn't be him.

***

It was coming down 'cats and dogs'; that was how his mother had described it, Tremayne remembered. It was early morning, and it was raining heavily, almost torrential, so much so that the rescue team had not been able to secure a chain to the sunken car.

'Confirmed?' Tremayne shouted out of his car window.

'It's a Bentley, late model,' one of the divers said. He was wearing a wetsuit, oblivious to the rain. Tremayne and Clare were not.

'Is there a body in there?' Tremayne shouted again.

'It's hard to tell.'

The phone call had come through three hours earlier. An early morning jogger, even before the sun had risen, and before the rain had set in, had seen the car roll down the boat ramp and into the river. He had watched it sink, unable to do much.

Ten minutes after his call, a patrol car had arrived, seen the car's tyre tracks, raised the alarm. The jogger's description of a Bentley, a make of car owned by a man of interest and in the police database, had caused the local police to phone Bemerton Road, Homicide. Clare had taken the call, picked up Tremayne at his house.

A two-hour drive, and now they waited.

'Give us another hour, and we'll try again. The conditions are too difficult for the divers,' a young constable from the local station said. 'With the rain, the river flow could pick up, make the conditions too dangerous. If it weren't for your interest, we'd mark the vehicle and come back when the weather's better.'

'How far down?'

'Twenty feet, more or less. The visibility's zero. Good car, was it?'

'It was, and very expensive.'

'Makes you wonder why people do it. Joyriders see it as fun.'

'Joyriders don't steal Bentleys. We can't find the owner,' Tremayne said.

The local police had checked out Colin Morrison's home, his office, all the regular haunts. His wife had not been able to help, nor his children.

'He was heading north, a business meeting in Manchester,' his wife had said.

'It's our man,' Clare said as she rubbed her hand over the inside of the windscreen. The vehicle was misting up; the heater was trying its best, but not coping.

'We can't stay here,' Tremayne said, knowing that he couldn't smoke in the car, and outside was impossible.

'We'll be back in one hour,' Clare said to the occupants of the vehicle alongside hers.

'Give it two. We'll not pull it out until you're back.'

Tremayne and Clare found a café; inside it was warm and inviting, outside it was sheltered and cold. Tremayne chose the latter. 'I needed that,' he said, as he exhaled the smoke from his first puff of the cigarette.

'Disgusting habit,' Clare said.

'I know, I know. I'm trying to quit. I hope you've packed an overnight bag.'

'There's always one in the car. You never know what's going to turn up. Why did they release him?'

'Not sure, no doubt a technicality, posted bail.'

'But he was involved with transporting drugs.'

'It was only that call to Wright that nailed him. Men such as Colin Morrison have access to the best legal teams, and if he was as big as we suspect, then who knows.'

'We'll check?'

'Once we know what's going on, we'll check with Serious and Organised Crime. A trip into Central London, maybe take in a show, get a few drinks, go dancing.'

'Your attempt at humour is lousy,' Clare said. 'I'll treat you to a hot chocolate.'

As the two sat in the café, a phone call. 'The weather's improved. We're going to attempt to get a chain onto the vehicle in the next ten minutes.'

'We need to go,' Clare said to Tremayne. 'Another drink to take?'

'Why not? I'll pay this time.'

At the river, the divers were already in the water when Tremayne and Clare arrived. The rain had stopped enough for the two officers to get out of Clare's car.

'I could have done with one of them,' the young constable said, eyeing the hot chocolates.

'Here, have mine,' Tremayne said. 'I've not touched it.'

'Just joking. We always make sure we've got hot drinks on days like this. Thanks for the offer. You'd be surprised how many stand gawping, but never offer.'

'What's the plan?'

'If they can, the divers will secure a chain to the underside; failing that, they'll smash the windows and run a cable through the car. The roof on a Bentley should be strong enough.'

'And then you'll pull it out?'

'Not with a regular tow truck. We've got a bulldozer coming from a local hire company. The car won't look so good afterwards, a write-off.'

'The car's not important.'

A local crime scene team was standing by. Two uniforms had secured the site. A few onlookers were gathering.

Tremayne paced around, taking out his packet of cigarettes, putting it away. The third time, he shouted over to Clare who was standing near to the front of her car, the heat of the engine permeating through the bonnet. 'I tried,' he said, as he took a cigarette and put it in his mouth.

Clare said nothing.

The bulldozer, once it had arrived, tensioned the chain the divers had secured the sunken car with, and then moved back. The sunken vehicle slowly emerged from the water.

'It's a mess,' Clare said.

'Have you phoned Jim Hughes?' Tremayne, who had finished his cigarette, said.

'He'll not come up until there's confirmation. The local CSE wouldn't appreciate an interloper.'

'That's what we are.'

'I'm surprised the local Homicide are not here.'

'They will be if we find anything.'

Another fifteen minutes, a couple of pauses while the bulldozer moved to one side of where it had been. There was a mud embankment, slightly lower on one side than the other. At the third attempt, the Bentley cleared the water and rested on the grass.

Tremayne moved closer, the water still coming out of the vehicle soaking his shoes and the bottom half of his trousers below the knees.

'Not until you've kitted up,' a voice close by said.

'It's Hughes. He's here already.'

'It's not,' Clare said.

'Nuttall, local CSE. I've had Jim Hughes on the phone. Apparently, you're a legend for entering crime scenes without following the correct procedure.'

Clare had liked the 'legend' reference. Indeed, that was what Tremayne was.

'We need to see if there's a man in there.'

Death by a Dead Man's Hand

'If there is, he's dead, unless he's got a pair of gills. I've not seen anyone around here with them, but back in your part of the world, maybe they do.'

'You're worse than Hughes,' Tremayne said.

'Some say better looking, but I'm not so sure about that.'

Clare liked the man's humour, and no, she decided, he was not better looking than Jim Hughes. For one thing, he was Tremayne's age, and he looked like a drinker. He was the sort of man that Tremayne liked.

'Yarwood, the rear of your car and be quick about it.'

'You've got your sergeant trained, I see.'

'Like a performing seal.'

'That's what he thinks,' Clare said, returning with two sets of coveralls, two sets of overshoes, and two pairs of gloves.

'Okay,' Nuttall said. 'Where do you think the man will be?'

'Try the boot. Inside the car, there's not much.' Clare looked, all she could see was a crayfish moving.

'American Signal crayfish,' Nuttall said. 'A failed attempt by our government to introduce them to UK waters. They thought they could export them to the Scandinavian market.'

'What happened?' Clare said.

'They were carriers of the crayfish plague. It's immune to it, our native white-clawed crayfish weren't.'

'And the exports to Scandinavia?'

'It never got off the ground.'

No more water could be seen coming from the vehicle. Around the back of the car, one of Nuttall's team was attempting to open the boot.

'I've got it,' he said. 'They make these vehicles tough.'

'It's yours. You can lift the lid,' Nuttall said to Tremayne.

Tremayne lifted the lid slowly, as the boot still contained water. Floating in it, some clothing. The CSI who had broken the lock put his hand in the water. 'There's a body.'

'Colin Morrison,' Clare said.

'Phone Hughes,' Tremayne said. 'I want him working with Nuttall on this one.'

'Fine by me. A major player, the body?'

'Drug trafficking, insurance fraud, and whatever else.'

'Shame about the car,' Nuttall said.

'Yes, shame,' Tremayne said, but his mind was elsewhere. A body in a sunken car was not there by accident. It was murder, and he had his suspicions.

Chapter 27

Tremayne and Clare were standing outside New Scotland Yard. Inside, Detective Chief Inspector Brian Constanza, the man they had come to see.

'The Mitchell family seem to be small fish now,' Tremayne said.

'Is Cosford the big fish?' Clare said.

'I'm not convinced.'

'Losing your touch?'

'How can anyone function on a starvation diet? The brain needs nutrition, cossetting, not macrobiotics or detox or whatever else.'

'You've been reading up,' Clare said. 'Do you intend to have a cigarette now or later?'

'You'll not tell Jean?'

'Not this time. We're heading into the big league. I don't want you standing there with your tongue hanging out, gasping for a smoke.'

'Be careful with these people, they're sharp.'

'Degree-educated?'

'Painfully so.'

'My kind of people,' Clare jested.

Clare had insisted on Tremayne sucking on some strong mints to conceal his ashtray breath. She had even paid for them.

'Tremayne, good to see you.' Costanza, a tall, imposing man, stepped forward and shook the detective inspector's hand vigorously when they met. 'Good to have you on board. And this must be Sergeant Yarwood,' he said.

'Clare will be fine,' Clare said. It was either a charm offensive or a good start to the meeting, she couldn't be sure which, and Tremayne had taught her well enough: reserve judgement for later.

'Pleased to meet you. You've both stirred up a hornet's nest. A cup of coffee? Tea? We've got it all here.'

'No budget constraints?' Tremayne said. He was glad of the mints.

'Some, but we're a growth industry, and the villains are getting smarter. Morrison came as a surprise to us. We keep a database, and he was down at one on a scale of one to ten. He didn't seem the type, and his background showed hard work and a capable mind.'

'We weren't investigating him,' Clare said. The three had taken a seat in the conference room. It was well equipped: video-conferencing, wireless connection to the overhead projector, internet.

'Better than what we've got,' Tremayne said.

'You're dealing with local crime. Up here, it's national, and nowadays, international.'

'A lot of travel?' Clare said.

'Some. We need to meet up with our counterparts occasionally. The phone and the video are fine, but face-to-face always helps.'

'Why are we here?'

'Some others are coming to the meeting. Give us ten minutes, and we'll kick off.'

Constanza excused himself and left the room.

'What did you reckon?' Tremayne said to Clare after the man had left.

'Full on.'

'That's Brian. We met a few years back. A drug syndicate were distributing into the west of Salisbury.

They used a factory unit out at Greenfields to store merchandise.'

'Homicide?'

'A nosey local. The criminals had found him inside the unit, it was late at night. The next day he was fished out of the river, his throat cut.'

'Rough justice.'

'Any rougher than what happened to Morrison?'

'Probably not.'

Two more people came into the conference room with Constanza. 'This is Inspector Ashcroft, and the man at the end, the one who looks as though he's had a rough night, but hasn't, that's Sergeant Johnny Johnson.'

'Take no notice,' Johnson said. 'I've been up all night keeping a watch on Morrison's trucking depot.'

'Anything?' Clare said.

'Nothing to report, although those involved will keep a low profile for a while. No point checking any of the man's trucks for the next ten days.'

'The drugs will still need to come in,' Inspector Ashcroft, a woman in her forties, said. Clare liked the look of her: professional, well-prepared, a laptop in front of her. It was clear she had been nominated or lumbered with keeping the minutes.

'They'll find another way, they always do.'

'No chance of stopping the flow?' Clare said.

'You've no idea who we're dealing with, or what lengths they'll go to,' Johnson said. Clare thought he was dismissive of her. He, the seasoned sergeant; she, the sergeant from the sticks.

Constanza knew that Johnson's reply was not as it should be. 'Take no notice of Johnny,' he said. 'He spent a few years undercover. He'll tell you it's a jungle out there, and any politeness or any weakness is tantamount to a death sentence.'

'Sergeant Johnson is correct,' Tremayne said. 'We've seen our fair share of murders, but organised crime, that's something different.'

'I had a problem with you coming on board. I've raised it with DCI Constanza,' Johnson said.

'Why's that?'

'Whoever killed Morrison didn't care about the police. He or they wanted to send a message to us, the drug syndicate, competitors, or whoever else. This is what we're dealing with. People who kill and maim with impunity. To them, we are no more than a mosquito that needs swatting.'

'If you're worried about us…'

'I am, and anyone else who gets involved. We've decided to fight these people the best way we can. Constanza, he's divorced, no children. Ashcroft, her children are grown up and have left the nest, and as for me, I'm single, always have been.'

'Yarwood and I are aware of the potential danger, count us in,' Tremayne said.

'That's cleared the air,' Constanza said. 'It's going to be a rough ride. Tremayne, an update from you.'

'We've put together a few slides. Yarwood, roll the slides as I speak.'

Tremayne stood up and moved over to the screen on one wall. 'Ethan Mitchell, just released from prison after serving seventeen years for the murder of his brother, a dispute over stolen gold. A successful security van hijack, forty bars of 400-ounce gold bullion. A lot of money in today's currency. He was shot dead in a church; a letter is found telling him to be there. It's from his long-dead brother. It's a good forgery, and whoever it was knew it would be enough to lure the brother to the church. After that, Gavin, the elder brother, was stabbed to death, close by to where half of the gold was hidden. Soon after, Tony Mitchell, a relative, is shot. He's got a detailed map to where some of the gold is buried. He's had it for eighteen years but had never used it. Betty, Ethan Mitchell's widow, also had a map, a rough sketch given to her by Ethan. Yet again, she had never used it.'

'Relevant?' Ashcroft said.

'It is. Let me continue. The gold was being shipped to Selwyn Cosford, a man I know. He's a local man made good. No doubt you've seen him on the television.'

'We have,' Constanza said.

'I had been the arresting constable for Ethan Mitchell eighteen years previously, by the way. We went out to see Cosford, he welcomed us in. He lives in a Georgian mansion, looks like Buckingham Palace. He was paid out by the insurance company for his loss on the stolen gold, but he's aiming to take them on again, as the value of gold has risen way in advance of inflation. Later on, he offered me a sweetener if I assist in his claim.'

'Anything specific?' Johnson said.

'Nothing specific, but I've known the man for long enough to know that he's generous.'

'Tempted?'

'I'm a plodding policeman. If I had wanted a bit extra on the side, there have been plenty of opportunities.'

'That's a no?'

'It is. We're suspicious of Cosford. That's when we decided that Morrison was worth a visit. It had been one of Morrison's trucks that had been carrying the gold.'

'You had your suspicions about the heist at the time?' Ashcroft said.

'Back then, I was a junior officer. I did, my DI didn't.'

'You could have followed up on your own,' Ashcroft said.

'It was forty bars of gold, and twenty had been retrieved. No one had died apart from Martin Mitchell, and we had his brother in custody for murder, a signed confession. One week after the gold had been taken, there was a double slaying at a farm not far from Salisbury. That was more important than the stolen gold,' Tremayne said.

'Point taken. No doubt you were understaffed as well.'

'We were, still are. It was only after Ethan Mitchell's death that we started investigating the case further. That's when we started to delve deeper, that's when Cosford and then Morrison became suspects. We started to apply pressure, find the weak spots, and then Morrison went and made that phone call, and you intercepted it.'

'It's not Cosford who worries us,' Constanza said. 'It's those who supply the drugs.'

'Russian, Bulgarian?' Clare asked.

'Them and others. We found drugs hidden in one of Morrison's trucks, and then we got a record of Morrison's phone calls. Not hard to get permission if drugs are mentioned. It was a coincidence that you were there in the man's office when he phoned Terry Wright. We knew about him, a middleman, but the connection between him and Morrison was tenuous, and Wright doesn't keep the same phone number for very long.'

'What do you want us to do?' Clare said.

Death by a Dead Man's Hand

'Your CSE is with Nuttall,' Johnson said. 'I've just got the word.'

'And?'

'A bullet in the head, his throat cut.'

'You see what we're dealing with,' Ashcroft said. 'If they can do that to one of theirs, what do you think they could do to us.'

'We've accepted the risk,' Clare said.

'We'll follow up here with Morrison's murder,' Constanza said. 'For your part, pressure Cosford. We'll have surveillance on him, though you'll not see it, and we'll be monitoring his emails, also his phone conversations. You just need to make him sweat.'

'We've still got three other murders to deal with,' Clare said.

'You can focus on them as well, but remember, Cosford's the mark. He could lead us to those who killed Morrison.'

'He's not one of them?' Clare said.

'Not with these people. He's still small fry, and if the whale senses the minnow is becoming too friendly with the law, you know what will happen.'

'Another murder.'

'Collateral damage can be expected.'

'Are you saying that if they attempt to kill Cosford, they'll go for us?' Clare said.

'Do you still want to be involved?' Ashcroft said.

'We're police officers. We'll do our job.'

'In that case, you'll both be issued with weapons before you leave, and advanced training. One day should be sufficient.'

'What show do you want to watch?' Tremayne said to Clare.

'What's that all about?' Johnson said.

'I've offered Yarwood a show and a dance, but she's not so keen on my size nines.'

'Humour, is that it?' Ashcroft said. 'You could have fooled me.'

Chapter 28

Tremayne had hoped to get back to Salisbury after meeting with Constanza and his team, but then he and Clare had stayed the night as planned. A decent hotel, well within Superintendent Moulton's budget directive, a good meal with Clare and him sharing a bottle of wine, and then an early night. There was to be no show and no dancing. Jean had dragged him along to a production of *The Sound of Music* in Salisbury once, and no matter how many mountains there were to climb, he had fallen asleep within ten minutes. And as for dancing, Jean, who could dance, always preferred to sit it out rather than to be dragged around the floor by a man with no sense of timing.

The following day, a further meeting with the Serious and Organised Crime team, and then to the shooting range. Yarwood proved to be the better shot, although Tremayne had done better than he had expected.

It was nine in the evening when Clare dropped Tremayne off at his house, another twenty minutes before Clare walked in the door of her cottage. Her cat was waiting for her. She picked it up and gave it a hug. A voice from over the fence: 'We've fed him.'

'Thank you,' Clare said. It was good to be home, she knew that. On her phone, a message: *This Saturday?*

I'll try, Clare texted back to the doctor.

A good night's sleep for the detective inspector and his sergeant, and then back in the office early.

'We need to pressure Cosford,' Tremayne said.

'Will he know about Colin Morrison?' Clare said as she sipped her coffee.

'He's got enough televisions out at his mansion.'

It was seven in the morning, and the traffic had been light on the way in from Clare's cottage in Stratford sub Castle. The date with the doctor still confused her. It had been a long time since she had met a man that she genuinely liked. She wondered if the night was going to be predictable, or whether it would end up with them together in a darkened room. Her two previous attempts at romance had ended badly. She didn't want a third.

'Are you coming or are you going to sit there daydreaming?' Tremayne said.

'It's early. Cosford might not be awake.'

'You know what they say about the early bird?'

'Catches the worm. Is Cosford the worm?'

'He could be the snake.'

'Handcuffs needed?' Clare said.

'We'll not catch him out that easily. His involvement in illicit drugs could explain the rags-to-riches and back to rags when he was younger. Stately mansions don't come cheap, and Cosford's wealth is not disputed, but how he came to have so much has never been clear.'

'I've seen him on the television. His advice: one hundred pounds a week invested over thirty years, and then with compounding and secured with real estate, the average person can fund their retirement.'

'Good enough for you and me, but it'll not give you a mansion and a garage of expensive cars, nor trips overseas.'

Tremayne and Clare were surprised to meet Paul Rudd of Gainsford Insurance when they drove through the entrance to the grounds surrounding Cosford's mansion.

'This is Maggie,' Rudd said. 'We were just going for an early morning walk.'

'Did Selwyn resolve his insurance claim?' Tremayne said sarcastically.

'We came to an agreement. Both Mr Cosford and Gainsford Insurance have signed off on it.'

'And the young lady?' Tremayne asked.

'Mr Cosford is my grandfather.'

As a romantic Clare saw it as lovely, but she had been trained by Tremayne and realised that something was amiss.

Like father, like granddaughter, Tremayne thought.

'We're engaged,' Maggie said. 'Paul's coming to work for Grandfather, deal with all his insurances, help him with his finances.'

Tremayne remembered the last person that Gainsford Insurances had tasked with dealing with Cosford. He had approved the insurance claim, and then subsequently joined Cosford, only to disappear some years later. The man was never reported missing, and no enquiries were ever made.

'Is Mr Cosford awake?' Clare said.

'He should be,' Rudd said. 'He's an early riser.'

Tremayne and Clare drove on. 'Check in your rear-view mirror,' Tremayne said.

'He's making a phone call.'

'Put your foot down. Cosford knows we're coming. I don't want him prepared, and I don't want his lawyer out here, not yet.'

Clare drove up to the entrance of the building; the front door was open. Inside they found Cosford.

'Tremayne, Clare, good to see you. What can I do for you?' Cosford said. In his hand, he had a piece of toast. 'I'm just having breakfast, do join me.'

'Thanks,' Tremayne said. Clare nodded her head.

At the rear of the house, in a conservatory, a small table was set for three.

'You were expecting us?'

'That's for Rudd and Maggie, but they'll be a while.'

'They're staying here?'

'Not always, but my granddaughter often comes over. They're a good match, her and Rudd. And before you ask, I do approve, and they're in love. Rudd's a smart man, knocked back my claim.'

'He said it was approved.'

'I've transferred all of my insurance needs over to Gainsford. Their giving me a win on the gold was one of the conditions. Believe me, they're ahead on the deal. You can't begin to understand how much I outlay on insurance each year, and rarely a claim.'

'The gold bars?'

'They're under lock and key.'

'Who brought them from the police station to here?' Clare asked.

'Morrison's. I've always used them.'

'Even after the gold heist?'

'Not for a while, but in time I went back to them. Colin Morrison was a man I always trusted.'

'He's a rogue, the same as you, Selwyn,' Tremayne said.

'A rogue never lets you down. He'll argue the deal, attempt to claim for extras, but he can be trusted.'

'Why?'

'His word is his bond. There are rogues out there who'll not take kindly to being cheated. Some of them will come at night and burn your premises down.'

'Or put a bullet in your head and dump you and your car in the River Thames.'

'Tragic,' Cosford said. 'We rarely met, only once in the last ten years.'

'Serious and Organised Crime Command had arrested Morrison. He was out on bail, not sure how. And you trusted him?' Tremayne said. Clare noticed he was on his third slice of toast, a liberal covering of butter and jam.

'A truck with drugs hidden under it doesn't mean that Morrison was involved.'

'His phone call to Terry Wright, a known criminal, confirmed his guilt. It was an open and shut case.'

'Nobody's guilty until the judge puts on the black cap.'

'We don't hang people in England anymore.'

'More's the shame,' Cosford said.

'Why's that?'

'I've met a few over the years who would have benefited from a hangman's noose.'

'Insurance accessors?'

'Financiers mainly, but we digress. Morrison, tragic. I'll make sure to go to his funeral.'

'Pleasant as this all is,' Tremayne said, 'there is still the matter of your involvement. Morrison was a good operator, but those supplying the drugs were gangsters out of Eastern Europe, and they're not Boy Scouts. Morrison has been murdered because they're worried that he'll talk.'

'Or because he cheated another trucking company. They're not Boy Scouts either. Tremayne, you're trying to make too much out of this. Morrison's dead and near to London. His murder is someone else's responsibility.'

'We're working with the police close to where Morrison was murdered, as well as the Serious and Organised Crime Command. They weren't focussing on Morrison, we weren't focussing on you, but now we are.'

'Don't go there, Tremayne,' Cosford said. 'I've always seen you as a smart man, but I've influential friends.'

Clare had seen it before, and Tremayne had told her it was coming. Influential friends only meant one thing; the person who said it had something to hide.

Rudd and Maggie returned and took a couple of chairs from the far side of the conservatory and brought them over to the breakfast table.

'Tremayne thinks I'm a crook,' Cosford said.

'Not you, Grandfather,' Maggie said. Clare could see similar facial features to Cosford.

'We've still got to solve the three Mitchell murders. Whether you're involved or not will be dealt with by Serious and Organised Crime Command. If you are, then remember what happened to Morrison. He was playing with fire, I hope you're not. I don't want to be there when they fish you out of your pond, or when this place burns down with you inside.'

'Tremayne, you've ruined a perfectly good breakfast,' Cosford said.

Clare could see that Tremayne was pleased. He had got Cosford rattled, and rattled people make phone calls, go and see people. And he would be kept under close surveillance.

As Tremayne and Clare made their way to the front of the house, Rudd came with them. 'He's a great man, you must know that,' he said.

'Maggie, she's very much like her grandfather,' Tremayne said. 'Are you sure you're not being fed a line? Women like her, they use men, spit them out when they've served their purpose.'

'You foul-mouthed bastard. I've a good mind to…'

'To what? Take a swing at me. Also, if you value your life and that of Maggie, I'd suggest you get some distance from this house.'

Rudd retreated.

'You were harsh with Paul Rudd. He's in love, she is as well.'

'I need Rudd confused and angry. Yarwood, phone up Constanza, ask him to put a trace on the young lovers.'

'You enjoyed yourself in there,' Clare said.

'It was an excellent breakfast,' Tremayne said. He walked around to his side of the car, the passenger's side. He was smiling.

***

Devlin O'Connor, no longer in hiding and with no crimes against him, resumed his position as estate manager at Longmore Park. His secret was known not only by Lord and Lady Linden, but also by half the village, which meant the other half would know soon enough. O'Connor, for so long a secretive man, did not like the sudden fame.

He had gone into the local pub early one night, only to be quizzed about what had happened all those years before. There were some, he could sense it, who no longer saw him as a tough man doing a good job, but now as a possible murderer of Gavin and Tony Mitchell. He drank his pint and left. He knew that if he wanted a quiet drink, he'd need to find another pub.

'Not you,' O'Connor said as he settled himself at the bar of the Swan Inn in Wilton, a small town not far from Salisbury.

'It's close to home,' Tremayne said. 'This is Jean.'

Jean realised that Tremayne wanted time alone with the man.

'A pariah, that's how they see me,' O'Connor said. He knew that Tremayne would not be prejudiced against him.

'You should have come into Bemerton Road and told us. You had done your time, and I'm not there to place judgement.'

'Hindsight, wonderful thing, isn't it?'

Tremayne had to agree. If he had known that the 'sure-fire', 'can't lose', 'the other horses are rubbish' recommendation he had been given by another of the betting fraternity had only three legs, he would be sitting at the bar, a free round for everyone in the pub. As it was, the loose change jangled in his pocket.

'Cigarette?' O'Connor said.

'No smoking in here,' Tremayne said.

'No law outside.'

Tremayne looked over at Jean, saw her talking to another woman. 'She'll be fine for a few minutes.'

O'Connor and Tremayne stood outside, their cigarette smoke wafting upwards. It was cold and miserable, but both men were enjoying a shared moment of blissful heaven.

'You don't look the marrying kind,' O'Connor said.

'I wasn't, but Jean, we go back a long way. We married young, then went our separate ways. I was difficult back then, still am, but I've mellowed. The bark's not as strong.'

'You must be feeling your age.'

'Between you, me and the lamppost, I am. They want to pension me off, but policing's what I'm good at, what I enjoy. It's as good as a hobby to me.'

'That's what it is with me. I always liked being out in the open, and Longmore Park was ideal. I turned up in response to an advert. Lord Linden took one look at me, showed me around the place, and that was that.'

'And you did a runner?'

'You would have found out about my past eventually, and my conviction for stabbing my friend had some inaccuracies at the trial. They stated that I was the instigator, but I wasn't. Also, they hid the fact that my friend had a knife as well. Supposedly inadmissible, just because he had thrown it away and he had been wearing gloves that night. It irked that I was in prison, not that I didn't deserve it, but it shouldn't have been that long.'

'You're a loner,' Tremayne said.

'There was a woman once, but she's not around anymore.'

'Any reason?'

'A drunk driving on the wrong side of the road. I don't talk about it that often, no idea why I'm talking to you. Maybe it's because you stood up for me, helped me to get my job back at Longmore.'

'You had served your time. Apart from a couple of youths that you roughed up, you've not been in trouble since.'

'It had been ten years since she died, to the day, and those hooligans are there in front of me, baiting me. Have you ever been that angry that you couldn't control yourself?'

'When I was younger. Kicked a few up the rear end harder than I should have.'

'Have you found out who's behind the murders?'

'We're close. Is there any more you can tell us?'

The two men lit their second cigarettes. O'Connor was enjoying the conversation, the most he had spoken to anyone for many years. Tremayne still had doubts about the man. Not that he was the murderer, but what he might know, what he might have seen.

'We were in London, fished a Bentley out of the river,' Tremayne said.

'I saw it on television. Is it tied in to Tony Mitchell?'

'Indirectly.'

'Selwyn Cosford?'

'You know the man?'

'He used to visit Tony. He would sometimes walk around the village with him.'

'How long ago?'

'It wasn't often, and the last time was almost a year ago. It was the day of the fete. Tony won a prize for his carrots.'

'Anything strange in their friendship?'

'Tony, a battler, worked hard all his life, and not much to show for it, and a man who had more money than the whole village combined?'

'They were in the army together. Tony was a war hero, saved Cosford's life.'

'I can't say they were happy with each other. I never saw either smile, and they always spoke in whispers.'

'Did either of them walk up near the gatehouse?'

'No problem if they kept to the road.'

'Did they look past the gatehouse?'

'Not that I saw, but Tony was trusted, at least by me, and Cosford was Cosford. They weren't likely to jump the fence and take a shot at a pheasant, were they?'

'Not at their ages.'

O'Connor left, Tremayne went back into the pub. It was warm. He ordered another pint.

'A friend of yours? Jean said.

'Devlin O'Connor. I don't think he's anyone's friend.'

'Murderer?'

'He's served his time.'

'And you introduced me to him.'

'Some of the most charming people are murderers.'

'That doesn't mean I want to meet them, and he wasn't charming.'

'He's not. I just hope he's honest. I'm going for bigger fish.'

'Selwyn Cosford?'

'We've no proof yet.'

Chapter 29

Clare was not surprised when Sergeant Johnson phoned her up. The man had been looking at her that day in Scotland Yard, and she hadn't appreciated it.

'An update for you and Tremayne,' Johnson said.

'We're busy down here, how about you?' Clare said in response. If the man kept it professional, then it would be fine.

'Terry Wright, Morrison's contact. He's dead.'

'No great loss.'

'It is to us. He was one of ours.'

'An informant?'

'No. One of us. That's highly confidential, only for you and Tremayne. And don't even tell your super. The man has a family, and we don't want those who killed him to find out.'

'Will they?'

'Not if you keep it quiet. We're only telling you as an act of faith. Ashcroft, she didn't want to tell you, but Constanza pulled rank.'

'How about you?'

'The fewer people who know, the better.'

'But you never knew about Morrison,' Clare said.

'Not until we wised you up.'

'Morrison wasn't the biggest player. We didn't tell you for your own safety. If you don't know, they can't get it out of you.'

'Torture?'

'Slowly roasting over an open fire.'

'They would do that?'

'The Russians, they're bad enough. The Bulgarians, they'd drink beer and wonder how long before the poor unfortunate tells them everything.'

'Wright?'

'He looks like a barbecued sausage.'

The thought of it made Clare's stomach turn.

'He was a tough bastard, tougher than me, but he would have told them all he knew.'

'Which was?'

'Terry Wright didn't know about you and Tremayne, only us. We're all carrying guns, although they could still pick us up.'

'Will they?'

'Who knows? Probably not. They'd not want the entire London Metropolitan Police after them.'

'Fear of being caught?'

'Fear of a downturn in business. They've got people to answer to, and they can make their fires hot where they come from.'

'Anything else?' Clare said.

'Selwyn Cosford. He's been checking real estate in the Caribbean. Not that it'll do him any good.'

'Extradition's always difficult.'

'I'm not talking about the police. The savage bastards can make fires down there as well. If anyone thinks they can get away from these bastards, they're living in cloud-cuckoo land. And they don't trust anyone who doesn't speak their language. If Cosford's involved, it would have been with putting up the capital, creaming off the top.'

'It sounds like the way Cosford operates,' Clare said.

'Are you up in London anytime soon?'

'No.'

'I thought we could get together, have a few drinks. Early night maybe.'

'That's sexual harassment,' Clare said.

'If they got Wright, I could be next, so could Constanza and Ashcroft, and we know you and Tremayne. I don't have time for subtlety.'

'Is that your best chat-up line?'

'That's not a chat up, it's a fact. If it's not this weekend, then I can't guarantee I'll be around for the next.'

'It's still sexual harassment.'

'Lighten up, Clare. You're dealing with the big boys. Your country bashfulness doesn't cut the mustard with the gangsters or with us. If they grab you…'

'You don't need to spell it out, and no, I will not be meeting you this weekend or at any other time, other than in a professional capacity.'

'Apologies, no offence intended.'

'None taken this time.'

'One more thing. Cosford's daughter-in-law, check her out.'

'We've met her daughter. We asked you to keep tabs on her and Paul Rudd. What is it with the daughter-in-law?'

'You'll figure it out. If I'm not here the next time, put a flower on my grave, that's if there's enough left of me. It may be best to keep off fish for a few weeks afterwards. I don't want you chewing on me, not in that way.'

'I should report you.'

'You won't. And besides, phone me up, let me know if what I've just told you was worth it.'

***

Tremayne could sympathise with Clare when she told him of her conversation with Johnson. If it had happened in Bemerton Road Police Station, he would have taken it further, but he had met men like Johnson before. Brave men who had been out in the field for years, detached from family and friends, always looking over their shoulder in case the group they had infiltrated would figure out who they were, or whether they would be a tip-off.

He remembered a young constable at Bemerton Road, one of those he had shared a house with. He had been ambitious, willing to get down in the dirt. Idealistic, wanting to stamp his mark. After three years in the north of the country, in Newcastle, he was number three in an extremely violent gang that controlled most of the serious crime in the city.

Two weeks after he and Tremayne had spoken by phone, a released prisoner that he and Tremayne had arrested but who was out on parole, and unbeknown was a cousin of the number two in the gang, had recognised the constable. A police-dredging operation after a tip-off, four weeks after he had last dialled a secure number, and his remains were dragged up from just off the pier.

Men such as Johnson, Tremayne knew, needed to be given some leeway.

'Apart from that, he said we should check out Cosford's daughter-in-law. Have you met her?' Clare said.

'I remember Cosford telling me the son was a waste of space, but there was no mention of the man's wife. Drugs when he was younger, doing nothing when he got older. Maggie is his daughter.'

'It's the mother we need to see.'

'Why didn't Johnson tell you what he meant?'

'He reckons he's got a chance with me. He thinks if I'm suitably impressed, I'll agree.'

'What are his chances?'

'He's a snivelling little toad. What do you think?'

'Not good.'

'Okay, so much for Johnson. It's a ninety-minute drive,' Clare said.

'Great, time for me to check my punter's bible.'

'More like a mug's bible.'

'It keeps me out of trouble.'

If Selwyn Cosford's son had not amounted to much, where he lived did not indicate it. On arrival, in front of the police officers, stood a large two-storey red-brick monster.

'Big enough for me,' Tremayne said.

'Too big if Jean expects you to help her clean it.'

Tremayne knocked at the door. Maggie answered it. 'We're down here visiting,' she said. She was dressed casually: a pair of shorts and a loose blouse. Her feet were bare. 'No shoes in here.'

Clare removed her shoes and placed them on a rack to one side. Tremayne removed his to reveal odd socks. Clare said nothing, the young woman sniggered.

'I was in a hurry,' Tremayne said, not bothered whether they were odd or not; they served their purpose.

'Max Cosford.' A hand stretched forward and grasped Tremayne's. A bear-like grip. The body behind the grip was tall, well-built, muscular more than fat. 'We met once, a long time ago.'

'We need to talk to you,' Tremayne said, shaking his hand free of the man. 'This is Sergeant Yarwood. We're investigating the murder of several people, Tony Mitchell included.'

'My father's army buddy.'

'Was he?'

'According to my father, not that I met the man that often.'

'He liked to keep to his own,' Clare said. 'Your wife?'

'She's out for a while. Not sure when she'll be back.'

'Do you have a photo of her?'

'We're not into photos.'

Tremayne noticed the man spoke fast, monopolising the conversation. 'Mr Cosford, Tony Mitchell has been murdered, so have two of his relatives. The matter is serious, and while we appreciate your civility, some questions must be asked.'

'Fire away, I'm all ears.'

Clare could see in Maggie, the daughter, an attractive, well-balanced young woman. She looked at the father and could only see a buffoon. She assumed the daughter's innate good sense came from her mother and her grandfather.

'We really need to talk to your wife as well.'

'She'll not be back today, maybe tomorrow. She has friends in London. They'll be up chatting for half the night, no doubt they'll drink a few bottles of wine as well.'

'Where in London?'

'Somewhere in Chelsea, not sure.' Tremayne was not convinced by the 'I'm a blithering idiot' routine.

'She must carry a mobile phone,' Clare said.

'I can give you the number. She's not good at answering, always diverting to voicemail. Damned annoying sometimes.' Cosford looked out of the window as he spoke. 'Looks like rain.'

Clare took the wife's phone number and went into the other room. She called Sergeant Johnson, a capable man, she knew, even if he was obnoxious.

'Interested in this weekend, is that it?' Johnson said.

'Not a chance. I've got a number for you. If I go through the official process, it'll take time. No doubt you've got contacts who can fast-track the search.'

'What do you want us to do?'

'Locate the owner of the phone, take her in, assisting the police in their enquiries. Don't use your pathetic chatter with her. I don't want her getting off on a technicality. Let me know when you've got her. We'll be up there within two and a half hours.'

'Professional is professional. I'll do what is right.'

'I knew you would.'

Clare walked back into where Tremayne and Max Cosford were sitting. Maggie was upstairs with Rudd.

'A meeting at Bemerton Road, we need to go,' Clare said.

Tremayne knew the code for let's go and now.

'What is it?' Tremayne said once they were outside the house.

'Have you packed an overnight bag?'

'Do I need one?'

'You might.'

'If it's important, I can always pick up some clothes on the way, change of underwear, a toothbrush.'

'Socks come in matching colours.'

'Very funny. Is this a secret or does everyone get to know?'

'I saw a photo in the other room. I've phoned Serious and Organised Crime, Johnson. They'll find Max

Cosford's wife if she's in London and bring her in for questioning.'

'Is she involved?'

'Describe Eileen Bleakes.'

'Brunette, five feet seven inches, blue eyes, short hair. That's the description we got, not sure how accurate it was.'

'How about blonde, five feet seven inches, blue eyes, long hair.'

'Cosford's wife?'

'Max Cosford may not be the sharpest tool in the shed, but his daughter is. And what's the bet that Max's wife is sharp?'

'Better odds than my current run on the horses?'

'Much better.'

Clare pointed the car in the direction of London, hoping that they would receive a call before arriving.

Chapter 30

'Some people take it calmly, others just stand their ground, protest that they've done nothing wrong,' Gwyneth Ashcroft said on Tremayne and Clare's arrival at Serious and Organised Crime.

'Katherine Cosford?'

'Calm. We traced her to an address in Tottenham. Not much of a place, considering who her father-in-law is. Have you met him?'

'I've known him for a long time,' Tremayne said.

'Have you ever taken his advice?'

'Never watched his programme, never sought his advice.'

'Do you want to see her?' Ashcroft said.

'Has she said anything?'

'We've not asked her anything. She's all yours. On the way here, she made a phone call. After that, not a word out of her.'

'Who did she phone?'

'Selwyn Cosford.'

Tremayne moved away and over to Constanza. 'Thanks for acting so quickly. What do you reckon?'

The two men were standing in a small cafeteria. It was complete with chairs, tables, brewed coffee, and biscuits in a glass container. Tremayne could only reflect on what they had in Homicide at Bemerton Road: a small alcove, the coffee in a tin, the milk in an old fridge that needed defrosting.

'Johnson found her. He's the one who should take the credit.' Tremayne liked a person who didn't hog the credit. He knew a few too many, some in Bemerton Road, who'd let their people do the legwork, and then would proudly stand up and say it was due to them. Not Constanza, though. The son of Italians who had come over to England when the economy back home was going through the floor, that was as much as he knew about him.

'Good man?'

'Rough around the edges. He was giving your sergeant a bit of lip. I could hear him on the phone to her, had to call him in here for a few words.'

'Any point?'

'Probably not, but the rules are clear.'

'The rules can be a pain sometimes. And besides, Yarwood's tough. Johnson wouldn't stand a chance with her, and if he tries it on up here, she'll have him on a charge.'

'He'll not cause trouble. He was undercover for a few years, not many can do that. I can admire the man, even if he can be a pig. Katherine Cosford is waiting for her lawyer to come. Until then, you'd be wasting your time.'

'We'll wait. Is it Barker?'

'You know him?'

'We've met.'

'Not a pleasant encounter?'

'Last time I gave him as good as he gave me. He'll not want me to break him again. We'll need to be on our toes when he arrives.'

'Do you want Yarwood in the interview room with you?'

'She knows the history of this case, and it was her who made the connection.'

'I only hope you're right. Men like Selwyn Cosford are apt to cause trouble if you're wrong.'

'He'll be here as well, mark my words.'

Tremayne found Clare talking to Johnny Johnson. 'We've got thirty minutes, not much more. We should grab something to eat. Do you want to join us, Johnson?' Tremayne said.

'Don't mind if I do. There's a place not five minutes from here. They're quick and cheap.'

Why do police officers always want to eat Italian? Clare thought. She was trying to cut back on the calories, and pasta was not what she needed, but in the spirit of teamwork she ordered a plate of spaghetti Bolognese, the same as the other two.

'Johnson was telling me about being undercover,' Clare said.

'We had this idiot, bragging down the pub about how he was a big-time gangster, and what he would do if he were running the show. Little did he know that he was shouting off to an off-duty policeman having a quiet pint. I'm in deep cover. I've been there a long time, and it gets to you. There are some days when you're not sure whether you're on the side of law and order, or whether you're a villain. It plays hell with the mind. Not many ever come back to regular policing. A few of us end up with psychological problems, a few end up turning to crime.'

'And you?'

'I was hyper for a while. In the end, I took three months special leave and went and spent time with a brother in Australia. After four weeks of sun, surf, and whatever else, I'm back on a plane to England, and straight into Serious and Organised Crime. I was one of the lucky ones.'

Death by a Dead Man's Hand

'You were telling us about this informer,' Tremayne said. The food had arrived promptly, as Johnson said it would. Clare could imagine the packet it had come out of, the microwave it had been heated in. Regardless, she had to admit it was tasty.

'It's not a pretty story, and I can't say I'm proud, but Clare wanted the truth,' Johnson said. 'The police start snooping on account of this foolish drunk, not that they've got anything to go with. Once the police are paid off…'

'Paid off?'

'Some were on the take, some were my contacts. If you're dealing with serious quantities of drugs, you've got to be willing to pay people.'

Clare checked her messages. 'We've got another twenty-five minutes. Cosford's coming, so are Barker and Maggie.'

'The idiot with the big mouth,' Johnson continues. 'He's trussed up tighter than a Christmas ham. He's panicking, not that he can do much about it. I'm there as one of the trusted lieutenants. I can't be seen to be weak with the man.'

'If you are?'

'They'll suspect, and then I'll be the ham.'

'What happened after that?'

'We start going to work on the man.'

'Hitting him?'

'And the rest. He's squealing, protesting his innocence. I know he is, but I can't let on. In the end, the boss is satisfied that the man was just an idiot and nothing more would be gained.'

'He was released?'

'Sort of.'

'What does that mean?'

'I wasn't involved, but six weeks later he was found where he had been trussed up, hanging from a beam.'

'Would you have killed him to protect your identity?' Clare said.

'That's what I was telling you before. You get messed up, a little crazy.'

'You would have?'

'I'm not sure. The line between right and wrong has blurred. It can never be that clear again.'

***

There was none of Selwyn Cosford's easy charm that was apparent on the television as he waited for Tremayne and Clare to return. The man was livid, and he was in reception.

Tremayne had seen his car outside. 'We're in for it,' he said.

'Tremayne, what is this? What right have you? I'll have you hung out to dry for this,' Cosford bellowed across the distance separating the two men as Tremayne walked in the door.

'I'm sorry, but this is a murder enquiry. Your daughter-in-law is a person of interest.'

'Are you intending to arrest my entire family to bolster your pathetic case?'

'Katherine Cosford is not under arrest. She is assisting us with our enquiries.'

'It may be best if I deal with this,' Barker said.

Tremayne could see that the man was ready for a fight. He was willing to give him one in return.

Maggie Cosford stood to one side, saying nothing. Rudd had his arm around her shoulders.

'I suggest we move somewhere else,' Tremayne said.

'I want to see my daughter-in-law,' Cosford demanded.

'We will interview her first. Mr Barker will, I assume, be present.'

'He will be.'

Tremayne and Clare left them and headed up the stairs to the interview room, and Katherine Cosford and her lawyer. The Serious and Organised Crime team were watching on a monitor in another room.

'Mrs Cosford, we believe that you used the name of Eileen Bleakes in the past.'

'I did not.'

Clare studied the woman's features close up. The descriptions of a 23-year-old woman and the woman who sat opposite were very similar, but not conclusive.

'On the day that we visited your house, you were not present. Why?'

'My client is here to answer sensible questions,' Barker said. 'There was no appointment scheduled with my client at her house. Do you expect her to be waiting there on the off-chance?'

'Not at all. Selwyn Cosford knew that we were getting close to bursting this case wide open, so did Mrs Cosford's daughter. How old is she?'

'She's twenty-four,' Katherine Cosford said. 'We were married young, Max and I.'

'Which means that you would have been a married woman with a child when you called yourself Eileen Bleakes, and when you seduced Aidan Farrell.'

'I did not seduce anyone. I have always been faithful to my husband.'

Clare wouldn't want to play poker with the woman, she knew that. She was attractive, but there was a hardness in her face, as if she was impervious to her surroundings.

'Your daughter has recently become engaged,' Clare said.

'To Paul, a good man. We are very pleased.'

'Your father-in-law approves of Paul. Is that what's important?'

'Are you implying that she has chosen Paul because of that?'

'Your husband, Selwyn's son, is not a capable man, is he?'

'He makes me happy.'

'Maybe he does, but he's not his father, whereas your daughter is Selwyn.'

'Are you insinuating that Maggie is her grandfather's daughter?'

'No, but she has his characteristics, his charm, his drive, his ability to bring in people as he needs them, to spit them out when he doesn't.'

'She is Max's child.'

'What is the point of this?' Barker said.

'Sergeant Yarwood is establishing certain facts,' Tremayne said. 'If Maggie is capable of manipulation, then so is her mother.'

'You have provided no proof. You've embarrassed my client in front of her friends, you've insulted both her husband and her daughter, and also you've impugned the reputation of a great man.'

'Katherine Cosford, we have your fingerprints. We also have fingerprints from the cottage that Eileen Bleakes was staying in at the time of the hijacking. Your daughter would have been six at the time, and you would have been married.'

'And with my husband.'

Clare studied the face in front of her. She could win a game of cards against the face she saw now.

'The fingerprints match. Katherine Cosford and Eileen Bleakes are one and the same person,' Tremayne said. 'At the time of the hijack, you were supposedly overseas with your husband and daughter.'

'I was.'

'But for a four-week period you were in England, using a false passport and a fake name. Your continued denial will not assist in this matter.'

'It doesn't make me involved,' the woman said.

'Your husband may well sit there and flounder, but you, Mrs Cosford, are not him. You are guilty of a crime. Was it that if Ethan Mitchell hadn't coshed Aidan Farrell, you would have taken him back to your place, slept with him, slipped him a drugged drink, and then left? And who was the woman for Vince Harding? What were you before you picked Max Cosford, or was that set up by Selwyn, the same way he has manipulated Paul Rudd to join the family.'

'I've nothing to…'

'You've nothing to say because whatever it is will damn you further. I suggest to you that you and your daughter use your bodies and your minds as needed to further Selwyn's empire, to cement your position with him, and that Max, your husband, and Rudd, your future son-in-law, are no more than pawns.'

Barker sat still. There was nothing he could say.

'Selwyn Cosford is a brilliant man,' Katherine Cosford said. 'My husband is not. He's not a bad man, but he will never emulate his father. I married Max out of love, and I do still love him, but I am ambitious. Selwyn recognised that in me, and I was a willing partner in several of his ventures. Max knows of some, others he doesn't. Selwyn cannot trust Max to take over the management of what he's set up. He's an old man, not long to live. I'm not capable, not with Max. But Maggie is, and Paul is the same as her, the same as Selwyn. She will be a good wife to Paul, the same as I have been to Max.'

'You have slept with other men since you married Max. Will your daughter be able to do the same?' Clare said.

'She will do whatever is necessary. I have committed no crime. I was meant to bring Farrell to the cottage, that was all. What Selwyn had planned, I didn't know.'

'What did he tell you?'

'He needed an inside man. He needed the man pliable. He needed to meet the man after I had worked on him. It wasn't illegal, not according to Selwyn, not according to me. Maybe it sounds reprehensible, but that's how big business operates. Selwyn was a winner, so was I. I didn't know about the gold.'

'Did you meet Aidan Farrell at a club?'

'Yes, and I slept with him. I was doing it for Max and Maggie.'

'And Maggie is doing the same with Rudd?'

'Paul and my daughter can maintain Selwyn's legacy. That's why Selwyn chose him, and why my daughter fell in love with him.'

'Mrs Cosford, no one was murdered by you,' Tremayne said. 'I'm willing to release you on your own surety after you have given a written statement. Charges may be laid at a later time. However, it doesn't answer how much Selwyn Cosford knew.'

'I'd prefer that Max did not hear of this.'
'Maggie?'
'She will understand.'

***

Outside, the mother and the daughter hugged. Selwyn Cosford muttered something to Barker, and then looked over at Tremayne with daggers in his eyes. Tremayne knew that the earlier invite to a party at the house was permanently cancelled. Not that it worried him, although Jean would be disappointed. After the Cosford family had left, there was a debriefing in Serious and Organised Crime's office.

'Not guilty?' DCI Constanza said.

'Not of murder. Whether she knew of the gold or not is probably not provable, and besides, it was a long time ago.'

'You don't think it's worth pursuing?' DI Ashcroft said. 'The morals of an alley cat, that one.'

'No, I don't. If she was just a phone number, and it was known that one of the Mitchells was going to cosh Farrell, and then tie them up, she wouldn't have needed to rent a house. The twins weren't great thinkers, more brawn than brain. They may have known what was going to happen, but happy-go-lucky Ethan can't resist hitting Farrell, and then the two of them thought they would help themselves to some of the proceeds. Little did they know who they were dealing with. Two things are certain. Firstly, that Katherine Cosford did not murder anyone, and secondly, Selwyn Cosford was involved, which meant that Morrison was as well.'

On the way back to Salisbury, Tremayne dozed for a while. After about forty minutes, close to the halfway point, he woke. 'We're back to the three Mitchell murders,' he said.

'What did we gain up there?' Clare said.

'We helped Serious and Organised Crime. They'll deal with Morrison's death. If Morrison was killed by criminals out of Eastern Europe, it doesn't bode well for Selwyn.'

'Is he important?'

'To them, we don't know, but he's still alive, and the Mitchell three are dead. Tomorrow it's back to focussing on them.'

Chapter 31

Selwyn Cosford was involved in the Mitchell deaths, whether directly or indirectly, Tremayne knew that. However, the focus had not been on either of the Cosford women. One was in her forties, the other in her twenties. Both, it had been stated by Katherine, the mother, were capable of duplicitous behaviour.

Selwyn, the patriarch, had admitted to cowardice once before. But was that an illusion he wanted to foster or was it true? Tremayne was confident that it wasn't; Clare was not so sure.

'Could it have been Selwyn that O'Connor saw,' Clare said. 'Tony Mitchell and Selwyn Cosford were of similar height, similar age, and they both moved slowly. And remember, they were both skilled in jungle warfare. Getting close to Gavin would not have been difficult. The man had a headset on, listening to the pings from his metal detector, and no doubt he was desperate, keeping a watch on the road to the front of him, not to what was behind.'

'It was Tony,' Tremayne said. 'It would be easy to place all the blame on the Cosfords, but it's not going to work this time. And Maggie, she must be some piece of work. If she accepted what her mother had done, what could she be capable of?'

'I hope it's not her,' Clare said.

'Yarwood, you've seen Rudd, you've seen her. What do you reckon? Matched pair?'

'They could be.'

'Okay, let's assume they are. Paul Rudd's admired by Selwyn who sees him as the son he wanted. He wants him close, but he can only let his empire be taken over by his family. Maggie plays her part, falls for the man, or the part of him that Selwyn can see.'

'You make it sound incestuous,' Clare said.

'It's not. Women marry men similar to their fathers. Was Harry similar to your father? The doctor, what about him?'

'I'll concede that point, but it doesn't get us closer to who killed who.'

'Let's go with Tony for Gavin. O'Connor's sure, so am I. If Tony had sat on the gold for all those years, then why? He must have known that Cosford wanted it.'

'Was Tony involved in the heist?'

'Not from what we've learnt. If what we're told by Katherine Cosford is true, then the hijack was not to be in a layby, but later, when the two men are drugged, or the women had worn them out.'

'In your imagination,' Clare said. 'They would have had to be drugged.'

'The other woman?'

'Not important at this time. Cosford expected to take the van, probably organised someone to take it, and to stash the forty bars at another place. Later on, when the insurance claim has been settled, Cosford ships it off overseas, the Middle East or India, the most likely.'

'Cosford would not have driven the van, so who?'

'We're certain it's not Tony Mitchell.'

'Why?'

'He was an honest man.'

'Set it up. All the key players,' Tremayne said. 'No need for the entire Mitchell clan, only Betty and Marcia.'

Death by a Dead Man's Hand

***

Clare commandeered the pub at Emberley. Instead of two in the afternoon, it was to be nine the following morning. A couple of patrol cars were to be outside to add credence to the meeting. Selwyn Cosford had not wanted to come, not until Tremayne said he'd have him arrested for his involvement in the hijacking of forty bars of gold. Katherine and Maggie agreed to be present, Max Cosford was not needed.

The pub was quiet that morning, and apart from a local strolling by, who on seeing people inside thought he could get an early drink, Tremayne and the assembled group were left alone. The landlord, not able to serve alcohol, only hot beverages, cold ones too, water if required, stood behind the bar. Tremayne had told him that what he heard was not for local gossip. He had agreed. Superintendent Moulton was also present, anxious to see Tremayne at his very best, as well as a couple of young officers from other departments at Bemerton Road wanting to learn from the master.

'Let me outline what we have,' Tremayne said. He was standing up close to the bar, almost wanting to lean over and pull a pint of his favourite beer. 'Ethan Mitchell is released after serving seventeen years for the murder of his brother, Martin. He meets a person pretending to be Martin, but it can't be. We now know who it was.'

'Who?' Betty said.

'Let me continue. We have three murders to solve. There is a murderer in this room.'

Those assembled looked around at each other, shook their heads, grabbed hold of their drinks. Nobody said a word.

'Is this drama necessary?' Selwyn Cosford said after a suitable pause.

'It is. Let me continue. Betty Galton had known where the missing twenty gold bars were. She eventually told us, and we retrieved seventeen. Three were missing. The crime scene investigators found a hairclip where the seventeen were. Sergeant Yarwood deduced that it could only have been Betty's. She confronted her, and the two women came out to Emberley and retrieved the three bars, stumbling upon Gavin Mitchell on the way out. He's dead, stab wounds to his back. He could have had the gold for the asking, as Betty had offered it to the family within the past couple of weeks. She is aware that withholding the whereabouts of stolen goods is a criminal offence, but we're not here to discuss a minor crime.'

'Aren't we?' Cosford said. 'It was my gold.'

'It was the insurance company's gold, not yours. Murder is what we are here for and murder we will discuss. Gavin's dead, and we know who killed him as well. That leaves one more to resolve, Tony Mitchell. This was more difficult. Selwyn had reason to want him dead, but he is an old man. It was someone else.'

'This isn't Agatha Christie,' Katherine Cosford said, 'and you're not Poirot.'

'I never liked his moustache, anyway,' Tremayne said. A few in the room attempted to laugh, most didn't.

'Who killed my father?' Marcia said, holding on to her mother.

'There are several possibilities. Bob, Betty's husband. He resented Ethan coming back, and he didn't want Betty to have to deal with divided loyalty.'

'It can't be Bob,' Betty said.

'If it were him, he would be here,' Tremayne said. 'Similarly, Eric Wilson, although he had no motive. He needed money, but he's not a murderer. Wilson would have been capable of melting the gold down and then selling it overseas. It may have taken him a long time, not like Selwyn Cosford, but he would have managed. This brings us to the present company. Selwyn is capable of murder and killing a man in cold blood wouldn't faze him. But he's not a man who does the dirty work himself. He has over the years coerced and seduced people into his web of deceit and lies, his criminal activities as well. Katherine was a willing inclusion, so is Paul Rudd.'

'I'll not hear my fiancé spoken about in such a way,' Maggie said.

'Be quiet,' her mother said. 'The man's right. And why should Paul or I be concerned? Your grandfather has looked after us well.'

'I always look after those I love,' Selwyn said.

'Even your son?' Tremayne said.

'I gave him Katherine. What do you think?'

'Tony Mitchell was more difficult. It took a few contacts, and the help of Serious and Organised Crime to pull in favours before we got the truth about him and Selwyn. It was hidden under layers of bureaucracy and the Official Secrets Act.'

'Get to the point,' Selwyn Cosford said.

'Very well. It could only be a Mitchell who lured Ethan to that church. The man knew it wasn't Martin, but the letter was too inviting, and Ethan had spent a long time in prison. His grip on reality had weakened, and he was clutching at straws. He must have known the reception he would receive in Salisbury, but where else could he go. He has been institutionalised. He's confused. The letter was written by a Mitchell, the execution committed by a Mitchell. No one else would have known what to write in that letter, or the impact it would have.'

'But there are only Marcia and me here,' Betty said.

'How often did you speak to Tony? How well did he know Martin and Ethan?'

'He knew them well when they were younger.'

'You see, he also knew where the gold was. He knew the twins were up to mischief. He would have seen them climbing the fence into Longmore Park, probably even saw them behind the gatehouse. Later on, maybe months after the hijack, and with Martin dead and Ethan in jail, he makes the trip out to the gatehouse. He was a perceptive man. He and Selwyn had trained in surveillance in Malaya. They were both experienced in deduction, and Tony deduces that the twins are predictable, liable to follow established patterns. He may have looked elsewhere, but eventually he figures it out. Tony, a skilled cartographer, army training yet again, draws a detailed map, keeps it in a safe place. He's a man of modest means. He has no need of the gold, no intention of letting on what he knows either. He knows Selwyn would want it, but he's not willing to let the man have the satisfaction of taking it.

'Ethan is released. Tony knows that he'll go for the gold, and then the Mitchell family would be involved, and he doesn't want Betty and Marcia to suffer. He knows what to do. It was him in that church. It was Tony that killed Ethan.'

'You can't prove it,' Betty said.

'Tony will never stand trial, but the facts lead to that conclusion. Tony knew Martin well, knew how he wrote, knew how he spoke. He was shorter than Martin and definitely older, but Ethan's not focussing, and the light in the church wasn't good. Tony gets close enough. Ethan may or may not have realised who it was, but it was unimportant. Tony pulls the trigger, there's no silencer, but he's an experienced man. He's killed before, isn't that true, Selwyn?'

'It's true. Sometimes we would be involved in one-on-one with the enemy,' Selwyn said.

'After he's certain that Ethan's dead, he walks out of the church. He doesn't look left or right or try to sneak away. He's just another person on the street, and some are looking around to where the noise came from, others are minding their own business, scurrying away.'

'It could have been Gavin,' Marcia said.

'He may have had the hatred to want Ethan dead, but you knew Gavin. He wasn't a decisive man, he had no knowledge of weapons. He must have been scared witless up where he died. No, it wasn't Gavin, it was Tony. But thanks, that brings us to Gavin.'

'Not Tony again,' Selwyn said. 'We fought together. He saved my life.'

Tremayne took no notice of Cosford's comments. As far as Tremayne was concerned, the man was vermin.

'Gavin's in the woods, it's late at night, mist swirling around his feet. He's frightened, not sure what he's doing up there.'

'What was he there for?' Betty said.

'He's a proud man, not willing to admit that he needs the money, not willing to ask for the gold. We checked his internet. He had been surfing a few sites, checking on how to melt gold, the temperatures involved, and how to sell it overseas. Gavin's not smart enough to put blockers on the sites he's visited. We've known about it for some time, but then Bob Galton and Eric Wilson had also been doing research. Neither of them is involved before anyone asks.'

'Tony Mitchell?' Selwyn said.

'Yes, Tony,' Tremayne said. 'He's killed Ethan, and it wouldn't have concerned him greatly. He's inured to taking a life, and as far as he's concerned, Ethan's death is a blessing to Betty and Marcia. He's not interested in Gavin or Gerry, never has been, and Bob Galton doesn't interest him, nor does Eric Wilson, a man he regarded as a good businessman but with no other redeeming features. Then he sees Gavin driving up through the village. He knows why he's there and he decides to follow on foot. Gavin knows the back lanes, and he finds a place to hide his car. Tony sees the car. Remember, Tony knows how to follow a track, how to make no noise. He sees Gavin, realises what he's doing. He keeps a watch on him, knows that he'll never find the three bars. He backs away and returns to his cottage, secret safe.'

'If he didn't kill him, then who did?' Katherine Cosford said.

'That's where it gets tricky. We had always suspected Tony, but we checked last night after we had gone through everyone's testimony. It is not possible in the daylight, even with the sun shining through the trees, to see a man's body standing where Gavin was. Devlin O'Connor had said he had. His evidence was false. We arrested him early this morning.'

'Did he admit to his guilt?'

'He had almost killed a man once before. He had seen Gavin in the woods, seen Tony come and go. He then went into the woods and found Gavin. O'Connor, a man who was plagued by nightmares, snaps. He always carried a knife with him. He killed Gavin. No doubt he'll be consigned to a psychiatric facility for the remainder of his life, or until he's deemed fit to re-enter society.'

'But why?' Moulton asked.

'The man had drunk himself into a stupor the night before. He had woken with a blinding headache and decided to walk it off, still badly hungover, not cognisant of who and what was around him. In the back of his mind, he knew that if Lord Linden saw him in that state, he'd be off the estate within the hour. Linden's an easy person to deal with, but he can't abide public drunkenness.'

'And Tony?' Betty asked.

Tremayne could see that everyone was wilting. 'Five minutes, get yourselves a drink or visit the toilet.'

'You're enjoying this,' Clare said as she handed Tremayne a mug of tea.

'Do you realise that O'Connor went back to Longmore Park on our say-so. The man could have flipped again, killed anyone. What if he had murdered Lord and Lady Linden?'

'He didn't, just be thankful.'

'Are the uniforms ready?'

'They are.'

***

Tremayne knew that he was flying blind on this one. He was confident he knew the reason and who, but the proof was not as tight as he would have liked.

'Here's what we know about Tony Mitchell,' Tremayne said when the group had reassembled. 'We know that he had fought in Malaya during the Malayan Emergency. We also know that he was awarded a medal when his unit came under fire. Selwyn Cosford was there with him at the time. That's the connection between two men of vastly different lifestyles. I'm sure that everyone knows this. We also know, courtesy of Serious and Organised Crime, and a few strings being pulled, that while in Malaya, both Mitchell and Cosford were involved in another skirmish. This is not in the official records, and neither man would be proud of what happened. I mentioned the possibility to Selwyn once in the past. He never admitted to it, but now we have proof.'

'It's not something to be proud of,' Cosford said.

'Do you want to tell everyone, or shall I?'

'Carry on. We have both spent our lives forgetting.'

'Very well. There was a village, Selwyn and Tony are on patrol. A shot hits one of their unit full on. One man is down. Sensing an ambush, the unit tightens ranks. Tony takes over the leadership, seeing that the dead man was the senior officer. The unit encircles the village. They're convinced the place is full of communists. The instruction is to wait and see, but Tony's keen to show his metal. He's forced to make a decision. It's either attack the village, attempt to subdue it or retreat and wait for backup.'

'I'll tell it,' Selwyn said. 'The sun's blazing down, the mosquitoes are driving us crazy. One of the men was suffering from dysentery, and the rest of us are worn out. We've done our bit and are in need of a rest. In the village, there's a well and some shade. Tony decides that we move in. After all, they're only communists, not worth worrying about. That's what we had been told, what we believed. The sun is relentless, and we're kitted up in gear more suitable for a colder climate, plus we're hungry, and chickens are walking around. Tony gives the command.'

'You could have phoned for backup,' Marcia said.

Death by a Dead Man's Hand

'We're in a war zone, decisions are split-second, and we know that backup will take two hours at least. We move in, Tony's at the front, I'm not far behind. The shooting from one of the huts starts again. We spray it with bullets. The shooting stops.

'I go in first, vomit at the sight of it.'

'What was it?' Betty said.

'It was a young boy, no more than ten. He had been shooting at us. With him are five other children, two girls, three boys. We had killed them all. We had followed the rule book, we had done our job, but we had killed children. Our superiors, aware of how this would be perceived, covered it up, gave us counselling, and sent us back to England, honourable discharges. None of us dealt with it well, but Tony, as you know, was more sensitive. In time I moved on, never truly forgot, but it was war, these sorts of things happen.

'But Tony, he became reclusive. Before that, he was into all the dens of iniquity we could find in the Far East. We were young lads out of England for the first time, and the lure of the Orient was irresistible. After our return to England, we kept in touch. I would have done anything for him, but he didn't want it. But there was a bond, forged not in battle, but in disgrace.'

'That is what killed Tony Mitchell,' Tremayne said.

'He was getting old. It was a secret he no longer wanted to keep. He came and saw me. He told me what he was going to do,' Selwyn said.

'And what was that?'

'He was going to tell the Mitchell family, give an interview to the local newspaper, whatever television station would take it.'

'But it was sixty years ago,' Maggie, Cosford's granddaughter, said. 'Surely no one's interested anymore. These things happen.'

'You've seen the photo I have of us in Malaya,' Selwyn said. 'Who did you see.'

'I saw you and Tony Mitchell.'

'How did you know it was Tony?' Tremayne said.

'Grandfather said it was him.'

'Why did you come to Emberley?'

'I was curious. I came out here and knocked on Mitchell's door.'

'What happened?'

'He invited me in. I told him who I was. He was very kind to me, asked if I'd look after his dog when he was gone.'

'How did you interpret that?'

'I thought he was an old man feeling his age.'

'Did he tell you who else was in the photo?'

'No, but one of them seemed familiar.'

'He's a politician now, Cabinet Minister,' Selwyn said.

'Did you contact him?' Tremayne asked Selwyn.

'I did. We agreed that Tony could not be allowed to talk. Sixty years it may have been, but mud sticks.'

'How much did Tony know about the gold bullion?'

'Nothing from me.'

'Maggie, why did you kill Tony Mitchell?' Tremayne said.

'How did you know?'

'I didn't, Devlin O'Connor did. He was a man who knew more about what happened in the village than anyone else. You shouldn't have parked your car in the lane that Gavin had used. When O'Connor confessed to murdering Gavin, he also revealed that he had seen you. He is a man who has spent his life keeping secrets. He was not about to reveal that he knew you to be the murderer of Tony Mitchell, but with nothing more to lose, he told us everything. He was not far from the cottage when you shot Tony. He will be a witness at your trial.'

'I had to. I couldn't let my grandfather suffer. Such a great man brought low by something that happened such a long time ago. I came out to Mr Mitchell's place, listened to what he had to say.'

'And then?'

'I left him and went back to my car. It was some distance away. I then returned, spent a few more minutes with him and then I shot him. I was sorry, as I had liked the man, and he was important to my father.'

'Maggie, it wasn't necessary. There was no way the government was going to let a Cabinet Minister be lambasted in the press. They would have dealt with it,' Tremayne said.

'I did it for you, Grandfather.' Maggie rushed over and flung her arms around the neck of the man she loved more than any other. Her mother sat quietly crying. Betty went over and gave her a hug.

Superintendent Moulton sat back in his chair, stunned. The other officers from Bemerton Road looked over at Tremayne in admiration. Clare sent a message to the doctor. *This Saturday, 8 p.m.*

Tremayne did not feel any satisfaction in what he had just done. Good and decent people were suffering, would continue to suffer. He wondered if he was ready for retirement.

Phillip Strang

The End.

ALSO BY THE AUTHOR

Death at Coombe Farm – A DI Tremayne Thriller

If it hadn't been for the circumstances, Detective Inspector Keith Tremayne would have said the view was outstanding. Up high, overlooking the farmhouse in the valley below, the panoramic vista of Salisbury Plain stretching out beyond. The only problem was that near where he stood with his sergeant, Clare Yarwood, there was a body, and it wasn't a pleasant sight.

Death and the Lucky Man – A DI Tremayne Thriller

Sixty-eight million pounds and dead. Hardly the outcome expected for the luckiest man in England the day his lottery ticket was drawn out of the barrel. But then, Alan Winters' rags-to-riches story had never been conventional, and there were those who had benefited, but others who hadn't.

Murder in Room 346 – A DCI Cook Thriller

A Downmarket Hotel. A Moral Campaigner. A woman who had killed her husband. Both Dead. Both Compromised.

On the bed, the naked bodies of a man and a woman. 'Bullet in the head's not the way to go,' Larry Hill, Isaac Cook's detective inspector, said.

'Do you recognise him?' Detective Chief Inspector Isaac Cook said.

'James Holden, from what I can see.'

'You know this will be all over the media within the hour,' Isaac said.

'James Holden, a proponent of the sanctity of the marital bed, man and wife. It's bound to be.'

Murder in Notting Hill– A DCI Cook Thriller

One murderer, two bodies, two locations, and the murders have been committed within an hour of each other. There's a connection, but what is it?

They're separated by a couple of miles, and neither woman has anything in common with the other.

Isaac Cook and his team at Challis Street Police Station are baffled as to why. One of the women is young and wealthy, the daughter of a famous man; the other is poor and hardworking and unknown.

Death and the Lucky Man – A DI Tremayne Thriller

Sixty-eight million pounds and dead.

Hardly the outcome expected for the luckiest man in England the day his lottery ticket was drawn out of the barrel.

Death by a Dead Man's Hand

But then, Alan Winters' rags-to-riches story had never been conventional, and there were those who had benefited, but others who hadn't.

Death and the Assassin's Blade – A DI Tremayne Thriller

It was meant to be high drama, not murder, but someone's switched the daggers. The man's death took place in plain view of two serving police officers.

He was not meant to die; the daggers were only theatrical props, plastic and harmless. A summer's night, a production of Julius Caesar amongst the ruins of an Anglo-Saxon fort. Detective Inspector Tremayne is there with his sergeant, Clare Yarwood. In the assassination scene, Caesar collapses to the ground. Brutus defends his actions; Mark Antony rebukes him.

They're a disparate group, the amateur actors. One's an estate agent, another an accountant. And then there is the teenage school student, the gay man, the funeral director. And what about the women? They could be involved.

They've each got a secret, but which of those on the stage wanted Gordon Mason, the actor who had portrayed Caesar, dead?

Murder is the Only Option – A DCI Cook Thriller

A man, thought to be long dead, returns to exact revenge against those who had blighted his life. His only concern is to protect his wife and daughter. He will stop at nothing to achieve his aim.

'Big Greg, I never expected to see you around here at this time of night.'

'I've told you enough times.'

'I've no idea what you're talking about,' Robertson replied. He looked up at the man, only to see a metal pole coming down at him. Robertson fell down, cracking his head against a concrete kerb.

The two vagrants, no more than twenty feet away, did not stir and did not even look in the direction of the noise. If they had, they would have seen a dead body, another man walking away.

Death Unholy – A DI Tremayne Thriller

All that remained were the man's two legs and a chair full of greasy and fetid ash. Little did DI Keith Tremayne know that it was the beginning of a journey into the murky world of paganism and its ancient rituals. And it was going to get very dangerous.

'Do you believe in spontaneous human combustion?' Detective Inspector Keith Tremayne asked.

'Not me. I've read about it. Who hasn't?' Sergeant Clare Yarwood answered.

I haven't,' Tremayne replied, which did not surprise his young sergeant. In the months they had been working together, she had come to realise that he was a man who had little interest in the world. When he had a cigarette in his mouth, a beer in his hand, and a murder to solve he was about the happiest she ever saw him. He could hardly be regarded as one of life's sociable people. And as for reading? The most he managed was an occasional police report or an early morning newspaper, turning first to the back pages for the racing results.

Murder in Little Venice – A DCI Cook Thriller

A dismembered corpse floats in the canal in Little Venice, an upmarket tourist haven in London. Its identity is unknown, but what is its significance?

DCI Isaac Cook is baffled about why it's there. Is it gang-related, or is it something more?

Whatever the reason, it's clearly a warning, and Isaac and his team are sure it's not the last body that they'll have to deal with.

Murder is only a Number – A DCI Cook Thriller

Before she left she carved a number in blood on his chest. But why the number 2, if this was her first murder?

The woman prowls the streets of London. Her targets are men who have wronged her. Or have they? And why is she keeping count?

DCI Cook and his team finally know who she is, but not before she's murdered four men. The whole team are looking for her, but the woman keeps disappearing in plain sight. The pressure's on to stop her, but she's always one step ahead.

And this time, DCS Goddard can't protect his protégé, Isaac Cook, from the wrath of the new commissioner at the Met.

Murder House – A DCI Cook Thriller

A corpse in the fireplace of an old house. It's been there for thirty years, but who is it?

It's clearly murder, but who is the victim and what connection does the body have to the previous owners of the house. What is the motive? And why is the body in a fireplace? It was bound to be discovered eventually but was that what the murderer wanted? The main suspects are all old and dying, or already dead.

Isaac Cook and his team have their work cut out trying to put the pieces together. Those who know are not talking because of an old-fashioned belief that a family's dirty laundry should not be aired in public, and certainly not to a policeman – even if that means the murderer is never brought to justice!

Murder is a Tricky Business – A DCI Cook Thriller

A television actress is missing, and DCI Isaac Cook, the Senior Investigation Officer of the Murder Investigation Team at Challis Street Police Station in London, is searching for her.

Why has he been taken away from more important crimes to search for the woman? It's not the first time she's gone missing, so why does everyone assume she's been murdered?

There's a secret, that much is certain, but who knows it? The missing woman? The executive producer? His eavesdropping assistant? Or the actor who portrayed her fictional brother in the TV soap opera?

Murder Without Reason – A DCI Cook Thriller

DCI Cook faces his greatest challenge. The Islamic State is waging war in England, and they are winning.

Not only does Isaac Cook have to contend with finding the perpetrators, but he is also being forced to commit actions contrary to his mandate as a police officer.

And then there is Anne Argento, the prime minister's deputy. The prime minister has shown himself to be a pacifist and is not up to the task. She needs to take his job if the country is to fight back against the Islamists.

Two government analysts have provided the solution. Will DCI Cook and Anne Argento be willing to follow it through? Are they able to act for the good of England, knowing that a criminal and murderous action is about to take place? Do they have any option?

The Haberman Virus

Phillip Strang

A remote and isolated village in the Hindu Kush mountain range in North Eastern Afghanistan is wiped out by a virus unlike any seen before.

A mysterious visitor clad in a space suit checks his handiwork, a female American doctor succumbs to the disease, and the woman sent to trap the person responsible falls in love with him – the man who would cause the deaths of millions.

Hostage of Islam

Three are to die at the Mission in Nigeria: the pastor and his wife in a blazing chapel; another gunned down while trying to defend them from the Islamist fighters.

Kate McDonald, an American, grieving over her boyfriend's death and Helen Campbell, whose life had been troubled by drugs and prostitution, are taken by the attackers.

Kate is sold to a slave trader who intends to sell her virginity to an Arab Prince. Helen, to ensure their survival, gives herself to the murderer of her friends.

Malika's Revenge

Malika, a drug-addicted prostitute, waits in a smugglers' village for the next Afghan tribesman or Tajik gangster to pay her price, a few scraps of heroin.

Yusup Baroyev, a drug lord, enjoys a lifestyle many would envy. An Afghan warlord sees the resurgence of the

Taliban. A Russian white-collar criminal portrays himself as a good and honest citizen in Moscow.

All of them are linked in an audacious plan to increase the quantity of heroin shipped out of Afghanistan and into Russia and ultimately the West.

Some will succeed, some will die, some will be rescued from their plight and others will rue the day they became involved.

ABOUT THE AUTHOR

Phillip Strang was born in England in the late forties, during the post-war baby boom. He had a comfortable middle-class upbringing, spending his childhood years in a small town to the west of London.

An avid reader of science fiction in his teenage years: Isaac Asimov, Frank Herbert, the masters of the genre. Much of what they and others mentioned has now become a reality. Science fiction has now become science fact. Still an avid reader, the author now mainly reads thrillers.

In his early twenties, the author, with a degree in electronics engineering and a desire to see the world, left England for Sydney, Australia. Now, forty years later, he still resides in Australia, although many intervening years were spent in a myriad of countries, some calm and safe, others no more than war zones.

Printed in Dunstable, United Kingdom